I have not forgotten thee

by *William P. Sexton*

I have not forgotten thee

by
William P. Sexton

O'Séasnain Publishing Co.
2002

Author: William P. Sexton
Cover art: Danielle Hughes
Typography and cover layout: Michael Höhne, Michael Höhne Design

ISBN: 0-9701310-1-1

Library of Congress Control Number: 2002113063

This is an historical novel with the main characters being fictional. Any resemblance to anyone living or dead is coincidental.

Other books by William P. Sexton
(aka Liam O'Séasnain)

Liam O'Connor

acknowledgements

To Marilyn Stangl, Ph.D., who for many long months gave her time editing and typing the book. Also, many thanks for her input into the story itself. To Danielle Hughes, the graphic designer who took my concept of the cover and made it a reality. Many thanks for the advice and encouragement of the following people: To Doug McClelland, author of *Hollywood on Ronald Reagan* and *Forties Film Talk*. To Michael Höhne, who as usual did a professional job in designing this book. To my son Brian, who followed up on the many details and loose ends of writing a novel. To my wife Rose, who helped proofread it. To my son Danny, who researched and added his ideas to the story. To Staci Backauskas, author of *The Fifth Goddess,* who has guided me through the minefields of publishing.

Mr. Connolly

Mrs. Connolly

Martin

Maureen

Grainne

Bridget

chapter one

he year was 1936. In the middle of Eyre Square in the county
of Galway, Ireland, a Catholic priest stood on the top of a
lorry appealing to the crowd

"How long will you let our Catholic priests and nuns be massa-
cred in Spain? The Communists are burning our churches and
slaughtering our clergy. I implore you to help us fight for our faith.
General Franco is leading his brave Nationalist Party against the
Communists. Will you, as Irishmen, not fight for Holy Mother, the
Church? The other counties are responding and signing up with
General O'Duffy, the courageous leader of the Irish Brigade." The
priest shouted, "The West Awake! The West Awake! It's for the
glory of God and the Honor of Ireland."

Among the crowd, watching and listening, was a 22-year-old
Connemara man of average height and weight. His dark hair and
blue eyes were no different from the features that were associated
with a typical Connemara man. His name was Martin Connolly,
and he had come to Galway City for the day to purchase a new suit
of clothes. He was well aware of the events in Spain. They were in
the papers, and even the radio had broadcast some of the latest
news from Spain. The crowd dispersed and moved away from the
lorry. There didn't seem to be much interest in what the priest had
said. Martin found this disturbing. He couldn't remember any
Galway man he knew that would shy away from a good scrap.

"My God," he thought, "this is for their own faith!"

He decided to drop into one of the local pubs in the square and
check out what the locals had to say about it. He thought he would

get plenty of comments on this subject, so off he went to the Old Salt pub, which must have been around for a long time because his grandfather used to swap yarns about it with his father. It was packed that day, and there wasn't even standing room. He ordered a pint and tried to maneuver himself into the conversation about what the priest had said. To his surprise no one was discussing it. The talk among the locals was all about Galway playing Limerick in a hurling match next week.

Martin had his pint and left. He had been into the clothing store to pick up his suit before he had stopped to listen to the priest. It was getting late, and it was a long way home. Martin had rode from Connemara to Galway City on horseback. It was not the most comfortable ride. Along the way he had stopped in to one of the smaller towns for his tea. He'd had a great dish of spuds and stew, and he'd swallowed it down with a pint of the old black porter. After his meal he had smoked like a chimney, puffing away for himself on his old, well-seasoned pipe. Oh, how he loved that old pipe! His mother was always teasing him about his pipe. The old fellah on the other hand was always serious. You could never get him to laugh. The mother used to call him "the old dry balls." This would set the whole house laughing. Martin had three sisters besides himself so he was used to having everything done for him. He was spoiled rotten. His mother often said to him, "I feel sorry for the lassie who marries you. She'll get no work out of you." That wasn't the case with his father. The old fellah worked him hard in the fields from sunup to sundown. He never let up on Martin. "Shake your leg boy," he'd say. "Let's not have another half day's work."

The old fellah never ran out of energy. Martin would be cursing him to hell all during the day for working the backside off him, yet he made sure he was doing the cursing under his breath. He was never quite sure, even though he was young and strong, if he could handle the old fellah.

It was pitch black when Martin got back to the farmhouse. There were no lights on in the house, and everyone was in bed. He was dead tired from the long ride, and he fell into a deep sleep. It seemed to him that he had just got into bed when he was awakened by the old fellah standing outside his room.

"Let's go, let's go, boyo. We lost a whole day's work yesterday, and half the morning's gone already."

Martin looked at the clock. It was only 6:00 a.m. He shouted out to the old fellah, "How much of the morning did we lose, Da?

"Don't be so sarcastic, or I'll give you a good whack that you won't forget."

"I believe you, Da," he said.

As usual the mother had the breakfast on the table. "Don't put too much on the table," the old fellah said. "We have no time for a big breakfast this morning. We've lost half a day's work already." Martin's sisters were giggling. "Shut up," the old fellah said, half kidding, "or I'll marry you all off to the old farmers here in Connemara."

Maureen, who was the oldest and who always answered him back, said, "Ah sure, they couldn't be any older than yourself. You're the oldest man in Connemara." They all started laughing, and the old fellah said nothing.

Grainne and Bridget were the two younger sisters, and both were very shy. Grainne worked for the local bank and was probably the smartest of the three. Mrs. Connolly often said that you never knew when Grainne was around. She would sit in a chair in the corner of the living room and read all night long, never making a sound. She was completely oblivious to her surroundings. Bridget and herself were very close. They did everything together. Bridget could not sit still. She was constantly in motion. She was in her final year of secondary school. Bridget's eyes were on the hotel business, and she would be going to culinary school after finishing her last term. Mrs. Connolly always said that Bridget was the best cook in the family.

Now Maureen was a real piece of work. She tended bar in the local pub and was always partying. If there was a dance in town, she was there. The old fellah would be waiting for her when she came home which was at all hours of the morning. Then he would start scolding her to no avail.

"Go away with yourself," she would say to him. "Ma is right. You are an old dry balls!"

"Go easy with that kind of talk," he would say. "I still can give you a good spanking on your bottom."

The devilment would dance in her eyes. "Come on," she would say, posing like a prizefighter in the middle of the floor. She would dance around him throwing punches in the air. The old man would finally break down and start laughing, a rarity for him. So life went on the little Connolly farm.

Martin was troubled over his trip to Galway City. One evening around the fireplace where the family often gathered, he asked his mother, "Do you remember me talking to you about the priest who was in Eyre Square the last time I was there?"

His mother replied, "Well, what about it?"

"Well, Ma," Martin said, "no one seemed to give a damn about what was happening in Spain. The priest was talking on deaf ears. God, Mother," he said, "he was talking about the priests and nuns being tortured and killed for the Faith. Would you believe that they were burning Catholic churches?"

"Mother of God!" his mother burst out. "If I were a man, I would go over there and kick their asses for them."

Martin saw his chance. "I'm a man," he said, "and I intend to do just that."

"A man!" the old fellah let out. "Don't make me laugh. You're lucky if you can finish a good day's work out in the field."

"Ah, shut up," Mrs. Connolly said to him. "You're very hard on the boy."

"Ah," said the old fellah, "it's a boy now he is. A few moments ago he was talking about himself in terms of being a man."

Martin said no more and left the house. He wandered out to the fields. Those Connemara fields always brought him peace of mind. Martin would sit for hours in the middle of the grass going over whatever problems he had. As a little boy after school, he would sit out there in the grass talking away to himself, usually about what had happened to him in school that day. He saw his sisters as miles away from his thoughts and dreams. To his way of thinking he was really an only child. What would girls know about his dreams of becoming an all Ireland hurling star? The old fellah kept him working in the fields every chance he could. He had missed so many hurling practices that he was nearly dropped from the team. Martin reasoned, even as a young boy, that the old fellah never liked hurling. The grandfather told him that his father wasn't worth a knob of goat's dung at hurling. As a matter of fact, he wasn't any good at all at any sports. His only interest was in farming, so Martin really had no one to rally to his cause. His mother had tried, but after a while she had given up and left him to the old fellah.

He was staring up at the blue Irish sky that was always full of clouds that seemed to come right down to almost touch him, when right then and there he decided he would enlist in General O'Duffy's Blue Shirts. No more talk. He would go into Galway City next week. What would he tell the old fellah? There would be a murderous confrontation. His father financially had enough money to hire a field hand. The old fellah had been socking it away for years. Maureen and Grainne were both working, so he saw no financial problems for the family. Even Bridget had a part-time job after school at the newsstand.

Before leaving the field, Martin asked himself the question, "Is this for the church and God, or am I doing this to escape the old fellah?" The speech in front of his Ma and the old fellah was not his true feelings. He wished it was. God, how he wished it was! The truth was, he didn't even want to reveal this to himself, he disliked the old fellah. There were times that, even though he was his father, Martin would have loved to hit him a good belt. The old fellah would never let up on him. Some days it was unbearable. He would start in the early morning and never stop all day, always telling him he was too slow, too awkward, and that he was no good to him. Martin had tried to curb his temper and to control himself all through the years.

Even during the hurling matches, which often created a good scrap during the game and afterwards, he would walk away from any confrontation. This left doubts about his guts among his team players. Martin was a fine hurler. The Connemara man had worked hard since he was a youngster. The Irish Fields in Galway were full of rocks and hard earth. The Irish Song, "Rocks of Bawn," tells it all. There were very few days in his life that he couldn't remember the rain pouring down on his head while he ploughed those Rocks of Bawn.

Hardened by his junior and senior hurling days, Martin was used to taking a good thumping on an Irish hurling field. To play the game itself you must possess strength, endurance, speed, and above all, you must have heart. The game of hurling itself is synonymous with the Irishman's character. It is often played with a busted nose or blood streaming across the player's face after being smashed with a hurling stick. This may be accompanied by a few broken bones. There is no quit to these players even though they play in pain and sometimes in agony. It would be a cold day in Hell when you would see one of them go off the field on his own accord. Martin was a typical team player, taking the ball right up to the bar and passing it over to one of his teammates to score. Even when he had the opportunity to score himself, he would still pass it to someone else.

Quiet people like Martin are capable of having a murderous temper if you made the mistake of setting them off. He never realized this in himself until the week before he went to Galway City where he was involved in a match against a strong Kerry team. The game was in Kerry, and Martin and his teammates stopped into the local pub for a pint after the game. The Kerry men, even after losing the game, were giving out to the Galway players with some good-natured codding. The evening was going great, and everyone was laughing and singing. Most of them were feeling no pain. Martin, however, was not a heavy drinker, and one pint was tops for him. No one ever saw him drunk. So between not drinking and not fighting, Martin was never really one of the lads. Not a good position to be in among his Irish countrymen. It was about closing time when one of the locals came in for a closing pint. He was a big Kerry man who went over to the crowded bar and ordered his pint. He shouted over the crowd, and with that he made a large opening for himself at the bar. In order to accomplish this he had to shoulder two Galway men almost to the floor. Little Timmy Burke, who played centerfield for the team, was the smallest man on the team, and it was often said about him that he wouldn't harm a fly. Good-natured and always in a good mood, no one could ever remember getting into an argument with him.

"Easy, easy boy," Timmy said to the towering giant next to him. "You're spilling good black porter on the floor. All the Kerry dogs and cats that wander in here will be lapping up the porter from the floor, and there won't be a sober cat or dog in the whole of Kerry."

It was never so much what Timmy said, but the way he said it that made people laugh. The Kerry man put down his pint.

"I suppose," he said, "that you think that's funny, little man." Grabbing Timmy by the throat, he said, "I work hard for my bread, and I lost £50 today because of you Galway bastards. I'm going to get my pound of flesh out of you." And with that he hit poor Timmy square in the face.

There wasn't a sound in the place for about sixty seconds. Then the whole place erupted. The guards (police) were called, and they quickly settled down the whole group. They took Timmy to the hospital. This left the group staring at each other. The silence was broken when a voice called out to the big Kerry man, "I'm going to kick your big ass all over Kerry."

The team turned to see who among the crowd was going to handle this Goliath. There was no one on the Galway team who could believe their eyes when Martin Connolly stepped out of the crowd and headed for the Kerry man. The Kerry man eyed him up and down with a sadistic smile. Martin was just about up to his chest, but there was something different about Martin. The talk later was that Martin had murder in his eyes. His mouth was quivering on one side of his face, and he was white with temper. The team said afterwards that they had never seen a beating bestowed on any man like that before. Martin came in with both fists swinging, landing one after the other on the Kerry man's gut. The Kerry man couldn't get a punch off with this tiger tank. Martin fired one punch after the other at his mid-section, and when the Kerry man bent over, he would punch to his head. Left, right, right, left, those punches came from all directions. He broke the Kerry man's nose and knocked his three front teeth out. It took five of his teammates to drag him away from Goliath. All the way home he wouldn't talk to anyone. It was the talk of the town. The old fellah was told about it when he went into town for a pint that night. He didn't believe it. When the old fellah came home afterwards, he was half jarred. He looked at Martin who was reading in the kitchen. "I heard all about you and your bad temper," he said. "Well, boyo, don't ever make the mistake of trying that on me."

Martin put his head back into the paper and smiled.

The incident gave Martin some sleepless nights as he worried about that terrible temper he had discovered within himself. He knew now that he was capable of killing someone, and it frightened him. Martin came to the conclusion that the anger that was building up in him from the old fellah made him take it out on the Kerry man. It was time to go. Some day the old fellah would go too far, and Martin knew that he would do some serious harm to him. This he could not live with. After all, this was his father.

A week went by, and that Sunday Martin was bringing home his mother and sisters from Mass. The old fellah was in the fields, working as usual. Not even for Sunday Mass would the old man stop his work in the fields. "Ma," Martin said when he was about half a mile from the house, "I would like to talk to you."

"Maureen, take your sisters home. We'll be along shortly."

When his sisters had gone on ahead, Martin took his mother in his arms and held her closely. Looking deep into her eyes, he thought she must have been a very beautiful woman when she was young. He never could remember her being young. She always seemed old to him. The hard Connemara fields had made her old fast. The wrinkles in her face were deep, and those beautiful Galway eyes had grown dim. Still, when she smiled, there was a glow that made one feel they were in the presence of a very young woman.

"Ma," he said, "I'm leaving in a few days for Spain, and I'm joining up with General O'Duffy's Blue Shirts. I have decided not to tell the old fellah. It will cause too much of a scene. So I will say goodbye to you now, and when I leave it will be quietly without anyone knowing I have gone. Ma, I will miss you dearly. You're all that has kept me here over the years. The old fellah is a hard man, and I often wondered how you ever put up with him."

She smiled at him. "Martin," she said, "the Irish woman loves her man beyond any reason, and under the most unusual circumstances. Come back to us safe and sound, and I will pray for your return." She held on to him tightly and then walked away. The Irish are not given to long emotional good-byes.

The house remained quiet for the next few days. It was as though everyone knew that something was about to happen. One sunny morning Martin left the house before anyone had risen. Even the old fellah was asleep. Standing on the top of the hill overlooking his house, he took one last look at his Connemara home. "God," he thought, "what a beautiful place my hills of Connemara are!" The words of the Connemara song ran through his head, "The Connemara lovely hills will call me back to you." He turned his back and walked away.

Karl Gunter

chapter two

Martin boarded the Galway Bay steamship leaving the Galway port on December 13th. It was to meet up with a foreign vessel that would take the Irish volunteers to Spain. The gale-force winds and rains were severe, and Martin, like many of his comrades, became seasick. He honestly believed he was going to die. He had never been so sick in his life. Finally, after a very dangerous trip, they reached the foreign vessel and went aboard. While heading for Spain, they seemed to regain their strength. The ship was a German registered cargo vessel.

After a very tedious journey, they landed in Spain at the port of Galica. From there they continued on to the town of Caceres, where they were to receive their training. This trip was about 600 kilometers. The volunteers arrived in Caceres a week before Christmas. The Irish, settling into their quarters, began their military training at once. The town was made up of small houses and a group of medieval buildings and churches. Caceres was a market town.

General Franco had placed the Irish volunteers in the "Terico," which was the Spanish Foreign Legion. The Spanish Foreign Legion was made up of career army Spaniards who were the cream of the crop. They were one hundred percent career men who were in for life. Their losses were high so eventually their replacements were coming from foreign sources. The Irish had the reputation of being well-known fighting men. So it was expected of them to perform with the best. The Legion's motto was "Long Live Death," and they called themselves the bridegrooms of Death.

There were problems from the beginning. The Irish felt that the Spanish training was a waste of time. Many of the Irish recruits had fought in the Big War (World War I) and were veterans of many trench battles. Some had fought with the IRA in Ireland during the Irish fight for freedom. They were well-schooled in general drill and were expert riflemen. The Legion was commanded by a Colonel Yagues who considered his men to be crack troops. He was against the idea of incorporating the Irish volunteers with his men.

The first few days of the Irish Volunteers were spent adjusting to the Spanish way of doing things. Martin's group was fortunate to have a Spanish NCO who had a fair command of the English language. While he shouted out the commands in Spanish, he would repeat them over again in English. At the beginning the Spanish officers had the same reservations that their colonel had. They looked down on the Irish Volunteers. Despite their personal feelings they soon realized that the Irish made good soldiers and were crack shots. On the firing range the Spanish were hard pressed to keep up with them.

It was at the firing range that Martin first met Karl Gunter, a German volunteer. A six-footer built like a seasoned athlete, blond and blue-eyed, he was the perfect example of the Aryan race. Both men were hitting the bull's eye one after the other, and it brought the attention of a Spanish officer in charge of the firing range. A match between the two men was arranged to see who was the best. This match was an excellent diversion from the ordinary intensity accompanying military training. The German had been well schooled in his German rifle and at the end won the match over Martin. The surprise came when Martin was asked where he received his training. To the astonishment of the officers and even Karl Gunter, the answer came back he had never before fired a weapon in his life. None believed him. Martin was a natural with a rifle. It came to him very easily. It usually takes quite a lot of training and skill to master marksmanship.

After the match, Karl came over to Martin and introduced himself. "That was fine shooting, my friend. I understand you have never fired a rifle before."

"Yes," Martin replied, "we don't have much use for a rifle in Connemara. We receive a lot of training with the old spade."

"Oh, I see," Karl smiled. "You're a farm boy. Where is Connemara?"

"It's on the west coast of Ireland."

"Oh, that explains it," Karl said. "You're an Irishman."

Martin looked at him and said, "What the hell did you think I would be in the middle of an all Irish Volunteer group?"

Karl laughed. "Well, I'm in this group, and I'm certainly not that, so how do you figure that one? You're an Irishman, and I have a healthy respect for the Irish. We have come up against them before, and they always proved to be formidable adversaries."

Martin was aware that there were Germans with the different Spanish brigades, and there were volunteers from other countries, too. Karl took Martin aside and explained to him how unusual it was to shoot so well without training. "It takes a good length of time and training to shoot like you did. I beat you because I've had such training. If the Spanish officers knew their business, they would have sent you to sniper school, although I don't believe they have such a place. Listen, Martin, I'd like to buy you a drink when you get some leave."

Martin liked Karl from the beginning. He was hesitant in telling Karl he didn't drink very much. At any rate, he decided to let it go with an agreement to meet Karl on the first leave that came about. The weeks went by and the training became more difficult, not because of the program itself, but because the tension was rising between the Irish Volunteers and the Spanish officers and NCOs. The Irish became discontented with what they felt was unnecessary training. They were anxious to fight.

Martin received a day pass and sought out Karl who had accumulated his passes for such an occasion. They decided to go fishing together, and there was a small river a few miles from the town. The local police officer was an avid fisherman and volunteered to lend Martin and Karl his fishing gear. Karl had approached him that day while he was patrolling his beat. "We'd like to fish today, but we don't know where to go, and there is no place to rent fishing gear."

"I'd be delighted," he said, "to lend you mine. After all, you have come over here to fight in my country for a Spanish cause." It was a lovely, warm Spanish day, although it was winter. They had gathered up the fishing gear from the Spanish policeman and were hiking towards the river, which was about three miles out of town. Martin felt very much at ease with Karl. The conversation was very interesting, and Martin soon realized that Karl was a highly educated man. But somehow, Karl didn't intimidate him. Both men had baited their hooks and thrown out their lines about twenty-five yards, which was about all the width of that river. Sitting on the soft grass, Martin lit up his pipe of joy, and following this gesture, Karl lit up one of his favorite big cigars. Peace and quiet reigned over the two men. They were a long way from the guns of war. Karl broke the silence, asking Martin why he came over to Spain to fight.

"I am a Catholic," Martin replied. "It's in defense of my faith."

"It has nothing to do with faith, my Irish friend. This is a political battle for the control of Spain. In my opinion the General is nothing less than a dictator."

Martin seemed surprised. "If that is so, why are you here?"

"I have other reasons, but I choose not to go into them with you right now."

"I believe you are a clever fellow," Martin said. "You find out what you want to about me, but you decline to reveal any information about yourself. I'm going to have to watch you." They both laughed.

The day went fast as they both basked in the warm Spanish sun. Neither man got even a bite, yet it was a peaceful day. Both men went away understanding a little bit more about each other. The bond was forming.

Training to Karl seemed boring because it was obvious he had gone through this before. Martin seemed to enjoy it. To him it was all brand new and certainly a change from his farming days in Connemara. No sergeant could be any worse than the old fellah. The training was nearly at an end when Martin received a letter from his sister, Grainne. It was the first letter he had received since arriving in Spain. Eagerly he opened the letter, but it carried bad news for him. Grainne told him that the old fellah has passed away. It seemed he got pneumonia and died. His mother was not well either since the old fellah has passed away. Martin was not able to finish the letter. He left the barracks and sat on top of one of the Spanish hills that overlooked the town. No tears came from him, just the feeling of despair. Martin had always believed that even though he never liked the old fellah, there would be a time when he and the old man would patch up their differences. Now it was too late. The chance would never come again. Instead of sorrow, Martin raged inside of himself at the old fellah for dying and leaving him without the only hope he had for reconciliation. He was very upset for his mother who he knew would not live long after her husband. He remembered what she said to him the day he said goodbye to her. "Martin, the Irish woman loves her man beyond reason and under the most unusual circumstances." Martin knew that this kind of love kills.

The orders came within a few weeks. They were to defend Ciempozuelos. A week before they left for Ciempozuelos, Karl and Martin were eating in the mess hall when one of the Irish lads sitting next to Martin turned and asked him, "What's with you and this Kraut? You got something going for you, lad?" The Irish lads at the table all started to laugh. "Since you landed here, you have never had a drink with the boys. Are we not good enough for you? Well, I think myself good enough for you and your Kraut friend," he said. "And if you'd like some satisfaction for my remarks, I'd be glad to accompany you behind the barracks tonight, bucko."

Martin seemed to ignore the remarks and kept talking to Karl. The German for the first time was quietly observing Martin and wondering if he had any guts. He was asking himself, "Is he afraid of this loudmouth, and why doesn't he respond?" In Karl's mind if he was to be his friend, he must react with strength to any challenge or threat.

Karl decided to bait Martin to see his reaction. Looking over at the loudmouth Irishman, the German said, "My Irish friend, I'll be more than delighted to accompany you tonight." And the Irish lad laughed at him.

"You and your gutless friend together would probably only take up a few minutes of my time." The Irish lads again started to laugh.

Karl said to Martin, "If you don't meet him tonight, he will think you're afraid of him, and from now on he will bully you. It is best, my friend, always to nip the challenges in the bud."

"Karl," Martin replied. "I don't like myself when I get angry. When I get angry, I have no control, and I'm capable of anything. So I choose to walk away from the confrontation."

Karl shook his head. "Well I'm sorry to say, Martin, this is not the German way of thinking. I believe the meek shall inherit the earth, but six feet under." Martin broke out laughing, and he put his arms around Karl's shoulders in a gesture of friendship.

That night Martin was reading in his bunk when one of the lads rushed in and told him there was a great fight behind the barracks. Martin knew what it was about but continued reading. He was about to put down the book and go to sleep when the barracks exploded with shouts and loud banging as they busted in. They were shouting about Karl and the young Irishman who had fought behind the barracks. Both men were covered with blood, and what Martin couldn't understand was why the German and the Irishman had their arms around each other as if they were comrades. Karl spoke first. "This lad can fight, and if all the Irishmen are like him, then this war will be over quickly."

Before turning in to bed, the young Irish lad went over to Martin's bunk. "I'm not finished with you yet. You're a disgrace to all of Galway. This German is a better man than you, and the first chance I get, I'll have a go at you."

Martin looked at him and said, "I'm not going to lose any sleep over it," and turned over in his bunk.

The Irishman would have hit him, but a few of the lads restrained him. "He's not worth hitting," one of the Irish lads said. "Go to bed. Tomorrow is a long day."

The following week they marched off for Ciempozuelos.

I have not forgotten thee

Contessa

chapter three

he Irish Brigade entered Ciempozuelos and took over the Moroccans' positions. They were immediately bombarded by the Republican artillery. To defend Ciempozuelos the Irish had to construct a defensive position that would be able to protect the town and enable them to observe the enemy's position, both north and south. As the fifteenth battalion dug in at Ciempozuelos, so did the whole Nationalist army along the entire battle line. One of the German auxiliary forces moved a battalion of big millimeter guns into the woods. The commanding German officer asked for an Irish platoon to guard the guns. Martin and Karl were members of that platoon. Each night after standing watch, Martin and Karl would sit around the campfire discussing the day's events.

One night Martin noticed that Karl had literally disappeared. Martin turned in early that evening but was awakened by Karl in the middle of the night. Karl sat next to his bunk and told him that he had met with the German General Von Stuben. Martin cleared his eyes from the sound sleep he had been in.

"What the hell are you talking about, Karl?"

"I will tell you something that I would ask you not to repeat. Yes, I am a volunteer just like yourself, but I am also an undercover German intelligence officer observing how this war is being fought." That caught Martin's immediate attention. "What do you know about our Führer, Adolf Hitler?" Karl asked Martin.

Martin replied, "Not too much. He doesn't get great coverage in Ireland."

They both started laughing. Karl continued, "He is a remark-able man who will lead Germany to great victories."

Martin studied Karl for a few moments and then spoke, "Victories over whom?"

"I can tell you he has plans to eliminate your old enemy England."

Martin smiled, "Well, he can't be that bad!"

Again they both laughed. "What do you want of me, my friend?" Martin said.

"After this war here is over, I will return to the Fatherland to accomplish an important assignment for the Reich, and I want you to come with me. I will see that you get your share of recognition. When Germany has defeated her enemies, you will want for nothing. This I promise you. I will always need someone to watch my back. Help me to attain my goals, my Irish friend. It will always be dangerous around me, for I have many enemies. There are men in Germany in high office who would like to see me eliminated. Will you be my eyes in the back of my head?"

Martin once again studied Karl's face as it reflected the light from the open tent. "Well, I was thinking of going back to Ireland after this war is over, but it has been very quiet over there now that the troubles have ended. Ah, what the hell? I'll have a go at it."

"Go at it?" Karl replied. "What does that mean?"

"It means," Martin said with a big Irish grin on his face, "that I will protect your ass."

The German started to laugh but quickly realized that they were disturbing the rest of the sleeping men. "We'll talk again," he said.

After a month of doing very little fighting, the Irish were ordered to attack the village of Titulcia. It proved to be heavily for-tified with many machine gun posts. Some of the machine guns were located on the crests of cliffs, and some were in caves. It was defended by elite Communist troops. It was during the fighting that Karl and Martin's platoon was pinned down by machine-gun fire. Karl could see that the forward machine gun nest had them direct-ly in their fire and was inflicting heavy casualties on them and that the platoon would have to advance or be wiped out. Without a word, Karl jumped up from his prone position and charged the machine gun nest with his bayonet, killing or wounding the entire machine gun crew. Martin followed him into the nest yelling, calling him "the craziest bastard that ever lived." While they stood there arguing with each other over the folly of Karl's charge, one of the wounded Republicans started firing at them. Martin flung himself in front of Karl to save him. The bullet meant for Karl hit Martin in the back. Karl was also hit in the arm but managed to put the wounded Republican soldier out of action with his rifle. The medics found Karl holding Martin in his arms. They had difficulty trying to get Karl separated from Martin.

"You crazy Irish bastard," he kept saying.

Martin could barely speak but was aware that they were loading him on the stretcher. Very quietly he said to Karl, "You told me to watch your ass, *dummkopf.*"

The stretcher-bearers were amused at the two wounded men giving out to each other. This war was over for both of them. The two men were sent to an army hospital in Madrid. Karl was up and around in a few days. His wound was not serious, but unfortunately it became infected, and it took a little longer for it to heal. Martin was hit in the back, but the bullet didn't pierce any of his vital organs. It went through his shoulder and out the other side.

A German in a dark business suit visited Karl one afternoon. Anyone could see from his bearing that he was a German military man. "*Guten Morgen,*" he addressed Karl, who was reading a local paper at the time. "You can read in Spanish, Leutnant Gunter?"

"Yes," Karl replied. "I studied it at the university."

"That was at Heidelberg University, was it not Leutnant?"

Karl had been given the proper password, and he replied, "Yes, it was quite a nice place."

The German pulled over the chair to get closer to Karl so he could talk to him quietly. "In a few days a German ship will be taking you home. You will receive the name of this ship in good time. You are to board her…."

Karl quickly interrupted the German before he had finished. " I have not finished my assignment here," he protested.

The German looked at him in a menacing manner. "You will do what you are ordered to do. *Verstehen Sie?*" Then changing his mannerisms, the German seemed to realize that he had over-reacted to Karl. "I bring you greetings from your uncle, Field Marshal Gunter."

"How is my dear Uncle?" Karl replied.

"He is in excellent health and awaits your return to Berlin."

"I have become friendly with an Irish Nationalist. He saved my life at Titulcia. He will prove to be a very valuable asset to Germany. He has courage, loyalty and a hatred for the English. It seems that during the Irish revolt against the British, his grandfather was shot by the English for no apparent reason. The British were taking hostages for an attack on their barracks. His grandfather was one of them. He will prove to be my good right arm."

Day after day Martin lay quietly on his Spanish hospital bed that proved to be very uncomfortable. He suggested to one of his doctors that the bed would make an excellent device to torture the Communist prisoners. It was obvious that he could not draw a laugh from that statement. All he ever got was a deadly stare that would have eliminated the crew of a machine gun nest.

One day Martin was awakened by someone behind him, but he couldn't see who, so he couldn't identify the figure. Soft hands started to untie his hospital gown. Although the hands were soft, they were strong, and they definitely belonged to a woman.

A musical voice spoke softly into his ear. "I'm going to change your bandages, so please lie quietly. I don't wish to hurt you unnecessarily. It is a bad wound."

What seemed to be forever and very painful was probably only about ten minutes. Anxiously he tried to see his tormentor. Turning on his side, he was met with a pair of dazzling dark Spanish eyes. Try as he may he could not see her full face and was forced to lie back on his stomach once again.

"Do not try to move, my brave soldier, you will reopen the wound." Then she walked away.

A few days later when Martin was finally able to sit up, the girl with the haunting voice reappeared. Walking towards him, she carried a tray of food. Even from a distance, she was a beauty. She sat down next to him and without a word started to feed him. Martin couldn't take his eyes off her. She raised a spoon containing hot potato soup to his lips, showing no expression on her face. Martin noted every feature of her face. He had never seen such perfectly chiseled features on any woman before. Her raven hair hung softly around her shoulders, and it had a silky shine to it that would light up a dark room at night. She had a perfectly straight nose that at the very end of it tipped upwards. Martin had never seen skin as white anywhere except on the Irish girls in Ireland. This beauty was their equal. Even her dark black eyebrows were tailored to fit her brow. He had yet to see her smile, and he awaited this moment with anticipation. Aware that she was being stared at, she smiled, both cheeks exposing her dimples that surrounded a small sensitive mouth. Her white even teeth reminded Martin of the Irish girls back home. Martin had always thought no woman ever smiled like an Irish woman. Once again he was surprised at what he had seen.

"Well," Martin said, "you are the best looking woman I have ever seen since I left old Ireland."

She said, "Haven't you met some nice Spanish girls since you arrived in Spain?"

"I have," Martin replied, "but not one of them could hold a candle to the Irish woman."

She smiled and said, "I suspect you are very prejudiced about your Irish girls."

"Ah," Martin said, "you'll have to come over to Ireland and see for yourself."

She reached over his shoulder and untied his hospital gown and started to remove it. Martin's reaction was quick. "Easy woman," he said. "Where I come from, the men do their own undressing."

She smiled at him. "Well, you're not in Ireland now, and I'm the boss here." Removing the gown completely, she stared into his face which reminded her of something she had read about the planet Mars. It was supposed to be completely red. Taking her washcloth she began to wash Martin. There was no doubt about it. She was teasing him with provocative washing. Finally she moved towards his lower body with the washcloth. Looking at him and seeing the anxiety on his face, she laughed aloud and threw the washcloth at him. Then she reached over and placed his face between her hands and kissed him.

"I think," she said, "that you are a special kind of man." Then she turned and walked away.

Martin remained in the bed with no hospital gown, and he was freezing, cursing and damning his nurse for all he was worth. Finally she returned with a clean hospital gown, and once again she started laughing. She bent over him and placed her hand across his mouth.

"There are others here besides you."

"Ah, go to hell!" Martin said, and he stopped talking.

During the next few days, they never exchanged a word. The time was drawing near for Martin to be discharged. The day before he said goodbye to Karl Gunter, they agreed to meet in Berlin, Germany, when Martin was released from the hospital.

Martin began his therapy, and part of it was walking around the hospital grounds for a few hours every day. His very attentive nurse performed her duties like a well-trained professional. Yet there was a tension between them that filled the air. Neither spoke very much to the other.

The day before he left, Martin sat fully dressed in the warm Spanish sun. Before he knew it, she was sitting down next to him on the arm of his chair. "I'm leaving tomorrow," she said, "and I'd like to say goodbye to you. I'm sorry we couldn't have become better friends."

Martin looked at her with a sinking feeling inside. He felt lost. He didn't understand these feelings that came over him. It was something he had never experienced before. He couldn't quite describe it. He wondered what kind of a hold that this woman had over him. Martin chose his words carefully.

"Where will you go?" he asked.

"Well, tomorrow I'm going into the city to do some shopping."

"I'm leaving also tomorrow," Martin replied. "I will be in the city too."

She smiled at him and placed her hand on his arm. "Well, maybe we could have lunch together. There is a small restaurant called El Toro's. Everyone knows it. I will meet you at 12 noon."

Martin barely touched the inside of her hand as she rose. "What is your name?"

"My name!" she said and shook her head. "I thought you would never get around to asking. My name is Contessa Garcia. What an unusual man you are! I'm beginning to understand now about the

Irish girls you speak of. God help them if you are the typical Irishman."

Once again Martin did not utter a sound. It was not what he usually expected to hear from a woman. "Will you be there or not?" he blurted out.

Again she disarmed Martin by bending down and kissing him on the forehead. "See you tomorrow," she said while turning around and walking away.

Contessa had walked about ten yards when she turned slowly and shouted out at him, "That's if you are in better humor than you are today!"

Martin left the following morning for the city center of Madrid. The hospital was in the suburbs of Madrid, and he hired a taxi to take him to the Alfonso Hotel. When he was being discharged from the hospital, he was given a note with the instructions that he would be contacted at the Alfonso Hotel at 10:00 a.m. Martin knew that this was Karl Gunter's contact for him. The arrangements were being made for him to leave Spain for Germany. During his ride to the hotel, he was thinking about his meeting with Contessa. Nothing now seemed more important to him than meeting her. When he got to the hotel, it was about 9:45, so he was early. He ordered breakfast at the hotel. It seemed to him that the restaurant was empty. Martin hated the hospital food and was anxious to eat a good breakfast. First of all he couldn't read the menu as it was in Spanish, and from the looks of it there wasn't anything near an Irish breakfast. Boy, how he missed the old brown bread, sausages and eggs in the morning. The waiter came to take his order and between hand signals and half Spanish and half English words he managed to order a cup of coffee and two slices of toast with some fruit tossed in. After breakfast he reached for his old pipe, but it was not there. Then he remembered that it had been lost when the medics were putting him on the stretcher at Titulcia.

"Oh," he thought, "this is the ultimate in suffering." For Martin no pipe after his meals would surely finish him. Sitting there at the table with no smoke, he was going through the tortures of the damned. From time to time as he had recuperated in the hospital, he had moments of need for a smoke, but this need had developed on a grand scale as he left the hospital. He was aware of a figure standing over him at his table. Looking up, he saw a face that was familiar to him although he had only seen it once. It was the German who had come to see Karl Gunter in the hospital, the one who walked with that military bearing.

"*Wie geht's?*" the German said.

"I'm fine," Martin replied. "How is Karl?"

The German seemed surprised. "You know about me and Karl?" he said.

Martin replied, "Only that I saw you in the hospital with Karl."

The German sat back in the chair and proceeded to light up a large cigar. "Would you like one?" he asked.

"No," Martin said. "What I need, you don't have."

The German smiled. "Maybe I have," and he bent over handing a small box to Martin.

Looking at the German, Martin took the box from him and opened it. He couldn't believe his eyes! It was his pipe, and with it was a note from Karl. It read, "I know you couldn't live without this pipe. When they were loading me on the stretcher, I saw it on the ground and asked the medic to give it to me. I waited to give it to you until now so that you would think of me and remember that I saved your most precious possession. Now you owe me."

Martin laughed but he couldn't wait to fill his pipe with tobacco, which to his surprise the German handed him. Sighs of joy came from Martin, as his lips puffed away like a steam engine on his old pipe. Seeing that Martin was completely relaxed, the German proceeded with his instructions for Martin.

"We are not going to be able to get you out directly from Spain to Germany. We will have to leave via Morocco. When I have finalized your transportation to Germany, I will contact you. You will stay in this hotel until that time. We will take care of all your hotel expenses." He handed Martin a white envelope. "You may use this for any other additional expenses."

The German stood up from the table and, looking at Martin with the most intense frown, he pointed his finger at him. "Be careful. Stay out of any trouble. We will meet again only when I have everything finalized."

Martin could have let this go with him, but he didn't like the way that the German was pointing his finger at him in a threatening manner. "Is it necessary to talk to me in that way?" Martin asked.

The German's reply was without hesitation "I am familiar with you Irish. You are not the most disciplined lot, and when a German officer gives you a command, you will obey it without question. *Verstehen Sie?*"

The blood rushed to Martin's head. "I wasn't aware I was speaking to a German officer. You looked more like a funeral director to me." Standing up face to face to the German, Martin put his finger up to his face. "Where I come from, you wouldn't be standing very long if you spoke like that to one of my people. However I am a peaceful sort of man, so I won't push this any further. Be careful when you meet with me again."

The German smiled. "We will meet again. I am a German. We consider this an offense, and this calls for a challenge to a duel of which by the way I have had quite a few. So my Irish friend, I will be looking forward to seeing you in Germany." With a click of his heels, the German was gone.

It was getting close to noon, and Martin was told that the El Toro was only a few blocks from where he was, so off he went at a quick pace that even surprised himself. Martin never rushed anywhere. He found himself unusually excited. "What the hell is wrong with you, Martin?" he said to himself. "She is only another woman." Martin arrived at the restaurant at exactly 12 noon. His heart sank inside of him. She wasn't there. The *maitre d'* approached and asked him if he would like to be seated at a table. Martin replied, "A table for two, please." It was a table at the restaurant window that faced the main street. The table gave Martin a full view of the activity that occurred on the street. The waiter came over to take his order, and Martin explained that he was waiting for someone. Meanwhile he ordered a cup of tea. The time to Martin seemed like it was hanging, yet there was no sign of Contessa. The waiter brought Martin his tea, and Martin asked him for the time. It was 12:20. Martin took a sip of the tea and nearly spit it out. This brought the waiter back.

"Is there anything wrong?" he asked.

Martin said, "Since I have been in Spain, I haven't had a decent cup of tea. Spanish tea tastes as if you washed your socks in it." The waiter spoke little English so he was not quite sure what Martin had said to him.

Where she came from, Martin never knew. She just appeared in front of him. His head pounded as she sat down before him. Contessa was wearing a short white dress with a white voile scarf, which she wore around her neck like a choker. The dress was simple yet he thought that whatever that woman wore, it would not look simple.

"Well, my Irish friend," she said, "I'm starving. Let's eat." She ordered a salad with a fruit drink.

"I thought you were starving," Martin asked.

She smiled at him and said, "Oh, I'm hungry, but I must keep my figure. How else could I get those wounded boys at the hospital to take their medicine?"

Martin was just staring at her. He had not yet composed himself. Every move she made, he watched with great interest. "Will you stop it," Martin kept saying to himself. "Why are you acting like a lovesick schoolboy?" His answer came when he happened to look around the restaurant room. There wasn't a man in the restaurant who wasn't looking at her.

Contessa finished her salad and looked directly into Martin's eyes. "You have the most beautiful blue eyes I have ever seen in a man. Are these the famous Irish eyes that are smiling?"

"Ah," Martin said, "I don't know what kind of eyes they are. They are the only ones my Ma gave me."

They both laughed, and it eased the tension between them. "Why would I not believe," she asked, "they are not your father's eyes?"

"The old bastard didn't have eyes. He had slits in his head."

"Ah," she said, "I see your father is not one of your favorite people. Tell me what he is like?"

Martin became tense, and she could see it. "I don't want to talk about him, you understand." She didn't press the conversation.

Martin had not ordered any food since he'd had his breakfast at the hotel. The waiter had brought him over a bowl of mixed fruit and while he was eating it, he happened to look up and caught

Contessa studying his face as if it were the first time she had seen it. Martin became very uneasy. Sensing his mood, Contessa reached across the table and caught hold of his hand.

"Martin," she asked, "have you ever made love to a woman?"

Well, if Martin could have disappeared from the face of the earth at that moment, he would have done so. "What in the name of Heaven is wrong with you, woman? I have never met anyone like you before. You ask the damnedest questions." Martin sat back in his chair and looked at Contessa. "Why," he asked, "are you so interested in my love life?"

"Well, I think, Martin, you have led a sheltered life. This is not Ireland," she said.

"You're damned right!" said Martin. "This is not the kind of every day conversation that is an Irish girl's priority. The Irish girls have a certain reserve about them that is known as class."

She rose quickly from the table and said, "I suppose that means I have none!"

Martin followed her out of the restaurant. "Please," he said, "I didn't mean that. It's just that you confuse me, and I don't know how to respond to you. I must go back to the restaurant and pay for the lunch. Will you wait for me?"

"Yes," she said. "I will."

Martin returned after paying the restaurant bill. "Let's take a walk," he said. "I see a small park over there. Maybe we could sit and talk."

Contessa slipped her arm under his. To Martin it felt so natural and comfortable. It was as though she had always belonged on his arm. They began walking and talking, and soon they broke into laughter. Eventually she asked what his plans were and if he was going back to Ireland and if so, when? Martin told her that he had some business to complete and then he was on his way to Germany. She didn't pursue that route any further.

"How about you?" he asked. "Where are you going?"

"I will remain here for a while and continue in the service of General Franco in my current capacity as a nurse. That is my profession."

They stood for a while looking at each other. Once again she made the advances. She reached up and kissed him on his lips. "I am very much attracted to you, Martin," she said, "and I would like to make love to you. I may never see you again, and I would like to spend whatever time we have left together."

Martin was stunned. He had to be careful that he didn't set her off again. This wasn't the way his Catholic upbringing was all about. He believed in marriage and love, and these were not the rules that he was taught. It was not only himself who thought that way. The Irish volunteers who came to Spain with him remained aloof from the Spanish women. They were not womanizers. Hardly a week went by that they were not at Sunday Mass. It was not that he didn't desire Contessa. She was such a stunning beauty that any man would be a fool to let her go. To feel no passion for this woman would leave one to question one's manhood.

Contessa stood there with those dark Spanish eyes looking for a response. "Well," Martin said, "I am in the process of arranging my transport to Germany. It will take a few days. Where can I get in touch with you?"

She said, "I'll be staying at the Alfonso Hotel. Where will you stay?"

"I'm staying there, too," and he smiled.

"I must go now, Martin. I have to do the shopping that I told you about. What about dinner tonight?"

"Great," Martin said. "How about eight o'clock?"

"That will work out fine," she said.

"See you then!" Martin said as he watched her move away. His eyes focused on her until she disappeared. He was nervous about their meeting tonight. Martin was not ready for any affair. He had promised Karl that he would watch out for him in Germany. This appeared now to him to be much more difficult than he thought at first, but he had given his word.

It was well into the afternoon when Martin returned to the hotel. The humid Spanish sun had gotten to him, so he ran a bath that he soaked in for over an hour. He left only because the water had gotten cold. Tired, he lay across his bed and fell asleep. When he awoke, it was late in the evening. Looking at the clock in the room, it had just struck 7 p.m. He had slept for hours. He was to meet Contessa at 8 p.m. for dinner, so he must hurry and get dressed. The only clothing he had was his Blue Shirt army uniform.

There would be time to buy civilian clothes tomorrow with the money that the German had left him. Feeling well rested and refreshed from his bath, he waited for Contessa in the lobby. Once again she was late. This annoyed the hell out of him. The annoyance left him quickly when he saw her coming toward him. She was attired in a short, black plain dress that fit her well-formed figure. She was dazzling in a Spanish black shawl that covered her shoulders. Martin smiled. It wasn't the famous Galway shawl that the songs were sung about, but after all she was Spanish and not Irish.

"Good evening," he said with a big Irish grin.

And she replied in Spanish, *"Buenas noches* to you, kind sir."

The waiter seated them at a table near a small dance floor. Martin noticed for the first time a small three-piece band in the corner of the room. "Good God," he said. "I hope I don't have to listen to that wild Spanish music. It gives me a headache."

Contessa was taken aback at his remark. She was angry, and looking at him directly, she let out a barrage of Spanish phrases that Martin knew couldn't be any form of flattery about him. "Is there nothing about me that pleases you? We are always in conflict." Martin felt bad and touched her hand.

"Please," he said, "this may be our last night, and I don't want us to part on bad terms." The music started, and the band played a slow Spanish air.

"Let's dance," Contessa said. "This melody should be to your liking. After all, these are the tunes my old grandfather used to dance to." Laughingly, she pulled him up from his seat, and before he knew it, he was on the dance floor. It didn't take Contessa long to realize that Martin couldn't dance. Very discreetly, she remained on the one spot, swaying back and forth, giving the impression they were dancing. Contessa brought her whole body as close as she could to Martin. She rested her head on his shoulder, and the scent from her freshly washed hair led Martin to forget he was on the dance floor. The warmth of her body next to him stirred up feelings he had never experienced before. She reached up on her toes and gently kissed him on the ear. Her feet performed this easily enough, especially as she was standing still on the dance floor.

Martin became conscious of other people around them and gently escorted her off the dance floor to their table. Martin told

Contessa to order the meal, which she did with the expertise of a woman who was very familiar with eating at the right places. A bottle of Spanish wine came immediately to the table and was opened by the waiter. The Irish volunteers didn't have a fond affection for the Spanish wines. As a matter of fact, there was no great love for the Spanish food, drink or customs. Spain's national pastime, the bullfights, appalled the Irish volunteers. They thought that the sport gave the bull no fair chance.

Martin waited in anticipation for the coming of his meal. After two glasses of wine it finally arrived. Martin couldn't make head nor tail of what was on his plate. Afraid to insult Contessa any further, he bravely attacked the unidentified mass of colored substance. "What in the hell is this I'm eating?" he said to himself. "Oh, it's killing me! I'm going to choke to death. My mouth's on fire. Merciful God, deliver me from this, and I promise I'll say the rosary tonight in gratitude for Your divine mercy."

He was brought out of his pain by Contessa's voice. "Do you like it, Martin? It's one of my favorites."

"Oh, it's grand," said Martin, choking on his words. Martin reached over for the pitcher of water and began to drink directly from it. This was a matter of some concern to Contessa. Her first thoughts were that the Irish used the pitcher to drink directly from, or maybe that Martin, being a country boy, had very unusual table manners. At any rate, it left her looking around the room somewhat embarrassed.

By now the Spanish wine had loosened Martin up. Contessa noticed he was talking less seriously than usual, and she began to enjoy his lighthearted conversation. He was making her laugh with the stories he was telling about his family in Ireland. The night passed quickly, but not before she got Martin up to dance again, this time to a lively Spanish folk dance. Martin took to this dance since it was as close as he could get to his beloved set dances in Ireland.

The night ended, and Martin brought her to her room. At the door she placed her arms around his neck, and this time she kissed him with great feeling. Martin was trying gently to back away from this long and passionate kiss. Contessa moved from his lips to his ear, breathing warmly into it. Softly she spoke, and at the same time she handed him the key to her room. "Please."

Martin thought to himself, "Well, that's the end of it, and at least I didn't make a fool of myself." But the night was not over for this Spanish beauty. Martin unlocked her door and turned around to Contessa to hand her the key, but she had proceeded to maneuver him into the room. In the dark room Martin could see the silhouette of her body against the light from her window. Warmly she kissed him, this time with her open mouth. Martin's head was spinning, not only from Contessa's kisses but also from the Spanish wine that didn't do much for his equilibrium. Martin became helpless while Contessa led him through the surrender of his youthful virginity.

The light from Contessa's window woke Martin in the morning. His eyes were full of sleep, and all he could make out was a head of dark black hair next to his pillow. He reached over and kissed her on the shoulder. It woke her, and she rolled over on her back. Looking at Martin, she smiled. "Well, how is my mucho, mucho lover this morning?" Martin wasn't quite sure if she was mocking him. Before last night Martin knew nothing about the art of lovemaking. Oh, he had three sisters, and from time to time he was made aware of the female body, but that was the extent of his knowledge about the opposite sex.

Martin was plagued with doubt about himself, not only with his sex life, but himself in general. Martin had always felt he was a loner, even when he was young. It always seemed difficult for him to be accepted by his school pals. No matter how he tried, he couldn't seem to get in with the crowd. When he grew up and played hurling, even then he was not accepted by the boys. The girls used to laugh at him and whisper in each other's ears about him. He never did find out what they were whispering about.

In school he was not a bad student, but he never excelled in any of the subjects. The only sure and confident ability that he possessed that no one could take away from him was that he was a fine hurler. When he was out on that open field, he was second to none. Running with the little ball on the top edge of the stick towards the goal, the wind blowing in his face and the bodies running beside him trying to take the ball from him, was the only time he felt himself alive and needed. Oh yes, the team needed Martin to put that little ball over the bar. The only time he was looked upon as a somebody was when he was playing hurling.

Martin's trips to the fields in Connemara were always alone and soul searching, always asking himself, "What is wrong with me? I don't seem to think like anyone else. Why are my thoughts different from the rest of the boys?" The old fellah would come into his thoughts. "How much," he asked himself, "has this man influenced my life?" Surely he couldn't blame him for his not getting along with the boys. Yet the hounding and constant bullying must have affected him somehow. Martin, after a little while, would dismiss these thoughts and would come to the conclusion that no one could blame someone else for what they turned out to be. Oh, surely these individuals have to a certain degree some effect on one's life, but at the end of the day you make the final decision on what kind of person you turn out to be.

Martin seemed to have one contact that he always felt close to, and when at the end of the day all had failed him, he turned to the One above all Who understood him, his God.

Martin rose and dressed quickly, not daring to look at Contessa for he felt ashamed of himself for what had happened. He would have to go to church to square it with his God. Finally Martin looked across the room at Contessa who had just come out from under the covers. He couldn't pull his eyes away from her naked body. She was a magnificent beauty. Contessa sensed his embarrassment and put on her clothing. "Martin, Martin," she said as she moved towards him. "I think you should have been a priest. What are you doing over here in this war and in the middle of all the temptation that accompanies the uncertainties of war?" Standing there fully dressed with her ruffled dark hair scattered all over her face and shoulders after coming out of the bed, she was beautiful. Martin knew at that moment he would never love anyone else again.

They ate breakfast in silence, Martin with deep dark thoughts to himself. When breakfast was over, Contessa asked Martin if he would like to go for a walk, which they did. It wasn't long before they passed a church. "Contessa," he asked, "would you like to go in with me?"

Martin noticed an unusual look that came over her face. He just couldn't make it out. "No," she replied, "you go ahead. I'll wait here for you."

As Martin walked to the altar, his thoughts ran away with him. Why did she refuse to come into the church? That seemed very strange to Martin. Kneeling before the altar, he spoke with his God. "I am very confused at this point, my God. I love this woman, but I know in Your eyes I have done wrong." Even then he couldn't take his mind off Contessa, so he blessed himself and left the church. Outside, his eyes moved in all directions, but try as he may, he couldn't find her. She had completely disappeared, and panic set in on him. Was she mad at him for going to church? Or maybe she was just sick and tired of his adolescent ways. She had spent the night with someone who was supposed to act like a man and didn't.

Martin made for the hotel. "That's where she's probably gone," he thought. "She got tired of waiting for me."

The hotel was not very far from the church, and Martin increased his pace. He was in view of the hotel when a voice behind him called his name. It was the German contact from Karl. "My friend, what's your rush? Sit down here on this bench with me. I would like to talk to you. It's very important." Martin wasn't in any mood for this man. He had to find Contessa, but he sat as requested. "I have news for you, my Irish friend." The German had made arrangements for him to leave Spain on a Spanish private boat that night for Morocco.

Martin started blabbering to the German that he wouldn't be ready tonight. He had some difficult chores to complete before he left. Annoyed, the German said, "You will go tonight. Otherwise it will be another week before I can make the arrangements again." Martin was very anxious to tell the German what to do with himself, but he had made his promise to his friend.

Martin reasoned that Contessa would be at the hotel, and he would straighten out the problems he had with her, so there would be no problem making the ship tonight. "What time are we leaving?" he asked.

"I will meet you at twelve o'clock tonight at the docks. There is a red building over there," and he pointed to a red building in the area towards the docks. "Meet me behind there at twelve. Do not bring your uniform. Stop in now at one of the stores and purchase some work clothes."

Martin was surprised at his remarks. The German had told him he was going on a private vessel. "It'll be much better to be wearing work clothes if you are stopped," he said. "They will assume you are a seaman aboard ship."

Martin asked, "Where will we dock in Morocco?"

"There are many places along the Morocco coast that are open for illegal crossing. I will see you tonight, Martin. Remember, twelve o'clock sharp."

Martin couldn't wait to leave the German. Moving at a lively pace, he got to the hotel. Racing up the hotel stairs, he headed for Contessa's room. The door was unlocked, and Martin walked into the room. It was empty. Looking in the clothes closet, there were no clothes on the hangers. Opening one drawer after the other, he found them all empty. He wouldn't let himself believe she had gone. Racing down to the hotel desk, he inquired of the clerk if he knew the whereabouts of Miss Contessa Garcia. "Her room is vacant," he explained to the clerk.

The clerk replied, "Miss Garcia checked out about an hour ago."

"Did she leave a forwarding address or a note for a Mr. Martin Connolly?"

"No, she left no note," the clerk said. "She just paid her bill and left."

Martin was stupefied. He walked over to one of the lobby chairs and sunk into it. Why, he thought? Did he offend her with his church visit? No, it couldn't be that. She promised to wait for him outside the church. Maybe it was the different events of the night. But he couldn't come up with a reason for Contessa's strange behavior.

He went to his room and lay across the bed and quickly fell asleep. It was about 11 p.m. when Martin awoke. He had failed to buy the work clothes as the German had told him. "The German will be angry with me," he thought, "for not following his orders. To hell with him," Martin said. He had brought over from Ireland an old sweater that he put on. A pair of beige slacks his mother had given him for his last birthday would be fine along with his brown-laced shoes. Everything else he had, he rolled up and tossed down the hotel laundry chute.

Arriving about five minutes to twelve, Martin waited for the German. Precisely at twelve o'clock the German appeared. "You seem to have trouble understanding orders," the German said. "Arriving before the designated time leaves you open for observation. It creates suspicion in the authorities' minds about why are you hanging around and whom are you waiting for at this hour of the night. I also told you to buy work clothes, not this mismatch of clothing you're wearing.

All Martin said was, "F__ off for yourself."

"I will be looking forward to meeting with you in Germany, my Irish friend. There I will take this Irish cockiness out of you. We Germans know how to deal with troublemakers like yourself." Martin just smiled at him.

As they spoke, a small craft pulled alongside the dock, opposite the red brick building that was about a hundred yards from the dock. "Come on," the German insisted. "We don't want to be spotted." They raced for the craft. Jumping aboard, they were out of sight in a few minutes heading for Morocco.

"What's all this secrecy?" Martin inquired of the German. "The Irish Brigade is about to be broken up, and we'll all be returning to Ireland very soon. So why are you smuggling me out?"

"We have plans for you, Mr. Connolly, and we don't wish at this time for your whereabouts to be known. We would prefer for our own reasons that you are thought of as being still in Spain." As he stood on the deck of this fast-moving craft, Martin wondered would he ever see Contessa again. As the Spanish coast moved slowly away from his sight, he felt the soft taste of her kiss on his mouth.

They were about a half an hour out when Martin, who had remained on the deck, noticed that the engines were slowing down and after a short while came to a full stop. Within a few minutes he noticed a disturbance in the water. There was no moon, and it was pitch dark. He could barely make out what was going on. It looked like the water was trying to part. "No," he thought again, "something is rising out of the water." He could barely see a small structural object breaking the surface. It grew bigger and bigger, and finally grew into what seemed to be a large craft in the water. "What do you know about that?" Martin thought. "It's a submarine." Martin's craft started up again and moved towards the submarine. Eventually it pulled alongside of the sub. There seemed to be a lot of commotion on his craft, men hurrying back and forth. Martin was surprised to see the hatch open. There were a number of uniformed men who came out of the sub and onto the deck. Lines were being thrown to the men from the crew of his craft.

Martin was taken out of his preoccupied trance with the submarine when his German companion came up to him and whispered in his ear, "We will board this submarine which will take us to Germany."

Martin looked at him. "What happened to Morocco? Am I so important that I am to be taken to Germany by submarine?"

The German smiled at him, "You're a bigger fool than I thought you were if you believe this submarine is for you. It is carrying very important cargo. It was decided to take you along with it. My friend, you will find that everyone is expendable to the Fatherland. Get ready. We're about to board it."

In about fifteen minutes the German and Martin had boarded the submarine. The disturbance of the water caused the German to lose his footing and fall between the sub and the craft. He was fished out quickly, and they were on their way. Martin was looking at him, and he looked like a drowned rat. The German could see that Martin was enjoying himself at his misfortune. "My Irish friend, my patience is growing short with you. I may not wait for our duel in Germany."

Martin moved towards the German. "Why are you wasting your breath with these threats? If you failed to show up without me, they would have your German nuts." The German nearly exploded, but he knew Martin was right.

Their trip to the port of Hamburg was many miles from Spain. Martin was allowed on deck for about an hour each night when the sub surfaced for air. The sub, Martin was told, was called the U-34 Schaefer, launched in 1936. It had a complement crew of 35 and could do 16 5/8 knots.

One night while heading for the tower, he passed by the open door of the captain's cabin. Martin looked in and saw a tall, gray-haired man standing alongside the captain, and on his left was a very small man. Both were engaged in conversation with the captain. Martin kept going and thought nothing of it, yet this was the first time he was aware of anyone aboard that sub except for the crew, himself, and his German friend.

The journey seemed to be very long and drawn out, and most of all, very confining. He spent most of his days and nights alone. His German friend hardly ever came in contact with him. Martin Connolly landed on German soil in late 1937 at the port of Hamburg. Two SS men in a long black car met him at the docks. They drove him directly to Berlin, and all the while they never spoke a word to him. Martin thought this was very odd and most unfriendly of them. He thought to himself that they didn't look to be the type that would enjoy a conversation. As a matter of fact it looked to him as though they did all their talking with clubs.

Leutnant Mueller

Fieldmarshal Gunter

chapteR fouR

Karl Gunter met Martin in the lobby of a four-story, white commercial building. They had their special training center on the first two floors. The first floor had a well-equipped gym with a stairwell that led to a small pistol range in the basement. The training director, Leutnant Mueller, had his offices on the second floor. The third and fourth floors were filled with commercial business offices. It was an excellent covert cover. The elevator would go directly to the third and fourth floors, and there were no stops at the first and second. The covert personnel would enter and leave through security doors at the rear of the building and use the stairs for access to the other floors.

Karl looked across the desk at Martin. "We will give you the best training that German intelligence could possibly give you. After I've finished here with you, Leutnant Mueller will brief you on the details, and then we have a couple of assignments for you. If you apply all we have taught you here, plus some strong instincts on how to handle the unexpected, you will do well, but this still will leave the odds against you. Martin, I have heard of this Irish luck. If what they say about it is true, then you will need every bit of it. It is my belief that luck plays a very important part in espionage.

"Your assignment is to return to your homeland in Ireland where you will prevent an Irishman named Sean McCarthy from delivering messages to the Russians. It has taken us nearly a year to find out who he really works for. We recruited him in Ireland because of his job. He is a seaman on the Holyhead ferry out of Dublin. He was to pass information on to us from our agents in

Ireland. Two of our agents that he helped smuggle out of Ireland were never seen again. He was to get them past the security in Holyhead as workers off the ferry. We know they got on the ferry, but they never got off. One of our deep cover agents has informed us that McCarthy is a double agent.

"In London we have an agent who works for British intelligence. His name is Olaf Pulaski. He is Polish and works as an interpreter in their code room in London. He is supposed to work for German intelligence, but we believe he is working for the Russians, too. You will get your instructions on how to neutralize him from Leutnant Mueller.

"Good luck, Martin. I know I can count on you." And he called in Leutnant Mueller, a young ramrod with the stand of a Prussian officer.

Mueller from the beginning had doubts about Martin Connolly. Martin appeared to him to be very ordinary with nothing special about him that gave Mueller the impression of confidence in him. A very important factor for espionage work is not to stand out in the crowd, nothing to indicate you are anything but what you appear to be. Mueller brought Martin to his office that was on the second floor of this four-story building. Sitting opposite Mueller, he noted he was wearing the Iron Cross, First Class.

"I see," Martin said, smiling at him, "you have done your bit for the Fatherland already."

"Yet," the German said, "there is much more to do, and we have many miles to go." He reached into one of his desk drawers and handed Martin two files with photos attached to them. "Study these men," he said. "Your life will depend on how much you can observe about them. Major Gunter, I'm sure, has given you the backgrounds on both men and what the assignment will be about. The next few months you will be put through a very rigorous program. When you leave here you will be in the best shape of your life and you will have received extensive training in small arms weapons, especially handguns. There will be no need to change your identity. All the documentation you have from serving in the Spanish Civil War is perfect. Your Irish passport will account for you staying in Spain after the war, and we can arrange that very easily with our friends over there. Your passport will well document the time you spent in Spain. Not to worry about it. We will also be able to account for where you worked during that time, and I'll have all this for you before you leave here. This will be very important to you in Ireland and England if you are to pass the security checks or if you are stopped and questioned. There should be no problem. This is your homeland, and it won't be easy to trap you on details from the land of your birth."

Martin was assigned to a very clean, comfortable room. He was by himself. It was not your usual German intelligence operation. There was no one there but himself. The physical training began at once, and the roadwork started at 5 a.m. the next morning. He ran up to five miles a day at the beginning, and in the last two weeks he was running between 10 and 12 miles a day. It was no bother to Martin, who was an athlete hurler,. The track work would be followed by hours of pistol shooting, and towards the end, a course in shooting with a silencer. He spent hours in the classroom going over his cover stories and detailed plans for the actual carrying out of his assignment.

At night he would go over the two agents' portfolios, and after a while he felt he had actually met them. Martin never left that building in Berlin for six weeks except to run in the morning. The track outside had been constructed with high walls around it. Martin ate his meals in a small cafeteria next to the gym. He never saw any of the other occupants of the building, and he was wondering how he was able to avoid the civilians eating in this cafeteria during their lunch hours. He was told that during his meals, the cafeteria was closed to anyone else in the building.

Martin also received some very special training in self-defense. He was not too fond of his instructor, a big bull of a German who kept tossing him around like a broken doll. It got so that Martin asked him one day, "You know, it looks to me like you enjoy yourself at my expense."

The German had never once smiled at him. He would come to the gym and proceed to knock the hell out of Martin. It was all commands with no talk in between. About the third week he informed Martin that from now on until he graduated, he would be trained in the art of killing his prey. At first Martin thought he was putting him on and started to joke about it. The German started to scream a long list of profanity in German, which Martin by now was proficient enough to understand. The German grabbed Martin by his throat, shoved him up against the wall and spoke to him in English. "You think this is some kind of a joke, you damned fool. I suppose you think you're going to Sunday school. I'm going to recommend you be dismissed from this program. You have no aptitude nor the mental capacity to pass this course." With that he left the gym.

Martin returned to his room. "What now?" he thought. "Ah, to hell with them all. If they don't want me, I'll go back to Ireland." At 6 p.m. that night Martin was summoned to Karl's office.

A very serious Karl Gunter greeted him at the door. "Sit down, Martin. I've gone out on a limb for you with the German High Command, and I understand you were making light of your training. This training may very well save your life. Maybe I have misjudged you. I need a man who will obey orders, and I can assure you that what you will accomplish by completing your assignment will be of great service to Germany. You do want Germany to defeat your natural enemy, Great Britain, don't you?"

Martin told Karl that the instructor was a head case. "He was talking about killing people."

Karl jumped up from his desk. "What the hell is the matter with you? What do you think you're here for?"

Martin looked at Karl and said, "You told me that I was to prevent these agents from operating. There was no talk about me killing them."

Karl could not believe his ears. Was Martin really that naïve or just stupid? "How did you believe you would accomplish this, Martin? Take them for walk and give them a ride on the merry-go-round and hope they would fall off?"

Starting to feel embarrassed, Martin could see that Karl was right. He should have understood what was expected of him. He rationalized to himself that his process of thinking was way off with the outside world. In the hills of Connemara, no one would ever think of killing anyone. Maybe it might happen in a fit of temper, but never deliberately. Planning to kill someone was not possible in the minds of the Connemara people. Their world was Catholic to the core, and they believed in every word that the Catholic Church told them. Martin was no different. He was devoted to his Church and believed thoroughly in what was taught. Did he not come over here to Spain to fight for the Church?

Karl was also thinking as he watched Martin across the desk. "I could lose him at this point. At this moment in time he is my only hope to complete this mission. No one would ever suspect him." So Karl decided to lie to him. "Listen. Go back and complete your training, and I promise that we'll find another way for you to stop these two men other than you having to kill them."

Martin felt at ease when he left Karl's office. After all, he trusted Karl. Karl was his friend.

Martin continued his training with the German self-defense instructor with great enthusiasm, sometimes giving the instructor second thoughts on this Irishman's strength. His courses became second nature to him towards the last few weeks of the program. There were some times when Martin even made the instructor look bad. The course ended, and he was prepared to leave. While he was packing his belongings, two of the instructors came into his room, and they both shook hands with him and wished him well. Standing back and clicking their heels, they smartly saluted with a "*Heil,* Hitler!" Martin did not know what to do after the salute, so he just stood there feeling foolish. Afterwards Leutnant Mueller came by to turn over to him the necessary documents he had promised him.

On his way to the car he felt a hand on his shoulder, and he turned to see his self-defense instructor with his hand out. "You will do well for the Fatherland," the German said. And with that Martin slipped under the German's outstretched hand, swinging him over his head and throwing him onto the sidewalk.

Martin was grinning from ear to ear. "Watch yourself with the Irish, boyo. We have long memories."

He entered the awaiting car and drove off to meet Karl in what appeared to be a sandstone building four stories high. The security was at its maximum. There were guards everywhere checking the papers of everyone who entered the building, even the generals. Martin met with a very jubilant Karl Gunter. "How are you, my friend? I'm pleased with your progress at the training school. Come, come. Sit down, Martin."

Martin noticed that Karl had been promoted to colonel. "I see you have done well for yourself, Herr Colonel."

Karl threw back his head and laughed. "Well, it's a lot better than being an advisor in Franco's army." And they both laughed. "Tell me, Martin. What happened to that little Spanish nurse you had big eyes for, *ja?*"

Martin wished he hadn't brought her up in this conversation. All the while on the submarine he had kept thinking of her. He was hoping for some distraction here in Germany. Karl could see that Martin wasn't having any of this conversation, so he suggested they go out to lunch.

Berlin was bustling with people. Walking along her streets, he noticed all the small sidewalk cafes were occupied with laughing and cheerful young people. There was a presence of many German uniforms. The city was alive with excitement. The stores were bright and well-lit, and Martin picked up the excitement himself. "What is it about this city, Karl?" Martin asked. "It makes me feel so up."

Karl was smiling at him. "It's not only the city, Martin. It's all of Germany. When Hindenburg died in 1934, Adolf Hitler became our president. And from then on Germany regained the dignity and honor we lost at the Treaty of Versailles. The Führer is doing wonderful things for Germany. Employment is up, and we Germans like to work, build and grow. The Führer will make us a strong Germany again."

For the first time Martin had reservations about the way Karl spoke of Germany. There was something in his voice that didn't sound sincere. It was almost as though he had rehearsed it. Martin brushed these thoughts away and got back into the pleasures of sitting at this table watching the large crowds going by. When they had arrived, the tables were all occupied, but when Karl showed the waiter some form of identification, an empty table magically appeared.

"My friend, after lunch we will go shopping at an unusual shop. It is not a German one, but a place that carries a brand of men's clothing that is very prominent in London. They carry a full selection of English and Irish clothing. As I have already informed you,

you will keep your Irish identity when you're in England and even in Germany. It's very important."

Martin asked him, "What part do you play in this new Germany?"

"I am a colonel in the Abwehr I, which is our intelligence group. We are under the command of naval Captain Wilhelm Franz Canaris. He became overall commander of the German navy, army, and air force intelligence at the age of forty-eight. The captain is a shy man, well liked, but do not fool yourself. This man will not show any weakness because of this shyness. At five foot four he is bigger in stature than most men of six foot or better. The captain speaks English, French and some Russian. Our office entrance is through an adjacent, four-story sandstone building at Tippitzuer on the north side of the Landwehr Canal. This is my permanent station. I use Leutnant Mueller's office for certain interviews and to oversee any intelligence operations that are of a special nature such as yours."

They finished lunch and headed for the English clothing shop where Martin would receive his Irish wardrobe. Approaching a very busy intersection, Martin suddenly stopped and pointed in the direction of a group of people heading towards a bus stop. "Karl, look," he said excitedly. "It's Contessa! It's her!" He started to run towards the bus stop and at the same time shouted her name. Karl ran after him, trying to restrain him, but it was to no avail. When Martin finally got to the bus stop, the bus had already left. Martin turned to Karl, who by now had caught up to him. "That was her!" he shouted excitedly. "I saw her. You must have seen her. It was her!"

Karl looked at Martin and smiled. "My Irish friend, you are having delusions. Forget her. She was a diversion at the time and nothing more."

Martin spoke very quietly to Karl, almost under his breath. "I love that woman, and there will never be another like her for me."

"Come, come, my friend," Karl said. "Let's go and purchase a brand new wardrobe for you."

Martin reluctantly moved away from the bus stop, but kept turning back, looking and hoping to see anything that would be a sign of Contessa.

The shop was crowded, but Karl produced his unusual identification, and they were immediately looked after. Karl could see that Martin couldn't care less for fine clothing, so he made Martin's decisions for him. Leaving the store, Karl put his arm around Martin's shoulders. "I can see," Karl said, "that you aren't much on fashion or the finer things in life."

"I'm a country boy," Martin replied, "and I don't give a good ball of goat's dung for your finer things in life."

Karl laughed. "What an odd expression about goat's dung. Where did you learn that?"

"I got that from my saintly mother," he said with sadness in his voice.

"She must be a jolly woman," Karl said. "Is she still living?"

"I don't know," Martin said. "The last letter I received was in training in Spain. As you well know, I'm not allowed to write. My father died not long ago. She took it badly."

"Well, maybe we can do something about that," Karl said. "Write your letter, and I'll see it's delivered to her by one of our couriers in Ireland."

"I hope it's not the one you want me to persuade to leave his present position!"

"No," Karl laughed. "We have other contacts, not necessarily agents." Martin's spirits rose after hearing this. "We have booked you at the Hotel Berlin. Remember that you're an Irish businessman trying to sell your cattle. You've been booked under your own name."

"What will I do?" Martin asked. "How will I spend my days here before I leave Germany?"

"We are making arrangements for you right now, but you must be patient. No one will bother you at the hotel. Remember, you're in Germany among your comrades."

The Hotel Berlin was a very comfortable place, not elegant, but clean and roomy. It was bustling with activity. Martin spent many hours sitting in the lobby watching all the goings on. It had its fair share of foreigners. At one time he was tempted to talk to an Irish couple who were over from Ireland on holidays, but he thought it over and realized that it was wiser to keep to himself. The sound of their Irish accents made him feel sad. He was reminded of the land of his birth.

Martin wrote a letter to his mother the next day. He found himself actually crying as he wrote the letter. "I'm terribly sorry that the old fellah died, not for myself but only because I know how much you will miss him. If I could come home, I would, but you know that I'm here in Spain fighting for our Church."

He felt a twinge knowing that he was lying to his mother for the first time. He stopped for a moment to take stock of himself. "I've certainly gone downhill," he thought. "The old fellah would have said, 'I knew it. You'd never be any good.'" Martin started to wonder maybe the old fellah saw something in him that he hadn't seen in himself.

Martin continued with his letter asking his mother how were his sisters and making inquiries on how the Galway senior hurling team was doing. "Oh, what I wouldn't give to belt that little ball over the bar!" His thoughts were running away from him, so he decided it would be best to end the letter and go to bed. He gave the letter to Karl the next morning in his office, and he thought no more of it. He had added a postscript to his letter, "When you answer this, Ma, don't attempt to mail it. It will be picked up by a special courier. This is wartime, you understand. You may tell anyone you like that you heard from me here in Spain." Again he lied, but he had to maintain appearances that he was still in Spain.

The days were growing long for Martin. He was waiting for his return to Ireland and further instructions on his assignment. He spent most of his nights sitting in the Hotel Berlin lobby watching the activity. One evening while he was having a drink, he glanced across the lobby and his heart sunk in his chest. There checking in was Contessa. He couldn't believe it. It was her that day after all at the bus stop. Moving across the lobby, he kept bumping into anyone that got in his way. "She's not going to get away from me this time," he thought. As he approached her, he noticed she was wearing the uniform of a German nurse. He came behind her and gently placed his hand on her wrist. She turned and looked at him with those dazzling dark eyes. He thought his heart would stop. "God, what a beautiful woman she is!" Martin thought. He was made aware of the presence of a German officer by her side. He hadn't noticed that before with all the excitement that he was caught up with at the time.

Politely she introduced him to the German officer. "This is Colonel Weiss. He is a medical officer with the German Wehrmacht, and this is an old friend of mine from Ireland, Martin Connolly." The colonel clicked his heels.

"It is apparent you are, of course, Irish."

"Yes," Martin said. "I'm afraid so."

"Ah," the German replied. "You have excellent hospitality in Dublin. I was there as an exchange student years ago. I lived there with the Irish, and they constantly made me laugh."

"I believe that," Martin said. "They even make the cows in Connemara split a gut."

The German wasn't quite sure he understood Martin. He believed his own English wasn't that good, and he probably missed the point.

Martin, of course, being Irish, could not resist pulling his leg. Impatiently, Martin tried to end his conversation with the German so he could be with Contessa alone. However, she seemed to be in no hurry. Suddenly, a disturbing thought came over him. Maybe she was registering with the Colonel. Unable to hold back this awful anxiety about her presence in the hotel, he finally blurted out. "Will you have a drink with me?" he asked her.

She turned to the colonel. "Would you like to join us?"

Martin held his breath.

"No thank you," the colonel said. "I want to unpack. I have many things to do."

Martin said to himself, "And I hope one of these things that you will do is to get pneumonia tonight."

Martin found a small table in the back of the room. "Let's sit down here," he said. He couldn't help but notice how trim she looked in her uniform. "Well, he said, "what are you doing here?" She seemed quite reserved, not at all like she was in Spain. She was more loveable when she looked at him with amusement at the things he would say and do, and her laughter had disappeared. She told him she had been wounded in the front lines after she had volunteered for the Spanish National Army after he had left Spain. And it was there that she met Colonel Weiss who offered her a commission in the German Army nurse's corps. She accepted and was now studying at the Berlin Medical University in Berlin. Once again Martin was blunt.

"What's with you two? Are this Kraut colonel and you lovers?"

Contessa's face turned white with Spanish temper. "And if we are, it's none of your damn business."

Martin became angry. "It's you the one that left me at the church that day in Spain."

The remark hit them both at the same time, and they both started to laugh. The laughter turned into serious looks at each other. They both knew it was time to go. He directed her to his room, and when they were in the room, he placed her directly with her back to the door. He kissed her gently on the mouth which she returned with such passion that he thought that the temples in his head would burst. Hours later, while she lay in his arms, Contessa told him how much she loved him. This time she was impressed with his great enthusiasm for making love.

"It looks to me like you've been practicing, Martin," she laughed.

He became offended. "I've never felt this way about any other woman but you," he said. "Don't mock me."

Contessa looked at him and realized that he was quite serious, so she stopped the teasing.

Martin was wondering where were the wounds she told him about in the lobby. He could see none. "Oh, why worry about that. I'm such an ass looking for trouble. Besides, who gives a damn. This woman most men would give their left arm to make love to."

Contessa received a seven-day pass from the German Wehrmacht, and Martin got Karl to grant him the time off to be with Contessa. Renting a car, Contessa drove around Berlin showing the sights to Martin. It was obvious to him that she hadn't been there long herself. As she drove to the prominent points of interest, she seemed to hesitate, and he noticed that she was constantly referring to the brochures. Martin said nothing about this, but it got him wondering. What was the reason for her trying to give him the impression she had been here for months when it was obvious she had never been there before?

They spent every waking hour together, day and night. Martin was clearly very much in love with Contessa, and she in turn was showing him every ounce of affection she possessed. Holding hands, walking along the countryside, they spoke of plans to come after the war. She expressed her love for Germany and how important it was for him to complete his mission, reinforcing at every moment the need for him to do a good job for Karl Gunter, whom he had identified to her as an Abwehr officer of importance.

They actually all met one evening for dinner. Martin waited patiently at his table at the Hotel Berlin for Contessa. They were to meet Karl Gunter at 8 p.m. that night. She was late as usual, and Martin tried to control himself. "God, that woman is always late." Then with her usual spectacular entrance, she suddenly appeared in a long, plain black evening dress to her ankles. To Martin's eyes, he could see no top on the dress, only her nearly exposed white breasts.

"Sit down," Martin said, speaking under his breath to Contessa. "Karl is on his way over here now."

Karl shook hands with Martin. "*Wie geht's*, my Irish friend?" And with him was a tall, gray-haired man. "This is my uncle, Field Marshal Gunter, my father's brother."

The Field Marshal smartly clicked his heels. "I've heard much about you, Herr Connolly."

Martin turned to Contessa and said to the Field Marshal, "This is my friend, Contessa Garcia from Spain." Again the Field Marshal smartly clicked his heels and bent down, kissing her hand. "It is a pleasure, Fraulein Garcia."

She smiled at him. "You may call me Contessa, Herr Field Marshal."

Karl bent over and kissed her hand. "And what may I call you?" he said in a very intimate voice.

"Oh," she said, "I think you're the kind of man who calls anyone whatever he damn pleases."

They all laughed, and as they sat down, the Field Marshal turned to his nephew. "I can see that this lady is a good judge of bad character." Again they all laughed.

The night was spent with good conversation and a very fine vintage wine. Martin could not help noticing that Karl every once in a while kept looking very intensely at Contessa. He couldn't interpret exactly what the looks meant. It was something he just couldn't put his finger on. At one time he thought they were looks of familiarity They had never been formally introduced, but he knew Karl had seen her in the Spanish hospital after they were both wounded. He was trying to concentrate on the Field Marshal's conversation that seemed to be directed to him all night. There were times it seemed that the Field Marshal was very interested in him, but he dismissed these thoughts. The Field Marshal would break off his serious conversation every once in a while to tell a joke. He had a fine sense of humor.

And one time the Field Marshal told an Irish joke that brought tears to Martin's eyes with laughter. "Did you hear the one about the Irishman who was talking to two tourists in a pub in Ireland? He was telling them about the problem the town had with the deceased in the town cemetery. Well, the Irishman said to the two tourists, 'Gentlemen, it's 11:30 p.m., and the bar will be closing shortly. We have time for one more pint. That's if that lot out there,' pointing to the nearby cemetery, 'doesn't get up and want to come in for a drink.' The Irishman, noticing the color had left the tourists' faces, continued with the conversation. By now a bunch of the locals had gathered around the group and could barely keep their laughter in. The Irishman continued, 'We had to hire a man with a shovel to run back and forth and keep hitting them down to stop them from coming in for the old pint. The minute the clock struck 11:30, they started to sit up, and I can tell you, some of them were quite nasty if they had to wait too long to be served. Well, the long and short of it was that the man that we hired to keep them down died of a heart attack, and now he's in here every night, yelling for service.' With that, the Irishman left the pub, leaving the two tourists hanging in the air."

Martin asked the Field Marshal if he had ever been to Ireland, and he said that he had. "It's a beautiful country, and I envy you your Irish countryside. I fished there for pike, and they were delicious."

"My God," Contessa said. "You didn't eat pike. That's an awful fish to consume."

Karl spoke up. "We Germans can devour anything and anyone if we have a mind to." The wine was going to Karl's head, and the look from the Field Marshal was enough to have Karl call it a night.

Afterwards Contessa came away saying to Martin how impressed she was with Karl and told Martin to not ever let him down or disappoint him. Martin could see that she was very interested in the mission. Martin told Karl he had discussed the mission with Contessa. He was surprised that Karl was not very concerned with him telling her about the mission; so one evening he asked Karl whether he was not a little apprehensive about Contessa knowing about this covert activity. Karl's answer was sufficient enough for Martin to feel comfortable. "She's a loyal comrade to the Fatherland, and she has risked her life time after time on a German battlefield to attend our wounded. Besides, I ran a security check on her the moment I found out you were seeing her again. I will forgive you for this indiscretion this time, Martin. But if it happens again that you inform someone about a covert activity you're involved with, I will have you shot."

Martin started to laugh, but stopped at once when he looked at Karl's eyes. This man was not joking, he thought. He would do what he said.

The time slipped away quickly for Martin and Contessa. To Martin he had never experienced such complete happiness. Never had he felt so close to another human being as he did with Contessa. Hopelessly and passionately in love, she had become his whole life. He tried to find an excuse to get out of his mission and have her disappear with him. He asked Contessa to consider leaving Germany with him, but to his surprise she made it quite clear that she expected him to complete his mission like a man and not shun his duties to Germany and his friend, Karl Gunter. It was quite evident to Martin that she was not quite as enthusiastic about him as she was about the mission.

The last night they spent together, after making love, Martin told her he thought Karl wanted him to kill two German agents, something he did not know if he could do. Karl had promised him he would find another way to have him complete his mission without the killing. Contessa's reaction was to take a quick jump out of the bed onto the floor. She went over to the table where she had a pack of cigarettes. Sitting down on the chair, naked, she lit up one of the cigarettes. Pulling it into her lungs with a deep inhale of smoke, she started to talk while the smoke exhaled from her nose and mouth. Martin couldn't take his eyes off her naked body. She was so desirable that it was hard for him to concentrate on her words. "Martin," she spoke, "what kind of a man are you? If you can't handle this assignment, why are you going on it? Must Karl hold your hand for you to do what you have to do? Martin, I must know that I am going with a man that is a man. You have disappointed me in the past. Are you going to do it again?"

At that moment Martin would have sold his soul to the devil for her. He could not lose her. She had possessed his very being. "I will do what is expected of me," he promised

And she waited for a moment. "And you will kill if you have to, won't you? I must know this," she said, "or we can't continue." Martin told her he could and he would. And she came back to bed, and she made love to him.

They got dressed and went down for breakfast. Neither said a word as they ate breakfast. Finally Martin reached across the table and took Contessa's hand. "Will I see you again soon?"

Not expecting his touch, her hand jumped. "I'm to be transferred to a hospital tomorrow, and I really don't know where until I report in."

Martin looked at her. "Will you call me and let me know where you'll be stationed?" he asked.

"I will, of course," she said.

"Do you know," Martin said, "I don't know anything about you?"

She smiled and said, "There isn't that much about me worth knowing. What do you want to know?"

Martin's first question was, "Who were your father and mother?"

"My father," she said, "I never knew. One evening he made love to my mother after a dance, and she never saw him again."

Martin was shocked. "My God," he replied. "What a bastard he was!"

Again she smiled at him. "Martin, Martin. That is the way of life for some people. Consider yourself fortunate to have known your father and mother."

"Ah," he said. "I might as well have had no father. He was no good to me and least of all to my mother. I mean, he never beat any of us or physically abused us. It was just that he was so cold, and he would never stop giving out to us."

Contessa said, "Martin, you have the damnedest expressions. I never know how to interpret them."

"Well, you haven't heard the best of them yet. What about your mother? What sort was she?"

Contessa lit up a cigarette and with a heavy pull on it brought it deep into her lungs and out through her nose and mouth. Martin enjoyed the way she smoked. She handled the cigarette like a man with all the movements of a first-class smoker. Martin hadn't been using his old pipe for a while now. He just couldn't get used to the German tobacco, and he was feeling the pain. So he asked her for one of her cigarettes. She watched him light up and could see he wasn't a cigarette smoker. "Better stick to your pipe, Martin," she said. "You smoke a cigarette like my old grandmother."

Once again Martin asked, "What was your mother like?"

Contessa withdrew from the conversation with another deep drag of the cigarette. Finally after a little while, she started to speak. Martin noticed that her eyes were filling up. "She was a woman who loved only herself, and I was a mistake. She never forgave me for that."

"Sure it wasn't your fault," Martin said with a touch of tenderness.

"She was stuck with me, and I was interfering with her plans for what she was going to get out of life. I was washing the neighbor's clothing at six years of age while she was in a local pub with whomever was available."

Martin said, "She must have been very beautiful to produce someone like you."

Contessa looked at him. "It doesn't take a hell of a lot to produce a baby."

"Ah," Martin said, "but they all don't come out like you. How did you become a nurse?" he asked. "And how were you able to afford an education?"

"When I was fourteen, my mother brought home her lover, and during the night there was a fierce argument. I was listening to it from my bed that was in the next room to my mother's. I heard a shot ring out in my mother's room. She had shot and killed her lover. 'Quickly,' she told me. 'Get your clothing. We're getting out of here.' As I ran to my room, I turned back to say something to her, and she was kneeling down next to her lover, going through his pockets. She pulled out a large bundle of Spanish bank notes. It must have been a large amount because we got to Madrid and lived on it for months. My mother was quite bright and got a job at a bank. Here the president of the bank fell in love with her and married her. I was in their way, so they sent me away to boarding school in Moscow, Russia. I was told later that was the furthest they could send me to get rid of me. My stepfather was a rich man and could well afford my room and board and education. I went to the University of Moscow which was an excellent university, and I learned much about medicine, but perhaps more about life and the unfair world we live in."

Martin was fascinated with her story. She was nothing like what he believed about her. It was the first time he had an appreciation for her intellect. She had accomplished so much more than he, it was humbling. "What time will you be leaving?" he asked her.

"I'm already packed, Martin," she said. "During the night when you were sleeping, I left the room and packed my bags."

They left the breakfast room with Martin holding her hand. She asked the hotel clerk to bring down her baggage. She would use the car they had rented to take her to the university for her orders. She reached up and kissed him softly and tenderly on his lips. "*Vaya con Dios*, my love," she said, and she was gone.

Martin was returning to his room when the desk clerk stopped him. "We have an envelope here addressed to you, Herr Connolly. Just one moment. I will find it for you. Here it is, Herr Connolly," handing Martin a small brown envelope. Martin went up to his room looking at the envelope. He saw no stamps on it. That was strange, he thought. When he got to his room, he opened it and found another white envelope with his name on it. He tore it open and was delighted to find it was from his mother. Sitting there on the chair, he began to read. Mrs. Connolly was writing with the demons of old Sergeant Death about her. Martin could see she was very depressed about his father's death. She never stopped saying in the letter she wouldn't have to wait too long to meet him. Mrs. Connolly raved on and on about this man being the love of her life. Martin was building up anger as he was reading the letter. "That old bastard did nothing but work her to the bones." Martin never recalled the old fellah saying a kind word to her all through the years. Her letter seemed irrational, and it would go off on different tangents. Maureen, she said, was seeing some fellow from Salt Hill, and Ma didn't like him. She thought he was abusing her. Martin thought to himself that that would be the day when anyone would abuse that lassie. Maybe Bridget or Grainne, but not Maureen. Mrs. Connolly also told him that he had played hurling against him with the Salt Hill team. His name was Mike Murray. That rang a bell with Martin. "Sure," he said to himself. "I know him. He was a dirty player, and he'd give you the shoulder for no reason. And if he could get a kick out of you when you were down, he'd try it. That's if the referee wasn't paying attention. Maybe Ma is right. It could be that Maureen has fallen in love with him, and like most of the Irish girls, they can't see anything wrong with their man. With the Irish girl, there's unconditional love all the way."

He finished reading the letter, and with Contessa gone, he became very depressed. He fell asleep on the chair and was awakened by a loud knock on his door. The room was dark. He had slept through the rest of the day into the night. Opening the door, he was surprised to see Leutnant Mueller. "Come in," Martin said. "How have you been?"

"I'm fine," he said. "I bring you some news about your mission." From his courier bag he took out Martin's Irish passport that Martin had surrendered to him along with his other papers when he had started training at the covert building.

Mueller informed him that he was leaving for Ireland via submarine. They had placed a German operative off the coast of County Kerry, Ireland, a few months ago. There was the feeling they would be at war with England in about a year, so this agent was put in place for if and when the war started. Their agent was doing fine in a coastal town called Dingle, County Kerry. He operated out of a farmhouse that was run by a widow with whom he was having an affair. She knew nothing about his secret radio transmitter that he used to broadcast to Germany on Wednesdays. This was the night the widow went out to play bingo at her church parish hall.

I have not forgotten thee

Sub Captain

Fritz Wagner

Tipperary Nun

chapteR fIve

artin left the next day for Hamburg, and once again
it was a nonstop by car from Berlin to Hamburg.
The two same SS men rode with him that brought
him to Berlin originally. Martin couldn't help but smile at his companions. They were so somber. Martin said to them, "How about it
lads? Will we stop for a good pint somewhere along the way?" No
answer from his companions. Martin tried again. Absolutely no
response, and it dawned on Martin neither of the two spoke
English. So the rest of the trip was made in complete silence.

It was dark when Martin arrived to meet the U-boat in the
evening. He boarded and was on his way in about fifteen minutes.
The sub captain asked him to come to his cabin. There he offered
Martin a drink, and to Martin's amazement, took out his pipe and
filled it with a very popular brand of Irish pipe tobacco. Martin
could hardly wait to ask him for a fill for his pipe. The captain saw
this and laughed and handed him the little green package that contained the Irish tobacco. Martin had to rummage through his bag
that contained his personal gear to find his pipe that was in the back
of the bag between his clothing.

The German captain had a sense of humor, and he sat back and
laughed at Martin who was crawling all over his cabin deck trying
to find his pipe. "I like a man who loves his pipe that much that
he'll make a damn fool of himself over it." And they both started to
laugh. With sighs of delight and pleasure beyond any imagination,
Martin settled back in the chair opposite the German captain and
puffed away to the delight of his pipe companion. The German

knew this love well. He told Martin that he had been a captain in World War I and had lost his pipe, and he nearly went mad without it. A bond formed between the two old pipe smokers.

All during the trip to Ireland they spoke at great length about sports. The German was well up on his sports statistics and showed an interest in the Irish sports. He had landed a German spy a few months ago in Dingle, County Kerry. The sub had experienced engine trouble and had to lay out about three miles at sea off the Irish coast. The repairs had to be done, or they could not return to Germany. Someone had to go ashore to secure the parts that were needed. There was no other way. They contacted by radio the spy they had just recently put ashore, but he knew nothing about what they were looking for. So the captain decided to go ashore himself, and he met with the agent. The captain told Martin that he spent two days in Kerry without being detected and got hold of the parts that were necessary. He contacted the German Chamber of Commerce or the German Trade Commission, he wasn't sure which one, and they were able to secure the parts for him. He bought the Irish tobacco at a Dingle tobacco shop. After that he found it hard to get used to the German brand again. He made Martin promise him that he would bring back a supply of that particular Irish brand when he returned.

His time had been short with this German captain, but Martin thought they would have been very close friends if they had met in any other time and place. Martin remembered how keen the captain was on football. He remembered a game where the Irish team came over to Germany and played them in a tied match. The captain told him he was impressed with the Irish sportsmanship. Martin had spent hours with him explaining the Irish hurling game. He could see that the German captain had great enthusiasm about the way the game was played. They had never spoken of war. The captain taught Martin how to play chess, which Martin loved. The captain had become a mentor to the young Irishman from Galway, something he missed from his own father. He had grown very close to the German captain. When the captain was dropping him off in Dingle, he gave Martin a closed white envelope that contained the name of the contact he was to meet in Ireland. They parted with the captain putting his arms around Martin and hugging him tightly.

This was new to Martin. No man had ever put his arms around him before in that manner. Not used to it, he felt a little uncomfortable, but he knew that with this man, he could learn to appreciate this gesture of comradeship. Years later in 1944 Martin was reading a casualty list of U boats. His pipe-smoking friend had been sunk off the coast of Norway.

One very dark night when there was no moon, Martin was put ashore at Dingle. It was the first time since he left home that he felt lost. Martin stood on the Kerry shore for a while, watching the sub disappear. His thoughts ran away with him, "Have I been so close to the Germans that I have forgotten my own? I am home now, and I'm on Irish soil." Once more he remembered the Irish song, "This is the land of my birth. There is no equal on Earth."

Martin headed for the farmhouse in Dingle. Leutnant Mueller had given him instructions about where he could contact the German agent. He remembered Mueller telling him that this agent was having an affair with an Irish widow who had no idea that he was a German agent operating a wireless out of her own house.

It was getting on to dawn when Martin was walking along the road to the farmhouse. As a matter of fact he could just about see the farm from his vantage point. The sun started to shine on the Irish patched fields, and Martin stopped to view it. "Ah," he said to himself. "There's no place like it. 'Mother Ireland always will be my land.'" The farmer came out in him, and the love of the land hit him very hard. It tugged away at his heart that morning as he stood staring at the green, green fields of home. From nowhere a fine young mare came galloping towards him. She stopped right in front of Martin and put her head down to be patted. It nearly brought tears to his eyes. What Irishman didn't love horses? Martin rubbed the mare's head down to her nostrils, which seemed to please the young horse. Martin looked up to the heavens. "My God," he said, "if You were to take me now, it would be the kindest deed You ever did for me." But God had other plans in mind for Martin Connolly, the man from Connemara.

Pulling himself away from that moment of sheer happiness, Martin headed towards the farmhouse. Before he got there, he met an old farmer with a horse and cart that was full of hay. "Good morning," the old man said to him. "It's a fine day."

And Martin replied, "It looks like a little rain."

"Ah," the old man said, "if it does, it will only be a soft rain."

"Goodbye to you sir," he said with a gesture of his head which only the Irish have mastered.

When he finally arrived at the farm, there was no one about. The first thought that came to his mind was, "If the old fellah was here, there'd be asses to kick all over the place. It must be at least 6 a.m. in the morning, and no one out working. How did the old fellah put it? 'Get up. We have missed half a day's work already.'" He stopped a while, and a tear came to his eyes. Coming back to old Ireland had brought up the Irish emotion that had been pent up in him for so long.

Martin entered the house, and there was no lock on the door. And why would there be? It was in Kerry. No need for locks in that county. "Hello," Martin called out, but got no reply. He examined the lower floor that consisted of a living room with an open fireplace and a kitchen that was adjacent to the living room. There was nothing else in the lower floor, so he walked toward a flight of stairs that led to the bedrooms. Opening the door to the first bedroom, he saw nothing in it but an empty bed and some furniture. Stopping at the second bedroom, he opened the door, and there in the bed was the Kerry lassie and her German lover. "Good morning," Martin said with a sheepish smile. "I see you two are up nice and early." Pulling down the sheet and trying to keep from laughing, he said, "Fritz, I see you have risen to the occasion."

The German was out of bed with his fists clenched. "Who the hell are you?"

"Easy, *boyo,* or you may make the wrong move, and the Kingdom County lassie will have to find herself another playmate."

Fritz Wagner was used to settling any disputes with his brawn. In Germany he had been a member of the Brown Shirts, Hitler's muscle men. He was on Martin in a flash, wrapping his brawny arms around Martin's waist. It took Martin by surprise. The German was exceptionally strong. Their heads being close together, Martin aimed his forehead at Fritz's nose. There was a very distinctive, sickening sound of Fritz's nose being broken. He followed this up with a well-placed knee in the groin, leaving Fritz in considerable pain. Fritz lay thrashing on the floor and bleeding. Martin sat on the bed and lit up his pipe. The Kerry woman was trying to find something to wrap herself in. "Ah," Martin said. "Don't bother yourself love. I'm a man that enjoys the beauty of nature."

"I know where you're from," she said, with her mouth foaming. "You're a Galway man, and I never met the Galway man that wasn't an awful rogue."

"Ah, I wouldn't say that, now love. You might find a few of us that are halfway decent."

Later Martin was sitting down in the living room smoking his pipe with Fritz. The Kerry woman came downstairs. Fritz was fully dressed, and the Kerry woman had cleaned him up. His nose had a bandage across it.

"Well, love, how about some breakfast? I'm starved," Martin said.

The Kerry woman threw one of the side lamps at him, just missing his head. "You Galway bastard," she said. "F___ off for yourself."

"Ah, sure, love, you'll have to forget all this unpleasantness this morning. Let's all make up and be friends."

It seems this needling by Martin was too much for Fritz, and he pulled out a pistol he had concealed in his pants. "I'm going to blow your big Irish head off."

"Please," the Kerry woman shouted at Fritz. "You'll bring the guards," (police).

Martin could see it was all getting out of hand, so he told Fritz in German that Karl Gunter had sent him. The German was in shock when he heard the Irishman speaking to him in German. "Make some breakfast," Fritz said to the woman. "I want to talk to this man."

"What in God's name," she said, "do you have to talk to this Galway bastard about?"

"I will explain later," he told her, and with that she left the room to prepare breakfast.

As she was leaving the room, Martin couldn't resist one more crack at her. "Listen, woman," he said, "I like my eggs well done, and make sure you don't burn the toast."

The Kerry woman went absolutely mad and started throwing everything she could pick up in the room. Fritz was hit with a pewter statue of an Irish football player. It nearly knocked Fritz out for the count. Martin was so weak from laughing that he couldn't escape being hit himself with several unidentified objects. When it was over, she could hardly walk into the kitchen, she was so exhausted. Martin looked at Fritz and said, "I don't think she would make a very stable and amiable wife. I'd hate to come home to her after a night with a few pints in me."

Fritz said, "What the hell kind of man did they send over here? You're a pure lunatic. She doesn't know anything about me, and I don't know what the hell to tell her about you. You're absolutely a head case." Martin knew he was right. It wasn't a professional way to handle such a dangerous mission. Martin was never one to act in such a manner. Whatever came over him was a new Martin Connolly than the man that had left Ireland. He thought being back in Ireland brought the Irish devilment out in him. Yet he had to be very careful. Fritz told him he had been notified through his wireless from Germany to assist him in any way that he could. The only assistance Martin needed from Fritz was to take him into Dingle to get the bus to Galway. He was to spend time with his family until he was contacted by Fritz, who would give him the timetable on when and how he was to take out Sean McCarthy in Dublin. Although Martin was instructed in German code, he was told only to use it to contact Fritz in an emergency.

The next morning Martin left with Fritz and his donkey and cart for the town of Dingle. Being outside of Dingle, the donkey and cart was a very natural way of getting around in Ireland at that time. He said goodbye to Fritz at the bus station and apologized to him, telling him he was sincerely sorry for breaking his nose. Fritz reassured him that if he had the chance, he'd break his nose and more. Somehow Martin believed him.

Martin sat at the back of the bus. He would have to make several transfers to go from Dingle to Galway. The road at times was very strenuous on one's back. He would have to go through Limerick where he would transfer at Limerick City to get the bus that went to Clare. And this bus from Clare would take him into Galway City. He would rent a horse in Galway City and ride to his home in Connemara. With good connections, he should be home by nighttime.

The patches of Irish green fields darted by as the old bus bounced along. He was a long way from the fine custom buses he had ridden in Germany. He was out about fifteen minutes when he thought his old ass would collapse. Yet there wasn't a man or woman on the bus that was taking any notice of it. They were all chatting each other up, even those that didn't seem to know each other. He noticed for the first time what a quiet speaking race of people they were, except for the laughter that broke out every so often. They spoke with a softness and sincerity that would make you feel you knew them all your life.

It was summertime in Ireland, and it brought out the beauty of this little island. All the types of flowers were jumping out at him as the bus went along the roadside. Looking at the cows and the sheep going by, he remembered the mornings that he had to get up to tend them. And he remembered that he would have hoped that during the night they all would have disappeared. Now they seemed to be magnificent animals. The sheep that would never stop baaing became magic to his ears. He laughed to himself. How many times when the old fellah wasn't looking, he would give the stupid ones a fine kick up in the ass to get them going. Looking at the cows in the morning sometimes made him sick, their old tongues hanging out of their mouths, dripping with saliva. He would repress the urge to grab the cow's tongue and separate it from its mouth with one big yank.

He made the mistake one day of feeling guilty about the way he tended the old fellah's stock, and he told the priest in confession about it. Well the priest let out a yell in the confessional box that would have brought back the dead from their graves. The priest, an ex-farmer, who had loved his animals before he entered the priesthood, went berserk, and at the top of his lungs, he yelled at Martin, which didn't go unnoticed by the members of the congregation. "You miserable excuse for manhood. In all my years I've never heard such a damnable sin." A pin could have dropped that moment in the church and you would have heard it. The priest's door opened, and he went over and opened Martin's door. "Get out," he said. "You're not getting any absolution from me," and catching hold of Martin by the ear, he whispered very quietly into it, "and if I ever see you in any part of this town other than the church again, I'll kick your ass all over Galway."

Poor Martin left the church in a state of collapse, and when he got outside the church, he had to sit down. Otherwise he thought he would faint. Some of the congregation were coming out of the church, and one of them, an old man, came up to him, bent down, and put his arms around his shoulders. Thinking he was going to get some support from the old man, Martin looked up at him with great expectations. But Martin was mistaken. The old man bent down and whispered into his ear, "Ah," says he, "go f__ off for yourself. You young fellahs have no honor at all. You're all alike. Nothing but trouble."

"But sir," Martin tried to explain, "you don't know what I did!"

The old man said, "I don't care. It must have been sacrilegious to get that lovely priest so upset."

When Martin thought about this, it was obvious to him that the Irish have no grey areas. With the Irish it's either black or white. One minute they can be laughing and singing and the next minute doing their level best to kick your ass for you.

Martin fell off into a deep sleep, but was awakened with a bump in the road that brought his head up with great speed and accuracy to the top of the bus. He thought that his skull had been fractured, but looking around he could see that it wasn't a bother to anyone but himself. "God," he thought to himself, "they must have some heads on them not to feel that."

The transfer to the Clare bus was no better. He bounced all the way to Galway City. He enjoyed the company of a very old Tipperary nun who was sitting next to him. Martin started to complain to her about everything from the bus ride to the way that the government didn't do anything about the roads. She looked at him, and he could see that her features were very wrinkled and her eyes, that he would imagine must have been very beautiful in her youth, were dim, and she was squinting to see him. "Too proud," he thought, "to wear the glasses."

He listened very carefully as she spoke in a barely whispered manner. Her voice was cracking as she spoke to him. "Young man," she said, "that's God's job to worry about that. It's not yours."

Martin became curious about her and asked her, "Where are you stationed, Sister?"

"I'm in a missionary order of nuns, trained as nurses, and I have just come back from Nigeria to retire. I've been there over thirty years."

"Well," Martin said, "I'll bet you're delighted to be back to old Ireland again."

"No," she said, "Nigeria is my home."

Martin was taken back with what she said. The old nun continued, "I landed there when I was very young, just out of medical training and after taking my first vows. I was assigned to a makeshift hospital in a small village in Nigeria, far from the main city itself. The Mother Superior was a staunch disciplinarian as most of them were in those days. If your mother and father should pass away, the chances were you wouldn't get permission to attend the funeral. They were very, very strict," she continued. "Well, I was there a few days when a little blind, black lad came crawling into the hospital. My heart went out to him, and he pleaded with me to let him stay. He claimed he had no home to go to. His parents had made him leave. They couldn't afford to take care of him. He had eight brothers and sisters. Well, I saw no harm in keeping him in one of the hospital rooms, and he was no bother to me. He was a lovely little man, and I grew fond of him in a very short time.

"One day, I was asked to report to the Mother Superior. It seems she found out the little fellah was not a patient and ordered me to get him out of the hospital immediately. I was young and full of love for my God and could not see the wisdom in the Mother Superior's decision. I brought him into my room and explained to him he had to go. The pitiful look on his face broke my heart, so I hid him in my room for months. The food I took from my own rations and whatever I could get from the other sisters. He made the mistake one day of walking out of my room, and the Mother Superior caught him. She warned me if this happened again she would send me back to Ireland. The Mother Superior pointed out to me, justifiably so, that there were hundreds of blind children who kept coming in all day to the hospital just to get something to eat, and the mission didn't have the resources to handle this overwhelming problem."

She told Martin that she prayed for many months to help her find a way to help these blind children. Meanwhile, she kept the little boy hidden between her room and some of the other nuns who, like herself, had grown fond of the little boy. One day, years later, she was told by one of the medical suppliers that a German entrepreneur was to come to Nigeria to build a school for young homeless children.

At this point the bus driver wanted to stop at one of the restaurants to have a cup of tea. He said to the passengers, "I've been up all night with the young ones, and I never got my tea this morning. I'll never last the day without my tea." Well Martin expected to hear all kinds of derogatory statements from the passengers, but to his surprise, the comments from the passengers ranged from, "Ah, sure the man has to have his tea; God love him, he looks very tired," or the woman who said, "I have five of my own. I know what that's like." And it went on and on.

Martin thought to himself, "Have I been gone that long that I have forgotten what fine, caring people I came from?" He wondered if there was any place other than Ireland that the passengers would worry about the driver having his tea.

Martin helped the old nun off the bus and took her into the restaurant for tea. She was very unsteady on her feet, and he kept looking at her. His admiration and respect for her grew, for she must have been at least in her seventies, and she so unselfishly had given her whole life to help others. "When she dies," he thought, "the Big Boss will smile on her, for she has stood fast in His ranks and has never faltered."

Martin was helping her with her tea when she looked cross at him. "I can do that myself," she said. "I'm not that old yet." Martin remembered that the old Irish people were fiercely independent, and many had been found dead near their fireplace rather than ask for help to bring in the turf.

They all returned to the bus after about a half hour, and the busman was delighted with himself. "Thanks, ladies and gentlemen, and I use the word 'gentlemen' lightly. I'm going to drive like hell now," he said, "just to show you my appreciation."

There were remarks from an older woman at the back of the bus. "Please don't show us too much appreciation. I'd like to see my husband one more time. Last night he came in two sheets to the wind, and I want to give out to him." That broke up the whole bus.

Martin asked the old nun to continue her story. "Ah," she said, "I'm probably boring the devil out of you. Oh," she said with her hand across her mouth, "I shouldn't be using the devil's name so lightly. Well," she said, "I went to the docks to see this German philanthropist, and he was very respectful to me after I apprised him of my situation. He said, 'I'm a Lutheran, not a Catholic, Sister, and I will not build this school for the Catholics. This is for my own religion. We want to educate these children to bring them into the Lutheran faith, not the Catholic faith.'" The old nun told Martin it was the most devastating letdown in her whole years of service to God. She had counted on this good fortune that she had heard about the German's arrival. She had been convinced that it was meant to be, a sign from God that this man was going to help her. Each year that the German came to Nigeria, she was waiting for him at the docks, pleading and even begging for his help. Finally, after many years, she wore him down, and he built her a school for young blind children.

She took from her robe a picture and showed it to Martin. There were about fifty young blind children sitting in the front of a schoolhouse, and in front of the children was a young black blind man dressed in a black suit. She pointed to him and said, "This is the school's first teacher. He's blind himself." And with tears in her eyes, she spoke with pride in her voice. "This is the first little boy they wanted me to turn away from the hospital," she said. "I often wonder if I had turned him away that day, what would the results be? Well," she continued, "I would have got a teacher with sight, but he would not be able to relate to the blind children as well as this young man who is blind himself. He understood what these children were going through. No, my traveling companion," she said, "it was God's will. And I have left these children in good hands."

She turned to the window and said no more until they reached Galway City. Martin wanted to reach out and touch her, but he knew well that she would want none of this. Any praise or admiration he would have shown for her would have embarrassed her. Martin knew her answer would have been that she did it for her God. Martin believed that was the reason for her turning away towards the window. She was afraid that Martin might give her a word of praise. The Irish cannot handle praise when they have done something good. The old nun's story stayed with Martin the rest of his days.

When they got off the bus in Galway City, he said goodbye to her and asked her to pray for him. She smiled at him and said, "I have already done this," and walked away from him. His eyes followed her until she boarded the bus for Tipperary. He stood in the middle of Eyre Square and remembered how the priest had stood up on top of the lorry, asking for volunteers to fight in Spain. It seemed to him to have been a long time ago. It was going on two years. He sat on one of the benches and reflected on what had happened to him since he had left here. He noticed a change in himself. Although he was disappointed in himself, morality-wise, he had grown in self-confidence. The German training school made him physically fit, and the self-defense course made him able to take care of himself. The awful rage of anger that he needed to display before he could have physical contact had left him. He could dispatch his adversaries without raising a sweat. Martin had witnessed death and destruction on the battlefield. He had proved his courage when he took the bullet meant for Karl Gunter. He had loved and still loved a Spanish beauty. Her face appeared before him with those flashing dark eyes. He thought of her nakedness when they made love together. The touch of her hand was almost as real as it could be. He actually felt something touch his hand. The very thought of her put him into a very deep depression. There was even pain in his gut when he thought of her.

He stopped into the Old Salt pub for a pint. It was crowded as usual, but Martin didn't seem to know any of the locals. He got the attention of the bartender and ordered a pint.

"I say, boyo, that you haven't made the acquaintance of a pint in a long time."

Martin laughingly asked him, "How did you figure that one out?"

The bartender said, "You drank that pint down like it was your last."

Martin asked the bartender, "What's new about town?" He told him he had been away for some time.

"Ah, nothing except that bunch that volunteered for that Spanish Civil War returned here last month, and they hadn't a good word to say about Spain or the Spanish people. They all looked pretty beat up. It's seems they weren't the heroes they thought they would be."

Martin finished his pint. "You know," he said to the bartender, "any man that fights on a battlefield is a hero."

Martin rented an old nag of a horse that looked like it was on its last leg. That was all that seemed to be available at the time. "What the hell?" he said to himself. "The ride couldn't be any worse than the one I had coming up to Galway." There were a few hours of light left when he sat on his horse overlooking his Connemara farmhouse, the place where he first saw the light of day. Mrs. Connolly had all her children in her own bed. Galway City was the nearest town to a doctor, and that was too far to go. Her neighbor, Mrs. Burke, little Timmy Burke's mother, delivered all her babies. It had to be done that way, and they had become great friends because of all the hardships they had gone through together. Both had the same kind of husband, not too interested in domestic affairs.

They had a lot in common. Their farms were about two miles from each other, and when the babies were ready to come into this world, they would send one of the older children, or if the husbands were around, they would ride on one of the plough horses to each other's farmhouse. Usually it was Mrs. Burke for she had only three, and Mrs. Connolly had six. Two of them died of pneumonia when they were very young. The Irish dampness took the lives of many Irish men, women, and children. Most of the causes were related to TB or pneumonia. When Martin was born, Mrs. Burke came riding to the Connolly farmhouse at great speed. The road was very slippery from the rain the night before. Just before she got to the Connolly farmhouse, the old horse lost its footing and threw Mrs. Burke into a ditch. Half stunned and bleeding, she ran the rest of the way. When she got to the farmhouse, she was out of breath and bleeding from her head wounds. She was met at the door by the old fellah. He started to give out to her, "Where the hell have you been? Look at the appearance of you, woman. You're a bloody disgrace."

Well, Mrs. Burke was a woman who was not known for her even temper. There were rumors that Mr. Burke would come into the pub from time to time with a dandy black eye. He would brag to the locals, "You should see the other lad." It is a fact that is hardly ever disputed that the Galway woman runs the house.

Staring at the old fellah, Mrs. Burke took a deep breath and proceeded to beat the hell out of him. Poor Mrs. Connolly struggled to get out of the bed to find out what all the commotion was about. She was wondering why all hell had broken out in her living room. Holding on at the doorway, she beheld the scene that cheered her old heart up. It was something to see. Mrs. Burke had the old fellah laid out on the floor and was beating the stuffing out of him. Mrs. Connolly started to laugh and her water broke. "Please, I implore you, Mrs. Burke. You can beat the hell out of him after you take care of me, and I'll even hold him down for you."

The two ladies proceeded into the bedroom with Mrs. Burke holding Mrs. Connolly. Being Irish meant that anytime, anywhere, under the worst circumstances, they'd break out laughing. All during the delivery, Mrs. Burke was calling the old fellah every name under the sun. Mrs. Connolly said, "Will you ever stop, Mary? I'll die laughing and lose the child. It'll be the first time that anyone died laughing in childbirth."

Mrs. Burke looked at her and broke out laughing. She could hardly deliver Martin with the fits of laughing that came over her from time to time. After Mrs. Burke had delivered Martin, an eight-pound bouncing boy, and after she had made Mrs. Connolly comfortable, she sat next to her on the bed, the baby in Mrs. Connolly's arms, wrapped in the blanket. They looked at each other, and you could tell they were as close as any sisters could be. Mrs. Burke, with tears in her eyes, told Mrs. Connolly, "You handled this like a trooper, and you never uttered a complaint all during the delivery. God," she said, "some of them would unnerve you with the roars out of them."

Mrs. Connolly's reply was, "I tell you there weren't any Irish women doing that."

Mrs. Burke said, smiling, "Ah, you can never see any fault in your own, can you?"

Just then the old fellah stood in the doorway. "I got to get back to the fields," he said. "I've missed a half a day's work already." Looking down at his newborn son, he said, "He doesn't look like he'd be able to plough the rocks of Bawn." Mrs. Burke was ready to renew the thumping, but after getting a good look at him standing in the doorway with his hair standing up on his head and the two red welts on his cheeks, she started to laugh. And when he turned to leave the room, his shirt was all but torn off his back, and the women both started laughing again. Mrs. Connolly was usually even afraid to smile, never mind laugh, when the old fellah was in a bad mood, but to her surprise he never said a word about what had happened. When Mrs. Burke delivered the last three children, the old fellah stayed away from her. Martin loved hearing the story, and he never stopped asking his mother to tell it over and over again.

Martin still couldn't stop looking at his Connemara hills, and the words kept coming back to him, "Still Connemara's lovely hills will call me back again." He put his head down, and all the emotion and danger that he had encountered ran through his mind, and he broke down and cried pitifully. Just then in the sky a beautiful Irish rainbow appeared and seemed to be there only for him.

Mike Murray

Katherine Hussy

chapteR six

artin reached the farmhouse and saw a fine figure of a young woman pulling weeds from the garden. She looked up at him and ran towards him. Throwing her arms around his neck, she said "Martin, Martin, is that you?" Martin was hard pressed to identify this young lady. Even though it was only a few years since he had left, Bridget had grown up to be a matured and beautiful woman.

"Is it you, Bridget?" he said.

"Yes, you eejit," and laughed. "I haven't changed that much, have I?"

"By God," Martin said, "you have. You're a fine young lady from the secondary student you were when I left. Did you ever get into culinary school?" He couldn't help but notice the disappointed look on her face.

"Ah, sure," she said, "Mom was not well, so I had to stay home and take care of her. Grainne and Maureen had to keep working to keep the wolf from the door."

Martin said, "Why?" with an irritated look on his face. "The old fellah had plenty of money sacked away."

"Well, we were never able to find it."

Martin was shocked, but he had no time to sort this out just now. He was anxious to see his mother.

The old house looked the same to Martin, and he made for his mother's bedroom. What he saw shook him up. He would never have recognized her. She got all excited when she saw him. To an

Irish mother there is no one that can come anywhere near to the love she has for her sons. This Galway mother was no exception.

"Martin," she said, "you look awful pale and thin." She made a motion to get up out of bed, but Martin gently eased her back down.

"Ma," he said, "you must stay in bed. I'll sit here next to you, and we'll have a good old chat."

She said, "No child of mine will come into my home without me making his tea." The tea in Ireland usually means their dinner.

"No, no, Ma, I'm fine. Tell me. How are you feeling?"

"Well, since I heard from you, I'm feeling much better."

"Did the old fellah suffer much, Ma?"

"Well, he coughed day and night, and he ran a high fever, and his old heart just gave out." She started to cry, and she tried several times to tell him something about the old fellah, but she just couldn't get the words out. They seemed to choke her all up.

"How is Maureen doing with her beau?"

"I don't like him, Martin," she said. "There's something about his face that seems cruel to me. He looks like an awful sneak."

Martin started to laugh. "I think you're dead on, Ma. I knew him from hurling against him."

"Well, he's hurling against the locals here next Saturday, and maybe you could go with Maureen and even get to talk to him.

"I will do that," Martin said. "Is Timmy Burke still playing?"

"He is," his mother said. "Many of the lads you played with are still here."

Just then Grainne came walking into the room. "Well, he said, "the banker is here. I'll be over to see you in the morning. I could use a few pounds (Irish currency)."

"Go away with yourself," Grainne said. "You haven't got a pot to piss in."

"Please," Mrs. Connolly said. "Don't use that kind of language to your brother."

"Ah, sure, it's all right, Mother," Martin said. "She's hanging out with a bad lot in those bankers. They would steal the last few shillings out of a dead man's pocket."

"My, my," Grainne said. "Haven't we changed? Something or someone has made a macho man out of him. Maybe it's one of those Spanish lassies gave him a good jump. Well anyway, it put some life into him."

Later Martin thought about what Grainne had said, and it was nearly all the truth. He had been a very boring man, who had appeared to the outside world to lack the strength to stand up to the challenges of life. To Martin that his sister thought that way of him made him feel bad. He wondered if Maureen and Bridget felt the same way.

Grainne and Bridget had prepared dinner, and Mrs. Connolly had to be taken out of the bed so she could sit at the table with them. She could barely manage to sit up, although she ate nothing, but drank a hot cup of tea. Martin looked around the table. Maureen was not home yet. She had gone in mid-afternoon to the bar, and she wouldn't be home before midnight, so her chair was empty. And the old fellah's chair at the head of the table was also empty. To Martin this made him feel sad. His little family was slowly breaking up. Bridget asked him in good humor, "Did you win any medals, Martin, in Spain?"

"No," Martin said, "but I brought home a bullet wound in my shoulder as a souvenir," and laughed. It was the wrong thing to say. He had no sooner got it out of his mouth than he realized he had disturbed his mother, and all through his stay, she never stopped asking him about it. "Ma," he would say, "I'm fine. Stop worrying about it." But it was a waste of time. Mrs. Connolly would put her hand on his back, making believe she was patting him, but he knew all along she was trying to feel the wound. "Ma, you're an awful devious woman," he would say, and they both would laugh.

One night he was sitting by the fireside with Bridget, puffing on his old pipe. "Listen Bridget," he asked her. "Do you know what the old fellah said to Ma when he was dying? I can't get it out of her."

"What he said to her was no compliment."

"What did he say?" Martin asked.

"Well, he caught her by the hand and looked at her with a look I had never seen before. 'Mrs. Connolly,' he said to her. 'You weren't a bad wife. I suppose I could have ended up with a worse one.' Well, you should have seen the look of happiness that came across her. She was going around the house for days, singing away to herself. Would you believe that, Martin?"

"I would," he replied. "The Irish woman adores her man, and for the damnedest reasons."

"If anything happened to Ma," Bridget said, "I would go up to Dublin. There's nothing here for me. There are fine hotels there, and I would get a job with one of the big hotels after I graduated from a good culinary school. Then I would go abroad and work in foreign restaurants for the experiences, and at the same time I could pick up another language."

"I see," Martin said, "you have it all worked out. Just don't bring us home some foreigner for a husband. I've seen what's over there, and you're better off with your own."

"How about you, Martin? Did you find anyone over there?"

"Yes," he said, "and she's beautiful. She's a Spanish nurse, and I love her."

"Oh, wait one minute!" she said. "Didn't you just tell me not to bring home a foreigner? What do you call this Spanish lassie?"

"Oh, it's different for me, Bridget," he said.

And she smiled and said, "How is it so different, my darling brother? The day will come in this country when Irish women will have the right to make up their own mind about anything they choose to do instead of being under the heavy hand of the Irish bucko telling them what to do."

Martin started to laugh. "You will never see that day, my darling sister.

"I'm going to the game Saturday. Are you going?" Martin asked.

"No, I have to stay home and look after Ma. Maybe Maureen can take you. She's going to see her boyfriend anyway. He's playing."

Saturday morning came, and Martin was up at sparrowfart. In some parts of Ireland that's another way of saying they got up early. Maureen got Martin up and made breakfast. They didn't want to wake up the other girls and Mrs. Connolly, so they moved quietly about the house. After breakfast Martin hitched up the old donkey and cart, and off they went. They were about two miles from the house when Maureen asked Martin to try to get along with Mike Murray, the man she told Martin she loved dearly.

"I know him," Martin said. "He'll bring you nothing but misery. He's not a good man. What does he do for a living, and is he much on the old drink?"

"Martin Connolly," she said, "I don't give a tinker's damn about what he does for a living or if he drinks too much. I'll sort him out quickly if he tries any rough stuff on me."

"My, God, Maureen, you never change, do you? You're still as tough as nails. You're like the old fellah. No wonder you were his favorite."

"Well, you sure broke his heart when you left without even saying goodbye to him."

"He was a man that didn't have a heart to break," said Martin. "Besides, the only thing he wanted me for was work."

"Be careful what you say to Mike. He has a nasty temper," she said.

Martin looked at her and said, "It would be a big mistake if Mike was to lose it on me."

"Ah," Maureen said, "you don't think much of yourself."

And they rode the rest of the way in silence. His sisters had turned into tigers.

Martin became excited when he saw the two teams on the field. This was his first love. Hurling had been his whole life. He was taken by surprise when the Connemara team ran toward him. They were all over him, hugging and patting him on the back, and he couldn't understand why. They hardly ever talked to him when he played with them. To them Martin was a hometown hero, returning home from the wars. "Would you like to play?" they asked him.

Martin was quick with his answer. "I haven't played in nearly two years." They all agreed he would be just fine. One of the fellows had been hurt on the field, so Martin went to the dressing room to change his clothes, and he was back in a flash. The whistle blew, and the game started again. The first time he got the ball, his drive was nearly the length of the field. His fitness showed among the other players, and many of them were surprised at the way he played. They remembered him playing as a very conservative hurler. This Martin Connolly was all over the field, and they had never seen him play that way before. Although he was an excellent player before he left, he had not been very aggressive. This Martin now was outrunning every man on the field. Making his way to the goal post, he put the first one right through the uprights. Towards the end both teams were tiring, but not Martin. He was coming on stronger than when he had first started to play. The result was that Connemara beat the Salt Hill lads thoroughly, Martin scoring himself ten points of the final score.

The whistle blew, and the game came to an end. Anyone could see that Martin was willing and able to play a second game. The team made a big fuss over him, and he loved it. Maureen came over with her beau, Mike Murray, who appeared to be exhausted.

"Well played, Martin," he said, extending his hand.

Martin caught hold of it and shook it warmly. "You played a fair game yourself," Martin replied. "If you don't mind my saying so, you've changed your game quite a bit since I last played you."

Mike laughed. "If you mean I've been using less of the shoulder, you'd be right. Some Cork guy straightened me out here last year, and I can assure you I learned my lesson. Will you have a pint with me?"

"I will," Martin said, and off they went, with Maureen chuckling to herself.

The days went by quickly for Martin. He spent many hours talking away to his mother, and he became very close to his sisters. He attributed that to the fact that the old fellah was not around. This man had intimidated everyone in the house but Maureen. There was a lot more laughter and fun in the house when they got together now. They were all gathered about the fireplace talking about the current events one night. His sisters expressed disgust with Adolf Hitler and his Nazi party. He sat in silence as he listened to one sister after the other condemn the Führer. Their opinion ranged from calling him a dictator that the world should look out for, to Grainne, the reader in the family, who had read *Mein Kampf*, Hitler's life story, and was after Martin to read it. She felt he would see that this man was a pure lunatic. This he did one whole day and into the evening in the Connemara fields. He was not able to put the book down. He was fascinated by the Führer's thinking, and he was excited about Germany's future. After all, he was playing a small part in it.

Martin became anxious with the summer coming to an end. It was late into the fall without any instructions from Germany. There was no word from Contessa. He had never had a chance to say goodbye to her. They had shipped him out suddenly on that U boat one night, and he was gone off to Ireland. The worst of his frustrations was not hearing from her. Each day without any word from Fritz made the situation worse. Many times he was tempted to disobey his orders and contact Fritz at the farmhouse in Kerry. His mother seemed to be getting worse, and he worried about the time he would leave. His presence was the only reason she had not died. She was fighting off old Sergeant Death because of him.

It was coming near Christmas, and Martin had still heard nothing from Fritz. Perhaps they had forgotten him. The Dublin papers had long articles on Adolf Hitler and how the Germans were rearming themselves against all the agreements of the Versailles Treaty. Just before Christmas he went into Galway City with Grainne to go Christmas shopping. They stopped at one of the local restaurants to have a meal. While they were eating, one of Grainne's coworkers at the bank came over to the table to say hello. Grainne introduced her. "This is my brother, Martin. He was away with the Irish brigade in Spain. Martin, this is Kathleen Hussy. She works with me over in the bank."

Martin stood up from the table and shook hands with her. She was definitely a Galway girl, dark raven hair with sky blue eyes. She stood tall with the posture of a model. "I wonder," she said. "Did you know a Patrick Tully? He was with the Irish Brigade in Spain."

Martin thought for a while. "I don't think so. There were around 600 men in that brigade. Is he back now in Ireland?" he inquired.

She turned pale. "He never came back," she said.

"Oh," Martin said, reaching out to touch her arm. "I'm very sorry to hear that."

She pulled back from his touch, a gesture by a woman that was obviously in love with another man. Grainne asked her would she be at the bank's Christmas dance that night, and she said she didn't feel up to it, but after much persuasion she finally agreed. "Will you be there?" she asked Martin. "I'd love to talk to you about what happened over there in Spain. I'd like to believe that Patrick's death was for a just cause." Although Martin had no intention of going to the dance, for some strange reason, unknown to himself, he agreed.

It was raining from the heavens when Martin and Grainne got to the dance that night. When they had started out from the farmhouse, the night was just overcast, so they had taken the donkey and cart that had no top. The Irish people are used to rain all their lives, and a rainwear shop that would open in Ireland would leave the owner with plenty of time for reading. So when they arrived at the dance, they looked like two drowned rats. Kathleen Hussy was there already. One could see she was not a very happy girl, but she burst out laughing at Martin and Grainne. "You're a well-matched lot," she said. "The both of you look like you just fell into the Shannon."

Martin couldn't help but notice how beautiful she looked when she laughed, but he knew she could never hold a candle to his Spanish beauty. They had a set dance together, and she was quite good. They tried a waltz, and in the middle of the waltz, she asked him to come outside. She'd like to talk with him. The rain in Ireland can stop as quickly as it starts. Although there was dampness in the air, it was still comfortable enough to stand outside the dance hall.

Kathleen started the conversation by apologizing for taking him from the dance. "It's just," she said, "that I have no one who can or would discuss what happened in Spain."

"That's fine with me," Martin said. "I'm not in the mood myself for dancing."

"Is there something wrong, Martin?" she said.

"It's a long story, and at this moment I'd like just to listen to you. I don't know if the Spanish cause was worth an Irish life. I came away disillusioned myself. We were not treated in the way you would expect for volunteers that went over to help them. My personal opinion is that they were not as interested in the defense of their faith as we were. It seemed more like they were fighting among themselves for power and control." Once again he realized his straightforwardness had given hurt. "I'm sorry," he said as he took hold of her. "I know you wanted a good reason for Patrick's death, but I can't give it to you. It would be deceiving you. I'm not very good at saying something I don't mean. Even though it will hurt someone, I just can't get myself to lie to them."

Kathleen smiled through the tears. "You're an honorable man, Martin, and the woman that gets you will always know where she stands with you."

Martin was a little embarrassed at her remarks and made light of them. "Sure," he said. "I'll be sleeping in the barn on my wedding night." And they both laughed.

When they went back into the hall, they danced the last dance together. It was a slow air, and Martin made note that Kathleen held on to him very tightly, something he didn't seem to mind.

The months dragged on and no word from Germany. It was March 1938 when Martin saw the headlines in the Galway paper. Germany had marched into Vienna, Austria, and had taken over with the consent of the Austrian people. Martin had been in Ireland nearly eight months, and he now believed that the Germans were no longer interested in him. During the eight months Martin had spent his time working on the farm. There was much to do since the old fellah died. Maureen and Grainne had full time jobs, and the only one handling the farm work was Bridget. She did the best she could, considering she also had to take care of her sick mother. Mrs. Connolly started to thrive on Martin being home, and after a while she was able to do light housekeeping and cook some meals for the family. During the weekend Martin played his beloved hurling, and Kathleen Hussy and he became great friends. Both were in love with someone else, so it didn't appear as though a romance was in progress. They went to the matches together and the Saturday night dances. They spent a great deal of time just sitting in the country-side talking.

Martin was working in the fields one day when he saw a figure of a man at a distance coming towards him. By the walk of him he didn't appear to be an Irishman. When the man got closer, Martin could see it was Fritz Schneider. Surprisingly enough, Martin was not glad to see him. He had fallen back into his old way of life. Although it was not as interesting as the spy business, it was a quiet and peaceful way of living, especially now that the old fellah was gone. He was his own boss, and he was enjoying it.

Fritz shook hands with him and told him the Fatherland had called him. He handed Martin a sealed white envelope that he told him contained his instructions from Leutnant Mueller. He was not to open it until he got to Dublin. That evening Martin told his mothers and sisters he was going to Dublin to see an exhibition on new farm equipment. He was hoping to get by Grainne because she read the papers from cover to cover, and she would know if there were such an exhibition. Somehow it got by her, and she made no comments. It turned at his insides to lie to them because he knew he might never see them again. Martin figured, and rightly so, he would go straight on to Wales and England after this assignment was finished. While they were having their tea, Kathleen Hussy stopped by. Bridget couldn't wait to tell Kathleen that Martin was going to Dublin the next day. Kathleen seemed taken back. "Oh," she said. "When did that come up?"

"I just heard about the exhibition yesterday, and I thought I might have a look at it."

"Funny," Kathleen said. "I never heard a thing about that from my father. He's always up on those shows. If you'd like some company, Martin, I could take time off from the bank and go up there with you."

Martin was completely trapped. There was no way of getting out of this. She would know he was lying if she went up with him, and he couldn't think of any reasonable excuse to give her for not taking her. "Kathleen," Martin said, "let's take a walk. It's a lovely night." They walked along the old stone wall that surrounded the farmhouse. Martin said, "I really would prefer if you were not to accompany me to Dublin tomorrow." It stunned her completely, and she stopped dead in her tracks.

"Oh, I didn't know that you felt that way. I really shouldn't be imposing myself on you. The last few months together have made me very happy. I just took it for granted you felt the same way, and I'm sorry. It won't happen again."

Martin at that moment wished that he could have disappeared from the face of the earth. "Kathleen, Kathleen," he said, "you're a very lovely person, and I have loved every minute we have spent together. I can't explain to you now, but some day I will tell you everything."

She never went back to the house. She left him there and went straight home.

His mother was up early to make his breakfast and as usual falling all over him. She came very close to feeding him. "Hurry back, Martin," she said. "I'll miss you while you're gone, but be careful of those Dublin jackeens. It won't be too long, will it?" she asked.

Martin noted to himself that it was coming much easier for him to lie. This change in him was starting to chip away at his insides.

Martin got his bus to Dublin in Galway City, and all the way up to Dublin he went over his stay in Connemara. He would miss the family and surprisingly Kathleen. He hadn't slept the night before, and he fell asleep towards the end of the trip. When they arrived at the bus terminal in Dublin, the bus driver awakened Martin. "Come on, young fellah, let's go. Culchies (country people) seem to need a lot more sleep than us city folks. Listen," the bus driver said to him, "I'll bet you a shilling that I can tell you what your mother said to you before you left. 'Be careful of the Dublin jackeens.' I can tell you this, lad," he said, "once you see Dublin, you'll never look at another sheep again."

Later on Martin got the message and chuckled to himself. Martin opened the white envelope in the bus terminal. The note read, "You are to go to Dun Laoghaire harbor. There you will find two long piers that are over a mile long leading out to Dublin Bay. You are to take the west pier. That is where most of the fishing takes place. Walk to the end of the pier, and there you will meet someone who can identify you." Martin was directed to the train that he was to take to Dun Laoghaire. It took him about ten minutes. He identified the west pier and proceeded to walk to the end of it. It was springtime in Ireland, and it was a bright spring day with a very gentle, blowing breeze. As he came closer to the end of the pier, he saw a figure of a man sitting on the top of the wall of the pier. It looked to him to be about ten feet upwards. The man jumped down next to him. "*Vie geht's*, Martin?" It was Karl Gunter!

"What the hell are you doing here?" Martin asked.

"Looking after you, my Irish friend," he said.

"I thought it was my job to look after you," Martin said.

"Your time will come for that, Martin, but for now I will need you to complete your assignment. It is most important. Well, you look fit to me, Martin. How was your visit to your family?"

Martin told Karl that he wished that he hadn't spent so much time at home. "Why was there such a delay," he asked him, "in contacting me?" The two sat down on the steps that led up to the top of the wall. There wasn't anyone around at the time, so Karl began to explain more about his mission to him. "There are great significant events happening in Germany. I'm sure you read that Germany has taken over Austria. I can tell you now that the Führer will invade Poland sometime next year. We think that France and Britain will not defend Poland, even though they have signed a pact with them.

"One week from today, you will take the ferry boat," and he pointed to it across the inlet. "It will take you to Holyhead, Wales, where you will travel on to London, England, by train to Paddington Station. You'll be met there by one of our agents, Greta Stein. She will take you to an apartment in Kensington, and you will receive further instructions on how to handle Pulaski.

"Martin, I'm afraid I have to break my promise to you about eliminating Pulaski. You're the only one we have at this moment to kill him. The English are discovering our agents faster than we can place them."

"I am ready," Martin said, "and I will do what is expected of me."

"Good man," Karl said. "I knew you wouldn't let me down.

"Now on the way over on the ferry you must eliminate Sean McCarthy." Karl handed him a German Luger pistol 08, 9 mm., with an eight round magazine. "It is equipped with a silencer. Wait until you're out at sea, and then shoot him and throw his body overboard. Do this only if you are not seen. If the target doesn't present the opportunity, then you will have to return to Ireland and try again on the way back." Martin shivered. Karl said, "Please send a telegram to Fritz when you have landed in Wales in care of the widow in Kerry. If you have completed your assignment, the telegram should read, 'Dear Hannah. Finally got your gracious gift of 50 pounds. Thank you so much. Your friend Mary Shea.' Then you may continue on your way to England. If you did not complete your assignment, send the alternate telegram. 'Dear Hannah. I'm still waiting for the money you said you sent me last Friday. I'm sorry to bother you again. Your friend Mary Shea.' If you haven't got the opportunity to complete your mission, then we'll know this by your telegram, and you are to return to Ireland on the ferry and try again to eliminate McCarthy. If it is impossible again, then Fritz will contact you with further instructions. The important thing you have to remember is don't risk being caught by being impatient. We will eventually get him. I've booked you into a B&B (bed and breakfast) in the building overlooking the harbor. So let us go over there now and get you settled in. We'll have dinner afterwards."

It was the typical Irish bed and breakfast, a small room overlooking the Dun Laoghaire harbor with a bed and a set of dressers and a wash sink. It had a comfortable easy chair next to the window. The bathroom was down the hall, and it was shared with all the other boarders. An Irish breakfast was served at 7:30 in the morning, which consisted of eggs, potatoes, black puddings, sausage, and rashers (bacon), with brown bread and tea.

After Martin checked in with the owner, a very slightly built Dublin woman with a huge smile, they went out to eat. They walked along the Dun Laoghaire streets until they came to a small restaurant off the main street. Martin was right at home with the menu, but Karl was looking for more than some plain food. It was obvious to Martin that Karl's background was much different from his own. One could see Karl Gunter was raised as an aristocrat. His manners were impeccable. His knowledge of food and wines was exceptional. Martin was fascinated by watching and listening to Karl order a meal. It was a sheer delight for Martin to be in Karl's company. Seeing that he wasn't pleased with the meal he was eating, Martin asked him if he would like to go somewhere else to eat. "No, this is fine," Karl said. "It doesn't do anything for my palate, but it fills the emptiness in my stomach."

A Dublin woman, sitting at a table alongside Karl and Martin, was listening to the conversation. Reaching over to Karl, she said, "Listen, sir. I would take it from your accent you are a German." Karl was taken by surprise.

"Yes, I am," he replied.

"Well, sir, I must say that I am perturbed at your reaction to good, wholesome Irish food. I would think, sir, you would have better manners in a foreign country than criticizing their food. And may I add, sir, that anyone that would enjoy pike, which I believe you Germans have a taste for, wouldn't be, in my opinion, able to tell the difference between a good filet mignon and horsemeat." This brought cheers from the all the patrons of the restaurant, who had a deep interest in this conversation.

Karl stood up, clicked his heels and said, "I'm sorry, and I apologize for my lack of sensitivity in your beautiful country."

"Accepted," the woman said, with sheer delight in herself.

Karl sat down and continued eating. "This is exactly what I meant when I told you to expect the unexpected. I have pinpointed myself to everyone in this restaurant, and I can guarantee you that two or three people from this restaurant will remember me and even you, although you're just sitting here. If the authorities are looking for us, they will have some good descriptions of us. I have broken the first rule in espionage. I have made myself known instead of keeping a low profile and just blending into the crowd. Let us hope we are lucky and can escape after this mission."

Martin was half listening to Karl. His mind was on other things. Patiently, he waited for Karl to finish. Finally he asked Karl, "Have you heard anything from Contessa?"

Karl, who was still trying to recover from his indiscretion, answered him in an irritated voice. "No, no, I haven't heard from her. Please, Martin, we must concentrate on your mission. This is not the time for you to be concerned about your lover.

"I think we must go now. We have spent enough time here." They paid the bill and left, and they sat on a bench at the entrance of the west pier. They were discussing the times in Spain that they had together, mostly the characters they had served with.

"Do you remember, Martin, the two Irish brothers who were always in trouble? What were their names again?"

Martin started to laugh. He knew which two Karl was referring to. "How could anyone forget them? They were some characters, Wacker and Hot Stuff Byrne. They came from Dublin."

Karl shook his head and said to Martin. "What kind of first names are they?"

Martin smiled. "These are nicknames used in Ireland, usually given to local characters. They have first names they're never called by all through their lives. They get so used to calling them by their nicknames that they hardly remember their first names. Their father was from Cork, and he's called them these nicknames since they were young lads. Mr. Byrne called the older brother Wacker because he was always whacking everyone that went by him. Mr. Byrne was called up one day by the guards (police). Wacker had hit a guard with a big stick while the guard was on patrol. Man, woman, or child, Wacker would belt anyone for no reason."

Karl interrupted Martin by saying, "And he's possibly still at it! Do you remember, Martin, we had a pass to go into Caceres? We were having a few drinks in the local bar with the Terico soldiers (Spanish foreign legion) when Wacker and his brother came into the bar. It took them about an hour to get drunk when Wacker went over to one of the Terico soldiers and told him he was acting like a maggot (acting foolishly). The Spanish soldier who was standing next to him spoke English and interpreted it to mean that Wacker was calling the soldier an insect. The soldier pulled out a knife and attacked poor Wacker. Wacker proceeded to beat the hell out of him, and then took on the whole Terico. The bar was wrecked, and Wacker was put in the guardhouse." What Karl thought was very funny was that his brother never raised his hand to help Wacker. Karl remembered asking him later why he let all those Spanish soldiers pile up on his brother without giving him a hand.

"Ah, sure," he said, "that's only a few minutes work for Wacker. Now in Dublin with that many, I'm afraid I'd have to give him a hand."

"I also remember we were on our way to Titulcia when Wacker hit the Terico sergeant a belt because he pushed Wacker along the march for not keeping up the pace with the squad. The commanding officer was going to shoot poor old Wacker, but we engaged the enemy before they could shoot him. Wacker and his brother disabled three machineguns the next day, and they were decorated. After the decoration, Wacker was standing around the parade grounds, and the sergeant that Wacker had hit walked by him. Wacker proceeded to kick him in the ass as he went by. Wacker was marched straight to the guardhouse, decoration and all. A few days later, his brother joined him in the guardhouse when they found him in bed with a captain's wife. Within three days the two of them broke out, and no one has heard of them since."

Martin said, "They were two wild men, and they were well-named."

Karl shook hands with Martin and wished him luck. "I will see you back in Germany when you have completed your mission."

Martin remained on the pier for a good while after Karl had gone.

Martin came every day to the pier until it was time to board the ferry. Those days were very peaceful, and it was typical Irish spring. It would rain for a while, stop, and the sun would break out, sometimes with bright rainbows. And later on in the day it would rain again. He caught some lovely fluke. Towards evening when it got dark, he was captivated by a blind fisherman who would catch conger eels. They would range up to 50 pounds at the pier. They actually barked. Martin couldn't believe how the blind fisherman would feel in the dark for this monstrous eel. This particular eel could take your fingers off with one bite. The chills went up and down Martin's back every time the blind man reached for an eel. One night Martin was going home, and he tripped over the blind man's line. "You eejit!" the blind fisherman called out. "Sure, I'm better off than you with two bad eyes than you are with two good ones."

The time came to leave Dun Laoghaire, and Martin felt sad. He had taken a liking to the old pier and the characters he would talk to all day fishing. Even into the evening they would share with him their last cup of tea or even their sandwiches. The old stories that were exchanged and the laughter he got from them would remind him once again that there was no place like Ireland.

Martin Connolly boarded the mail and passenger ferry from Dun Laoghaire heading for Holyhead, Wales, with the intention to commit murder. What had he become? He was about to kill another Irishman like himself. This act was not for the defense of his church or his God. This was being a spy for a foreign country whose cause he was not sure he believed in himself.

I have not forgotten thee

Greta Stein

Olaf Pulaski

Sean McCarthy

chapter seven

martin watched as the Dun Laoighaire shore started to disappear. Once again he was leaving the land of his birth. This time it was for a different reason. It grew dark, and the passengers were going below deck to the ship's bar. Martin remained on deck watching for McCarthy to appear. The Luger with the attached silencer was in his inside coat pocket. He had not seen McCarthy yet, and he wondered if he was aboard. Martin filled his pipe and lit it. It calmed him down. The members of the crew came by now and then to attend to their particular duties, but no McCarthy.

Martin was deep in thought, looking out at the sea when he felt a sharp pain in his back. It was the muzzle of a gun, and his nostrils were filled with the heavy odor of drink. "Don't turn around, you dumb culchie. Oh, yes," he said. "I'm McCarthy, and I wouldn't make the wrong move, boyo, or I'll give you a quick trip to Fiddler's Green."

McCarthy saw that two women passengers were approaching them. Otherwise Martin would have been dead without any warning. McCarthy, being the professional, smiled at the two ladies going by. "Lovely evening, ladies," he said, "but don't stay too long on deck. The sea has a way of being very bad for your complexion." The ladies giggled as they went by. When the ladies were out of sight, Martin heard a zip, and the gun that McCarthy held to his back fell away. Turning around, he saw McCarthy lying on the deck. He was dead. Martin saw that McCarthy had been shot in the back of the head, so he raised him up to the deck rail, and with one swift motion, threw him overboard. He was shaking all over, and cold sweat dripped from his forehead. Whoever it was, was gone. Martin went below for a stiff drink of whiskey to steady his nerves.

Feeling better, he went back up on deck, and once again he lit up his pipe and began to go over what had just happened to him. Why was McCarthy shot, and by whom? Who else knew about this mission? All these questions he might never get an answer for. The only positive outcome to this mission for Martin was that he didn't have to kill McCarthy. He tried to tell himself that he could have done it, but Martin had a hard time convincing himself. Another question went through his mind. How did McCarthy know that he had come to kill him? It was obvious that McCarthy had been tipped off, for he had known what Martin looked like, and he had been waiting for him. Martin was becoming less and less intrigued with the espionage game.

The ferry docked at Holyhead, and there was some random searching of bags by the customs, but nothing of significance. After all, it was still peacetime. When Martin got off the ferry, he sent a telegram to Hannah, telling her that he had received the fifty pounds. A little way from the customs in Holyhead, Martin found the train bound for London, so he boarded it. He fell asleep at once. He was mentally exhausted from his ordeal on the mail and passenger ferry from Dublin. He was awakened a few times by the conductor collecting tickets and by the man with the sandwich cart that roamed through the train between Holyhead and London.

Martin got off at Paddington Station in London. Still half asleep, he looked around to see if he could spot Greta Stein. Karl had told him that she would find him. He waited for about fifteen minutes and then went over to the coffee and tea stand and ordered tea and a biscuit. He was eating when he felt a touch on his elbow, and turning, he saw a tall, stout woman with hair graying at the temples under a mop of blond curly hair. She had a jolly look about her, and it was hard for Martin to relate to her as a spy. Karl said she had served in World War I with a German espionage group, and she had been decorated for bravery. Karl had also told him that no one would ever suspect her of being a spy.

"Mr. Connolly," she said, "I am Greta Stein. I have been sent by my travel group to show you the sights of London, and I'm sure you'll be well satisfied with our escort service. We hope you will then refer us to your friends. Come," she said, taking him by the arm. "I have a car waiting to take you to your hotel. It is in the Kensington area of London." She directed him to the car that was parked outside the station. Martin got the impression that she was trying to feel the muscles in his arm as they went towards the car. She seemed to be all physical with him. She clung to him every chance she could. This made Martin feel very uneasy. She was quite pleasant, so he thought no more about it, thinking to himself that she was just a touchy person who was trying to be friendly.

When they arrived at the Hotel St. John, she took him to his room. She had already checked him in and gotten the key for him. She asked him for his passport. The hotel wanted to have him registered. It was standard procedure. Martin was unpacking when she returned with his passport. "Come, come," she said, "take off that jacket and relax." She walked over to him and started to untie his tie. She smiled at him. "You must relax, Martin," she said.

Martin thought that she had the look of a half-starved wolf that was about to consume her prey. Martin gently removed her hand from his tie. "I can do that myself, thank you," he said politely. No sooner had he removed her hand from his tie than he felt her hands sliding up and down this legs.

"Martin, Martin," she said, "may I call you that? We must all get to know each other better. In our work it is a great pleasure to share some intimate moments together. This work is quite tedious and dangerous, so we must have some relaxation in between. Don't you agree?" she said, coming even closer.

Martin thought of running. "My God, she'd kill any fair-sized man by turning over on him in the bed." Moving away from her, he told her he was tired and he would like to go to bed. She reluctantly moved towards the door and turned to him. "We will discuss this further, *mein Liebchen*. You must just get your rest now. You will need it." And with a mischievous smile, she left.

Martin felt a wave of cold sweat come over him. The mere thought of this woman trying to seduce him gave him chills up his spine. He thought to himself there would have been a few Galway lads he knew who would have loved to take her on, just for the old craic (fun).

The next day for breakfast he met with Greta. He found her to be quite intelligent when she kept her mind on business, but every once in a while she would give him a look that made him feel like she was going to have him for supper. She handed him a big yellow envelope across the table, and she advised him not to open it until he was back in his room. Greta further explained to him the contents of the envelope. There was a picture of Olaf Pulaski and the address where he lived. It also contained the address of the building that he worked in. There was also a picture of his girlfriend along with the address where she lived. There was nothing left undone—typical German efficiency. After hearing what the envelope contained, Martin asked Greta who had come up with this information. It was quite thorough. She smiled at Martin and told him she had spent nearly six months tracking Pulaski around London. Trying to locate where he worked had been the most difficult. He would go a different route to work every morning. She laughed when she told Martin how Pulaski would take different buses to work and jump off the bus before it came to a stop. "As you can see, this was quite a feat for a woman of my size to keep up with him." Martin could well understand that.

Greta reached across the table and caught Martin's hand. "*Mein Liebchen*, I'm quite a versatile person, and I'm used to getting my man." The blood had left Martin's hand from the squeeze that Greta put on him. Even in Spain in the days when the fighting was the hardest, he never remembered being that afraid. "God," he thought, "I am more afraid of this woman than of completing the mission." When they rose to leave the restaurant, Martin couldn't help comparing Greta's behind with a German half truck. He couldn't figure out which was the bigger.

They stood in the lobby of the hotel for a while talking quietly to each other. Greta told him to spend some time following Pulaski to get to know his habits. This mission was not to last too long, but he was not to rush the job either. The wrong timing could be disastrous. "If an opportunity occurs for you to make friends with Pulaski, do so. This will make it much easier to kill him if he doesn't suspect you." The words "to kill him" deeply disturbed Martin.

Greta took him around London the next few days. She familiarized him with the different bus routes. She pointed out to him the building in west London where the British code room was located. They had lunch in Covent Gardens where there were many food and craft stalls. This is where the merchants sell their wares. She told him that this was a highly trafficked area where they could meet and would not stand out in a crowd. There were many groups from all parts of England in this area of the gardens. Later she showed him the flat where Pulaski stayed. Martin was very impressed with London. It was a beautiful city with tall buildings and many historical sites to see. He loved riding on the buses that covered every part of the city.

After a long day of traveling around London, Greta told him to take a few days off and look around by himself. "Try as best you can to familiarize yourself with the different ways to get in and out of the city. This way if you are discovered, you'll be able to make a fast exit."

Martin went back to his hotel and went directly to bed. His head was spinning with facts about all the places he had seen and the different bus routes he must familiarize himself with. But before he left, Greta had handed him a letter from Karl Gunter. Martin was too tired to open the letter, so he left It on his dresser until morning.

Martin was awakened about 12 noon with a loud pounding on his door. It sounded like the housemaid trying to get in to clean the room. Martin got up and told her through the door that it was not necessary to clean his room today. A voice said that would be fine, but she would have to leave some towels. Martin had slept that night in the nude and opened the door only halfway to get his towels. Too late, the maid turned out to be Greta Stein, who was more than delighted to view Martin's manhood. Before he could close the door on her, Greta was in the room chasing him around the bed. Poor Martin was petrified. The room was so small, and she had the advantage because she occupied half of it. Finally cornering poor Martin, she proceeded to push him to the floor, and with all Martin's skills of self-defense, her weight overpowered him. Pleading for all he was worth, he tried to calm her down. But Greta would have none of that. Martin was near capitulating when the door that was half open from Greta's charge, suddenly opened all the way with the hotel maid standing there. The maid had been with the hotel for many years, but had never seen such a spectacular event as she now beheld. Greta released her exhausted captive and got off the floor. Martin ran for his trousers and stuffed some English pounds in the maid's hand. "God love you," Martin said, "and may you be blessed with a rich and long life for saving me from a hideous fate this day."

When the maid had left, Martin got dressed while Greta sat in the chair near the bed. "Well," Martin said, "if we were not supposed to call attention to ourselves, this wasn't the way to do it. My God, woman, how did you ever survive at this game?"

Greta was clearly disturbed. "It is my one weakness. All my life I have loved men. When I was eleven..."

Martin cut her short. "Good God, woman, don't tell me any more. At eleven!" he shouted back at her. "I've never heard anything like it in my entire life. I don't want to hear anymore. We must leave this hotel at once. The maid will tell everyone on the staff what has happened."

"*Ja, ja,*" Gertrude said, "you are right. Please I beg of you. Don't report me to Germany. They will shoot me for this"

"Don't worry," Martin said. "I won't tell. They might shoot both of us if I do. They would probably think that I was participating in this folly." Martin asked Greta if there was anything else she was supposed to do for him.

"No," she said, "just help you if you need anything else."

"Fine," Martin said. "Then let's make this our last encounter. Give me your telephone number to call if I have to get in touch with you. I will find another hotel myself and let you know where I'm staying, but you are not to contact me unless it's an emergency. *Verstehen Sie?*"

"*Ja, ja,*" she said, and left the room.

Martin packed and left after a little while. He went down and checked out of the hotel, and he could tell by the clerk at the desk, whose face was lit up like a Christmas tree, that he had heard about the incident. Martin was right. The maid had spread the word. As he left the hotel, he wondered if this would come back to trip him up. Martin found a bed and breakfast that was still in the Kensington section of London. It was small and off the main streets. It was managed by an Irish woman from Mayo. Her name was Kitty Dougherty. She was about the same age as his mother, and they hit it off right away. They were both from the west of Ireland, and they spoke often about home. They were two strangers in a foreign land, and they had much in common. She hadn't been there too long herself. She had come over to England after her husband died. They had no children. She wound up running the B&B for the owner. For the short time Martin was there, Kitty looked after him as though he were her son. She had two other elderly boarders who stayed much to themselves, so Martin never saw too much of them except at mealtimes.

It was about two days after Martin had found Kitty Dougherty's B&B, and he was going through his clothes, when from in between his shirts the white envelope fell out. It was the letter that Greta gave him from Karl Gunter two days ago. He tore open the envelope and began to read the contents. Karl was hoping that Greta was working out well for him. She was one of their most capable agents. "Oh, yes," said Martin out loud. "If you only knew how capable she is!" His eyes suddenly focused on a name in the letter. It came right of the page to him. Contessa! His vision blurred for a moment as he tried to focus on the script. Karl was telling him that she was in London on a sabbatical at St. Mary's Hospital in south London. She'd be there for two weeks. Martin's heart pounded over the thought that he had wasted two days already. He hurried out of the B&B and headed for a taxi rank. The taxi driver delivered him right to the visiting section of the hospital. There he made inquiries at the desk for a nurse named Contessa Garcia. They found no such name. Disappointed, he sat in the waiting room while he pondered the situation, not knowing where to go now or how he could find out where she was. Then it hit him. She was here on a sabbatical, and they were probably working at the hospital, but they were not on the personnel lists. Excitedly, he approached the desk again, explaining his problem. Once they knew the situation, they found that the particular group was taking courses at the other end of the hospital and directed him there.

Sweating profusely, he found the classroom that the group was in. Straining his eyes, he searched the length and breadth of the room, looking for his love, but she was not there. He turned away from the window that looked into the classroom and buried his head in his hands. He was brought out of this position with the sounds of a woman's high-heeled shoes coming towards him. He looked up and there she was. She had left the classroom to go to the W.C. (bathroom). She ran towards him with her black hair bouncing in the air. When she fell into his arms, he thought his heart would leap out of his chest. He held her for a long time and said nothing. The scent of her hair had numbed his senses. God, how he loved this woman! She pulled herself away from him, looked at him, and then moved closer to him, kissing him gently on his mouth. Once again she pulled back and spoke, "I see Karl got in touch with you. I met him in Berlin and told him I was scheduled to come over to England. Karl must have broken all rules in the book by telling you where I was."

Something flashed in Martin's mind at that explanation. Martin couldn't understand that Karl would reveal and jeopardize the operation by Contessa seeing him and knowing where he was. He had remembered that he told her about Karl asking him to kill two men on a special mission for the Abwehr. But once again Martin ignored all doubts in his head when it concerned Contessa. All he knew was that she was here in his arms, and to Hell with everything else. "How long will you be here?" asked Martin.

"I have ten more days, but I finish my classes at 4 p.m. every day, so if you wish I can be with you at 4 p.m. for the next ten days."

"It's not enough," Martin said, raising her up from the floor.

"Martin," she said, "the whole class is looking at us. Put me down."

"Ah, sure, let them look," he said laughingly. "All they can see is that there's a fine-looking Irishman with you."

"You don't think much of yourself," she said, smiling at him.

"I'll wait for you outside the hospital at four, and we can have dinner together. Where do you stay at night?"

"We are all quartered here in the hospital building."

"Well," Martin said, with a devilish look in his eyes, "you just checked out."

"No, no, Martin," she said. "I can go back to your hotel with you every evening, but I can't stay overnight. We have bed check at 11 p.m. If we don't eat, we'll have about six and half hours to make love," she said laughingly, throwing her head back. "That should be enough for you."

"I don't know. I never get enough of you."

"How does that Irish expression go?" she said. "Go away with yourself!"

"Ah, Contessa. You're starting to become an Irish woman." Once again he hit a bad note with her.

"I am Spanish," she said, "and proud of it, and I will never become your Irish girl. I'm your Spanish love."

"All right, all right," Martin said. "I won't try to convert you. God, woman! You have a fierce temper. Sometimes I don't know if I could take fifty years of you."

She smiled at him and said. "Is that a proposal, Martin Connolly?"

"Ah, go away with yourself!" he said, and they both broke into laughter.

It began to rain on Martin as he stood outside the hospital waiting for Contessa. Across the street from him stood a man in a raincoat whom Martin paid no attention to. He thought he was probably waiting for someone. Just for a fleeting moment he thought he recognized the man. He thought it was Karl Gunter, but when he looked again the man had disappeared. He was taken by surprise when Contessa came swiftly up to him. "Let's go, lover," she said to him.

When they got to Martin's hotel, Martin asked Contessa if she would like a drink. "Let's go, boyo," she said with a very good imitation of an Irish accent. Entering his room, they both charged for the bed. Both landed together at the same time, and under the weight of both of them, it collapsed on the floor. They were both shaken up, and they had difficulty in trying to get up. There was nothing but laughter could be heard from the room. "What will we tell the hotel staff about what has happened?" Contessa asked.

"I'll tell them that you're a wild woman who sexually attacked me in my room."

"Well," she said, "if I get the blame, I might as well have the gain," shoving him to the floor. This time they made love with great intensity. Martin also noticed that Contessa was exceptionally passionate, and he became unsure of himself. When they had finished, they both stayed on the floor, Contessa smoking a cigarette while Martin was looking at her and trying to determine if she had noticed his poor performance. She made no comment, but went directly into his mission. "Have you finished your mission, Martin?"

"No," he replied, "part of it is over, and the second part is to be completed here in England."

She asked him if he still had any concerns about killing someone. Martin spent over an hour on the floor explaining to her his concerns about killing anyone. Contessa continually questioned him about would he be able to complete his mission or not. Martin's replies were always that he wasn't sure if at the last minute he'd be able to kill someone outside of war.

They traveled all over London, even outside of London to Shakespeare's country which was located about two hours away in Stratford-on-Avon's lovely countryside, where they explored William Shakespeare's birthplace. Martin was surprised at her knowledge of Shakespeare, and she even quoted many lines from his plays. She was able to inform him about the complete story of Shakespeare's life. Poor Martin was lost in this culture. All through their travels she never let up on his completing the mission. Once again he had broken the rules and discussed the mission with her. Martin certainly didn't have the aptitude for a spy.

They were gone about three days when Martin returned to his hotel and Contessa returned to the hospital and was severely reprimanded for being away from her classes. There was a message from Karl at the hotel asking about Martin's progress with Pulaski. That evening at dinner he told Contessa that he would not be able to see her for a few days. He was a little surprised at her callous reaction. He had expected her to be more emotionally upset about not seeing him, especially because her time in England was going by quickly.

The following morning Martin was standing across the street, watching Olaf Pulaski's residence. Greta Stein had given him the address and also said that Pulaski was a very punctual man. At exactly 7:30 a.m. in the morning he would leave his residence and catch one of the London buses to his office. He never left his office building until he had to return to his residence at night, and that was anywhere between 8 p.m. and 9 p.m., depending on what work he had to complete. Martin's eyes became blurry from trying to identify the coming and going of that building's residents, and one time he thought he had missed him. That particular morning Pulaski was about five minutes late and came running out of the building to catch his bus that was about a block down the street from his flat. Pulaski was a short, stocky man with a mop of blonde hair. Martin figured him to be older than the portfolio picture that Leutnant Mueller gave him. Trying to keep up with Pulaski while still not showing himself, he managed to jump on the bus after it stopped at the first light. That was just a little way from the bus stop where Pulaski had boarded.

Pulaski was sitting in the front of the bus alongside a very attractive blonde woman. Martin found a seat directly behind him. The bus had been traveling a short distance when it picked up a bunch of school teenagers. They looked to be in their secondary classes, and they were acting up on the bus. The bus driver told them he'd put them off the bus if they didn't settle down. During this commotion Martin lost his concentration on Pulaski, so later he wasn't quite sure if he saw Pulaski passing something to the young blonde woman who sat next to him. Whatever happened had escaped him. The blonde woman left the bus at the next stop. She was trying to make her way to the door, when the rowdy teenagers knocked a brown envelope out of her hands. She picked it up in a hurry and left the bus. Martin made note of the stop where she got off. He wasn't sure that she had the brown envelope when she got on the bus, or had Pulaski given it to her on the bus? When it was time for Pulaski to get off the bus, Martin made no move to follow because he had Pulaski's work address in his pocket. The next stop wasn't too far from where Pulaski had gotten off. Martin got off there and slowly walked back to the building. Well, as far as Martin was concerned, there was nothing else he could do because he knew Pulaski wouldn't leave until eight or nine that night.

He made a telephone call to Greta Stein to find out if there were any messages from Karl Gunter for him. Greta answered the phone and informed him that there was no word for him from Berlin. Making inquiries as to how he was doing, he felt that she was not too happy with his progress. After all, he was away three days with Contessa. Martin asked if at any time Pulaski left the code room during the day. Martin told Greta that he didn't think it was all that impossible for Pulaski to leave the building once in a while. As a matter of fact Greta said that one time when she was trailing him to his office, he had come out briefly for a smoke and met an attractive blonde woman. "But it seemed to me," she said, "to be a chance meeting, and it didn't last very long." Martin asked her if Pulaski passed anything to this woman. "Not that I could see," she answered. Martin told of the attractive blonde on the bus and about the envelope. "Maybe she is his Russian contact," Greta said. "I will ride that bus myself to see if he meets her again, and I will get off the bus and follow her when she leaves the bus. It would seem to me he would not risk too many meetings with her."

Martin said, "I believe that Berlin should have a team surveillance on this building. You and I cannot spend all day and into the night watching that building. It would certainly bring suspicion."

"Martin," she said, "do you know that the English have caught nearly every one of our agents, and now we're not quite sure which agents they haven't turned, and we might be already compromised."

"I have to go now," Martin said, "and I will call you the same time next week. If you discover anything new about this attractive blonde, let me know. We may run into each other on that bus, and I know you know enough not to make eye contact with me."

"Listen, Martin," she said, "I'm a professional, and I don't need a country hick like you to tell me my business."

"Ah, sure," he said, "you proved that to me, especially back at the hotel. That remark about a country hick will give me some serious consideration to remind Berlin how professional you are." There was a silence at the other end of the phone, followed by a series of pleading and crying and even some begging not to inform Berlin. Martin just hung up the phone. He wanted to leave her in suspense.

Contessa was in his mind, and she would be leaving soon, and he was trying to concentrate on this important assignment. Once again he took a chance to see her. In front of St. Mary's Hospital at 4 p.m., he patiently waited for his love. To his delight she exited the hospital at about 4:10 p.m. Saying goodbye to her classmates, she moved towards him. Martin happened to look to his left, and there again was the same man who looked like Karl Gunter watching him. Contessa was in Martin's arms before he knew it. She was holding onto him tightly, which made him lose sight of the stranger.

"I was getting very bored here at the hospital," she said. "I missed my Irish love. Did you finish your assignment, Martin?"

Martin said, "Contessa, it will take some time." He noticed her reaction to him not having completed his assignment. It seemed to bother her. "Let's go eat," he said. "I'm hungry. How about you?"

"Yes," Contessa replied, "and then let's go back to your hotel. I want to show you how much I missed you."

Martin was delighted with himself. How lucky, he thought, that this beautiful woman wanted to make love to him. They ate at a small restaurant at Trafalgar Square in the heart of London. Just standing in the middle of the square was exciting. Crowds of people passing by, stores all lit up, one would be hard pressed to find a retail business that was not represented in this area. After dinner despite Contessa's pressing invitation to go back to the hotel, they spent a good few hours wandering about the square and the surrounding stores. They had browsed about in quite a number of stores when they realized it was already going on time for Contessa to go back to the hospital. "Remember, by the time I get to the hospital for bed check, it will be 11 p.m." Martin was disappointed, but realized Contessa was right. The time had clearly slipped away from them. While they were walking together towards the bus stop, Contessa informed him that she was to attend certain meetings at the hospital in the next three days and would not be able to see him. Martin stopped on the street. Sounding frustrated, he said, "Why, that will only leave us about two more nights before you go back!"

"I'm sorry, Martin," she said. "There's nothing I can do about it." They had walked a long way from the bus stop, so it took them some time to get back to it. On the way back she kept encouraging Martin to complete his assignment. Martin could no longer handle this pushing. "Why are you so interested in my assignment? You never stop. You're becoming like a picking wife." The words hadn't left his lips when he knew he was in for trouble.

"Well," she said, with that fiery Spanish temper, "you'll never have to worry about the wife part. This is your big chance to move up in this new German society, and with Karl Gunter at your back it would mean a premier spot in the Nazi Party. If you fail, there'll be nothing in Germany for you. And if you think I'm going to live in old Ireland with you, you've made a mistake. It would seem to me your women are servants to their men in Ireland, and I am not an Irish woman."

Martin found himself shaken by Contessa's attack. Within seconds Contessa realized she had gone too far. Placing her hands on each side of his face, she pulled him close to her. "I am only trying to encourage you to do your best so you will be successful."

"Well," Martin said as he removed her hands from his face, "there are other ways of getting this done than nagging me." They kissed in the middle of the street and then continued on their way to the bus stop.

"I'd like to go back to the hospital now," Contessa said, and Martin made no attempt to change her mind. He took her back to the hospital, and she kissed him goodnight, and she told him she would see him in three days. On the way back to the B&B, Martin kept pondering the evening.

There was a message from Greta Stein. He was to meet her at Covent Garden the next morning at 11 a.m. Martin was intrigued with all the goings on at the Garden. There were different ethnic groups all over the place, and it was buzzing with activity. Greta sat down next to Martin on a small bench and proceeded to pass on instructions from Karl Gunter in Berlin. The *Abwehr* (German Intelligence) has made arrangements to meet with Pulaski at his flat next week. "They told him he would receive a visitor on Monday at 11 a.m. who would bring him money and new orders. He was contacted this way in the past, so he will not suspect you. You will kill him in the apartment, and they have assumed you still have your Luger with the silencer."

"Yes, I do," Martin replied.

"Well," Greta said, without a trace of emotion, "then use it, *mein Liebchen.*" Greta also informed Martin that she had tailed Pulaski on the bus. "Last week I spotted the attractive blonde woman who was on the bus when Pulaski got on. Later I saw him pass a brown envelope to her as she got off the bus. I followed her to her place of employment. It was a Russian commerce business office that was marketing Russian dolls." Greta had passed this information on to Karl in Berlin, and she heard no more about it.

The weekend was long for Martin. He got no sleep, waking up all hours of the night and smoking one pipe full of tobacco after the other. He ate very little during this time. Kitty Dougherty at the B&B noticed that he was looking very pale and nervous. "What's wrong with you, Martin?" she inquired. "You hardly ever finish your breakfast, and these last two days, you hardly ate any dinner."

"Nothing really, Kitty," Martin said. "I have some business to conduct, and it has me a little worried. I will be fine. Don't worry about me. I suggest you watch your bottom from the old geezer that sits next to me at mealtime. He's been eyeing it for the last few days."

She laughed at Martin. He was always good for a laugh. After a little while she looked over at Martin and said, "It's been a while since anyone looked at this old bottom. Do you think the old geezer could handle it?"

Martin nearly choked on his pipe. She had caught him off guard with her delayed remarks. As it happened, she hadn't got the words out of her mouth when the old geezer walked into the kitchen where Martin and Kitty were talking. Martin looked over at him. "We were just talking about you. Kitty was telling me that you're a man who can tell a good piece of meat when you see it." Kitty was choking trying to keep in the laughter.

"Well," the old man said, "I would consider myself a good judge of bottom round meat." This was too much for Kitty. She had to leave the room or she would burst out laughing at Martin's codding the old man. That was the only laugh that Martin had for the rest of the weekend. Martin was up very early Monday morning for his meeting with Pulaski. He left the bed and breakfast house without eating his breakfast. His stomach was in knots. He stopped on his way to church and knelt down at the altar, trying his best to convince his God that he was going to kill a man today for a good reason. In essence he was saying, "I am a soldier, and I am obeying my orders. This man is the enemy of the army I serve in." It wasn't coming out right. He knew that he was not in the German Army. He was a spy. And he wasn't even sure that this Polish agent justified being killed. He blessed himself and left the church, and by his pure will refused to think about what he was about to do.

Exactly at 11 a.m. he knocked on the door of the flat of Olaf Pulaski. After what seemed to him to be eternity, the door finally opened. Face to face with Pulaski, his legs began to feel like jelly. Pulaski offered his hand, and Martin reached for it. Pulaski was very strong. The grip told Martin that spying wasn't the only kind of work this man had done in the past. The room was exceptionally clean. Everything in the room seemed to be in its proper place. At least that's what Martin believed to be the case. Pulaski wasted no time. "Did you bring me the money? I am running out of English pounds. It is costly living here in London."

Martin was uncomfortable in the room because he had the feeling this morning he was being followed. He hadn't seen anyone that would prove his suspicion. It was just a feeling. Pulaski went to his dresser to take something from the drawer. In a split second Martin drew his Luger with the silencer attached to it and aimed it at Pulaski's back. Martin's hand started to shake, and cold sweat poured from his forehead. Try as he may, he wasn't able to pull the trigger. It was impossible for Martin to kill an unarmed man. The answer to his church visit was given to him.

Martin put the Luger back in his jacket. The next few seconds would leave Martin with a blank memory for what had happened to him. A heavy blow to the back of Martin's head left him unconscious on the floor. There was no way of knowing how long Martin was unconscious, but when he finally got to his feet, there were some sharp pains in his head. He staggered around the room, lost his balance, and fell between a chair and the wall. Martin nearly passed out again with the fall. Still dizzy and not being able to focus too well, he sat down in the chair. After a little while his head started to clear, and he started scanning the room when he saw too legs protruding from behind the couch. Martin knew before he examined the body who it was. Olaf Pulaski lay dead, jammed between the wall and the couch, a small hole in his head that looked to Martin to be the work of a small 22 caliber round, an assassin's tool. Martin moved to the door in great haste and found that it was slightly open. It would seem to him that the assassin had come in through the door and left the same way. The only way Martin could believe the killer could get in without them hearing him was if Pulaski had left the door open, or else the killer was in the flat all along.

The cold air hit Martin's face as he stepped out of Pulaski's building into the street. "Dear God," he thought, "You have spared me again from committing murder. Why?" It was like a heavy weight off his shoulders. He stopped at a little tea and pastry shop and ordered some tea and scones. His mind was working overtime. Who was killing these men? First it was McCarthy on the ferry and now Pulaski here in London. Why was someone doing his killing for him? It became too complicated for Martin. There were no answers forthcoming. "I'll probably never know, at any rate," he said to himself, "and I will go back to Germany and tell Karl that I want no more part in this spy game."

Waiting for orders form Berlin, he remained in England a couple more months enjoying the English countryside and drinking in the pubs at night. He found a section in London where mostly Irish immigrants lived and felt much at home with the Irish lads that worked in the area. The newspapers in England were talking war. They were asking what would happen if Hitler decided to invade Poland. The English and French had signed a treaty with Poland that stated if Poland were attacked, the English and French would come to her aid. Hitler continued to build up his military forces. A telephone call from Greta told him that they would have to meet the next day in Trafalgar Square at a small restaurant for lunch. She had orders from Berlin for him. The telephone call had brought him back to the reality that he was still connected to the Third Reich. Greta seemed nervous when she met him, and she never stopped looking over her shoulders as if she had been followed.

Martin asked her, "What's the matter? You seem on edge."

"I don't know," she said. "I feel someone is shadowing me."

Martin wanted to take her mind off her fears and asked her, "How long do you know Karl Gunter?"

"Well, I met him through his uncle, Fieldmarshall Gunter, who I had the pleasure to serve with during World War I. The Fieldmarshall was then Colonel Gunter, and he and myself were sent over to Ireland to see if we could recruit some of the Irish as agents. We knew that there would be bitterness and deep hatred against the English for the crushing of the Rising in 1916. The Irish could have proven useful to Germany, having the advantage of living next door to Mother England. The Fieldmarshall and I worked well together, and when the armistice was signed, we returned to Germany."

Martin knew now why the Fieldmarshall was so knowledgeable about the Irish that night in Spain.

Greta handed him a long white envelope, and she told him that it contained money and instructions for him. He was to leave England by a German freighter that was docked at South Hampton. Martin was to go aboard the freighter the following night, and he would meet one of the crew who would escort him aboard. There were security guards on the dock watching for any smuggling or for members of the crews that would want to jump ship. Greta bid Martin goodbye and left him feeling a little sorry for this woman who spent her time deceiving and lying in another country far from home.

The next morning Martin sat quietly eating his breakfast and reading the papers, Kitty as usual fussing over him like his mother. He would miss her. She was a fine woman, and in another time and another place, they would have become great friends. His eyes darted to a small article at the bottom of the paper. Last night an English constable was summoned to a flat in the Kensington area. The body of a large blonde woman was found dead on her living room floor. Her throat had been cut. There was no evidence of a struggle, and it didn't appear as if robbery was the motive. The neighbors said she was German born. Martin knew by the description that it was Greta Stein. She had spoken to him about the area she lived in when they first met, and the description of the body was too close to be anyone else but Greta. He never finished his breakfast. He went directly to his room and sat down on his bed. "Poor Greta," Martin thought. "What a way for her to die!" England was making Martin quite nervous. Since he got there, two people had been murdered, Pulaski and Greta Stein. And whoever did it had the same chance that morning in Pulaski's flat to kill him as well. "Why, why?" he said to himself. "What the Hell is going on here?" He started to pack his bag for his departure that night for Germany. It still was quite early, and he went for a walk in Kensington Park. It was a brisk and windy day, and his mind was asking all kinds of questions as he walked along in the park. Towards the afternoon he stopped by a post office and wrote a letter to his mother explaining that he had to leave Dublin after the trade show to go to England on personal business. He knew the term personal business would confuse her, but he could think of no legitimate reason for being in London at that time. He also informed her that he might be away for some time and not to worry about him. "Please, Ma," he wrote. "Do not try to write to me. I'll be traveling quite a bit, and I will have no permanent address for a while for you to contact me." He posted the letter and left.

Martin went straight to his room and finished packing. It was time for dinner. Instead of sitting down at dinner, he went straight into the kitchen where Kitty prepared the meals. Surprised to see him, she asked him if the old geezer was seated yet. Martin hadn't seen him yet. "I suppose," he said jokingly, "he's out bottom watching. I've been thinking that he's probably the right man for you on a cold night. At least your bottom will be kept warm."

Kitty started to laugh again but stopped dead in her tracks when she observed a look of depression on Martin's face. "What's wrong, Martin?"

He just handed her some mixed English pounds, ones and fives. "I'm leaving tonight. I have business to conduct in Wales. I don't think we will meet again, Kitty Dougherty, but it was lovely meeting you, and I enjoyed my stay with you. I hope you will meet someone again, for it would be a shame if some decent man missed out in life by not having met you."

Tears filled her eyes. She had grown very fond of Martin, and since she'd been in England, she was never as happy as the last few months she had spent with Martin. He made her laugh, and this made it easier for her to deal with her husband's death. She walked over to him and put her arms around him. "God love you Martin. I hope you will find whatever you are looking for."

Sergeant Keppler

Wilhelm Strauss

Mannheim Krueger

Heinz Schroeder

chapter eight

artin had a few hours left before he was to board the German freighter, so he decided to see Contessa one more time before he left. Leaving Kitty Dougherty's bed and breakfast with his traveling bag, he took a taxi to St. Mary's Hospital. Approaching the information desk, he asked if they might give Contessa Garcia a message that he was in the waiting room. After a slight delay he was informed that she had left the group and gone back to Germany. "There must be a mistake," Martin said. "She had two more days before this sabbatical ended." He was informed that he was correct, but Contessa Garcia had left the class before she had finished her course. Martin was stunned. Once again she had disappeared without telling him of her plans.

Martin headed for the pier, and because he had some time before boarding, he stopped at an unsavory eating-place a block away from it. He could see the old freighter from the place. He ordered a cup of tea and some English biscuits. While he was eating, he looked around the room, and there were some seamen in a group, talking among themselves. They were obviously from some of the ships that were docked at the pier. There were also a few down on their luck characters that made him think to himself that they'd cut your throat for a few shillings. The place gave him some thoughts about being there in the first place. Finishing up quickly, he went out into the cold night air. There was a man waiting outside who spoke directly to him. "Martin Connolly, I'm your contact. Follow me." Martin was relieved because he had thought for a brief moment that he was about to be mugged. The two men headed for the security gate where they were stopped to check their identification. Martin's companion spoke quietly to the security guard, and to Martin's surprise, both men went through the checkpoint without any incident. It was a long walk to the German freighter, and Martin thought he'd never get there without someone or something stopping them, but both men boarded the ship without a hitch. Martin was placed in an isolated small cabin at the stern of the ship. During the trip he saw no one except his contact who brought him his meals. Martin slept almost the entire trip away. There wasn't much else he could do.

The old freighter finally lumbered into Hamburg's docks. The two SS men came aboard and escorted Martin from the ship. He rode in the same car that had brought him to meet Karl Gunter the first time he came to Germany. The trip from Hamburg to Berlin was the usual routine with the two SS men sitting in the front, never speaking a word for the entire trip. Arriving at Gunter's headquarters, he was escorted to Karl's office where he waited for over an hour for him to arrive. The welcome was not as warm and cheerful as the first time he had arrived there. He sensed that Karl was not very pleased with him. Karl sat down opposite him and lit up a long German cigar. Martin, as usual, lit up his old pipe and sat back to relax. "Well, my Irish friend, how are you after your trip?" Karl asked. Martin began to explain what had happened, and Karl interrupted him. "The past is the past." No more was said about it. "An important event in history occurred last night. Poland violated our borders, and they attacked a German outpost. We are now at war with Poland. It remains to be seen if England and France will honor their commitment to defend Poland. Martin," he said, "I haven't forgotten that you saved my life in Spain, and I have secured a commission in the German Wehrmacht for you."

Martin seemed taken back. "I thought I would still be working with you, Karl."

"I'm afraid, my friend, you are not suited for the Abwehr. Germany will need every combat experienced man like you to lead our young men into battle."

"If I am to be in the German army," Martin replied, "I will not accept a commission. I will go as a private. I don't much care for officers, and I would like to be with the common soldier."

Karl seemed to be losing his patience. "Whatever you wish, my friend. You will report for duty tomorrow to the *Fall-schirmjaeger* regiment (paratroopers)." Their meeting was over. There was no warmth in Karl's goodbye or any indication that they were the same friends that had fought together in Spain. Martin left Karl Gunter's office with the feeling of being betrayed. This man had used him all along, and when he hadn't completed his mission, the German had no further use for him. Martin thought of escaping, but couldn't see any way out of it at the moment. Reporting the next morning to the transport unit, Martin was taken to the Fallschirmjaeger in Alten. Two days after the Germans invaded Poland, England and France declared war on Germany. The world was at war, and far away from his Connemara Hills, Martin was in the middle of the fray.

Martin was met at the Fallschirmjaeger school by Sergeant Keppler, a tall blonde German with the appearance of a Prussian officer, not your everyday noncommissioned officer. Martin was dead on with his appraisal of Sergeant Keppler. He had been a commissioned officer and had been reduced in rank for questioning the Führer's experience to command because he had only been a corporal in World War I. Keppler was overheard just once at an officers' club. He was just expressing his concern, and immediately he was reduced in rank and made a squad leader. He was fortunate that he wasn't shot. When Sergeant Keppler finished reading Martin's file and his orders to report to the Fallschirmjaeger school, he spoke to Martin in German and was surprised that Martin fully understood him and also that Martin spoke German fairly well. "This is very unusual, Private Connolly. We have never had a foreigner in this Fallschirmjaeger brigade. We have only the best of the German manhood. Do you have some special qualifications?"

"No," Martin replied.

"Your orders are signed by a Colonel Gunter. Who is he?"

"Colonel Gunter is attached to Abwher I in Berlin."

"That is German Intelligence," Keppler said. "Were you in the Abwher?"

"For a while," Martin replied.

Sergeant Keppler seemed vexed. "What the Hell are they sending me? A spy for a fighting man? Never mind. You probably won't last through the paratrooper training. We have a high percentage of failure. Report to the Quartermaster for your uniform. Are you familiar with our MP40 machine pistol? It's a 9 mm caliber, and it can shoot up to 500 rounds per minute. It is used by our paratroopers because it's small in length, an easy weapon for us to carry when we jump."

Martin told him he was not familiar with the MP40, but was an expert with the Gewehr 98 and with its attached grenade launcher.

"Where have you used it?" Sergeant Keppler replied.

"I have fought in Spain with the Spanish Terico."

"You were in good company, my friend. They were dedicated soldiers. Well, at least you have some combat experience. This is a fairly new experimental unit, and it's made up of all raw recruits, but they are exceptionally enthusiastic for being chosen and belonging to such an elite unit. Our commanding officer is General Kurt Students."

When Martin had put on his Fallschirmjaeger uniform and received his MP40 machine pistol, Sergeant Keppler marched him over to meet his new platoon. They became interested in Martin the moment Sergeant Keppler told them he was Irish born. They were apprehensive about Martin not being one of their own. Could they trust him at their backs? After all, he wasn't German. They whispered quietly into the night of their concerns about Martin.

The training was grueling, and they were pushed to the limit of their endurance. Martin was up to the training, and his Irish rugged health was equal to the task. Where Martin was having trouble was mentally. He was not sure that he could jump out of a flying plane. On the ground he had no trouble with the wooden platforms where the squad practiced to jump. Every time he thought of that open door on the plane and being so far up, his feet would grow cold. The training lasted for many weeks until they actually were taken aboard a plane to make their first jump. The first time up at the door Martin froze. The sergeant pushed him out, but because he was the last to jump, it saved him the embarrassment of the other men seeing that he froze at the door. When they landed, Martin thanked Sergeant Keppler and promised him that it would never happen again. The next time they went up, Martin started to freeze again at the door, and nothing but pure pride in his Irish birth forced him to conquer his fear, and so he jumped. He would never show that kind of fear to anyone again. Martin received a marksman's badge for his MP40. During the year of 1940 Germany had occupied Denmark, Norway, Holland, Belgium, Luxembourg, and France.

Although Martin got along well with the whole platoon, he was particularly fond of Heinz Schroeder, Mannheim Krueger, and the funny man, Wilhelm Strauss. Heinz was perhaps the one man in the squad he trusted the most. He wasn't afraid of anything. Tall, blonde, and handsome, he was the delight of all the ladies. When the four men would go on leave together, Martin was always amazed at the way the German girls would come on to Heinz.

Martin spent three days at Wilhelm's farm and laughed for the whole time he was there. Wilhelm was stocky and burly, and he never stopped eating. The only son of his parents, they seemed to be very affectionate toward him. For the time Martin was on the farm, he worked alongside Wilhelm's father in the fields. It felt good again to be working on Mother Earth. Wilhelm's father reminded Martin of the old fellah in the way he worked, but he wasn't all over Wilhelm like the old fellah would have been. The difference was there were times he would show him a moment of affection. That was enough for Wilhelm to know his father loved him. Martin had never got this from the old fellah, and so he envied the moments of affection that were shown to Wilhelm by his father.

Mannheim was a different story. He was a good man to have alongside you on the battlefield, but between the fighting he was a brooding, deeply disturbed young man and highly suspicious of any gesture of kindness or the showing of any sign of friendship towards him. It would trigger an angry response from him. So Martin went to war with his newfound comrades.

In April 1940 the German airborne Fallschirmjaeger jumped into Norway, and Martin Connolly and his squad were part of the invasion. The object was to capture the main ports and secure the airports. Sergeant Keppler stood at the open door of the plane, his men all lined up ready to jump. He said to them, "Don't delay when you land. Regroup and get away from the drop zone as fast as possible." Martin's group was to secure the main airport at Oslo. One could feel the tension among the men. One by one they jumped, and the last man out was Sergeant Keppler.

The Norwegians stood in amazement as the paratroopers came out of the sky. When they landed, Martin's squad moved quickly and, with little resistance, took over their assigned positions at the airport. Martin, Heinz and Mannheim were together, but there was no sign of Wilhelm. There was some small arms fire, and they fell forward into a prone position. "Where is it coming from?" Heinz asked.

Mannheim pointed to a second-story window in a small building near the runway. There was rifle fire coming from that window. Martin's reaction was spontaneous. He jumped up and ran towards the building. Mannheim shouted out to his comrades to give Martin fire cover. Within seconds he followed Martin out and was about a hundred yards from the building when he was hit in the leg. Down he went, losing his MP40 machine pistol.

Martin knew the firing was coming from the second floor and proceeded very carefully up the stairs. When he got to the landing, he cautiously looked around. His eyes focused on the room where the firing had seemed to be coming from. The firing had stopped, and he burst through the door. Lying near the window were two fallen bodies. They appeared to be dead. He turned over one body at a time, and he could see that both had caps on. As Martin looked closer, he could see that one was an old man with white hair, and the other was an old lady who appeared to be the same age. Martin went over to the other side of the room and threw up his guts. He had killed a very old couple that looked to be just about the age of his mother and father. Bending his head down, he asked his God for forgiveness. Meanwhile Heinz had come up behind him and asked what had happened.

Heinz examined the bodies and told Martin to forget about it. It was war, and those things happened. There was no consoling Martin. He would spend the rest of his days remembering that incident. Weeks later Martin Connolly stood at attention when he received his Iron Cross Second Class for bravery, not for killing the old couple, but for some time later risking his life to save Mannheim in another encounter with the Norwegians. The Major who decorated him had one arm and deep scars all down his face. After he pinned the Iron Cross on Martin, he spoke quietly to him. "Don't you remember me?"

Martin studied his face. "Yes," Martin said, "I do. You're the German officer who took me out of Spain to Germany."

"*Ja, ja,*" he said, "and I'm afraid I will have to postpone our duel. As you can see, my dueling days are over." He had lost his dueling arm.

Wilhelm Strauss had landed in a tree and received some cuts and bruises. They patched him up and sent him back to his squad for active duty. Martin's squad was to jump again on May the tenth into Holland and afterward Belgium. They were assigned to secure airports and bridges in Holland and Belgium. Once again the Fallschirmjaeger led the way for the famous *blitzkrieg* invasion of Europe. Martin and Heinz were both decorated with the Iron Cross First Class for bravery in Holland. They held back a company of Dutch soldiers at the risk of their own lives so that their comrades, who were trapped in a building, could escape. During the fight a squad of Dutch soldiers, who outnumbered Martin and Heinz five to two, overran their position. Martin and Heinz killed three with their rifles and, in fierce hand-to-hand fighting, killed the other two. Martin felt proud of winning this Iron Cross. His thick Irish blood proved equal to the task.

The constant use of the Fallschirmjaeger in this campaign had taken its toll. Out of Martin's platoon there only remained Martin, Heinz, Wilhelm, and Mannheim. The friends were still together. Wilhelm was wounded in Belgium, but quickly recovered and was reassigned to his squad. They were returned to Germany for rest and recreation. Wilhelm went home to his farm where his concerned parents drove him crazy over his wound. He was battle tested, and the days were over for his parents to coddle him. Martin and Heinz left Mannheim in a run-down *biergarten*, brooding over a beer. "Go on," he told them. "I don't need your company. I did fine before I met you, and I'll do better without you two." Try as they may, there was no changing Mannheim's mind. After all they'd been through together, he still rejected any form of kindness or friendship shown to him.

Martin and Heinz got to Berlin at the end of their seventh day of leave. Heinz made contact with an old girlfriend and said good-bye to Martin. They would meet back at the base three days later. Martin walked along the streets of Berlin. This time he noted that although the cafes and restaurants were still bustling with activity, the laughter and merriment had toned down a bit. He ordered a beer and sat quietly looking out onto the street. At first he thought he was imagining what he saw walking towards him. Was it possible? "My God," he said out loud. "It's her! Contessa!" She stopped and smiled at him. His heart pounded inside his chest the same way it had the first time he had met her in the hospital in Spain. She was in the uniform of an officer of the German nurse corps. "Well," Martin said, "doesn't this call for a salute. I'm only a private, and you're an officer."

She looked at the decorations on his chest. "No, I think I should salute you, my brave Irish soldier. I see you have fought well." Martin became embarrassed and asked her if she would like a drink.

"That would be nice," she said and sat down at his table. It seemed like time had stood still. Martin hungrily looked at her. She smiled and said, "You look like you're about to devour me."

Martin reached over the table and caught hold of her wrist. "You have not changed. You still are the most beautiful woman I have ever seen."

Throwing her head back she started to laugh. "More beautiful than your Irish girls?"

There was no hesitation. "Yes," he said, "and more so. So where are you stationed, Contessa?" he asked.

"I'm attached to a combat company in France." Martin for a brief moment looked over her head, and once again he thought he saw Karl Gunter standing in the distance. He stood up and shouted across the table, "Karl, Karl!"

At this point Contessa stood up and looked behind her to see where Martin was pointing. "I don't see Karl," she said. "Where do you see him?"

Martin started to point in the direction that he had seen Karl, but there was no one there. So they both sat back down at the table. "The last I heard about Karl," she said, "he was attached to a combat unit, but no one knows where." Martin asked what happened to his assignment with the Abwehr. "He was transferred from his duties there to a combat unit," she replied.

"That sounds to me," Martin said, "like he stepped on someone's toes. After all, he is the nephew of a Fieldmarshall who had a strong connection with the Abwehr high command and also, I understood, the Führer himself."

"Oh," she said, "the Fieldmarshall fell out of grace with the Führer, and he is now commander of a division stationed in Berlin." They left the café arm in arm. Martin said, "I have two days left of my leave, but in order to get back to my base in time, I will have to leave tomorrow night. Where would you like to go now?" he asked.

Contessa looked directly into his eyes. "I must get back to my quarters tonight. I'm on duty tomorrow, and there is no way I can avoid it. I will meet you tomorrow night at 6 p.m. after I get off duty at this park bench," pointing to a small green bench in front of a very large tree.

Martin was disappointed, but at least he was going to see her for a few hours tomorrow night. "I will take you to your quarters," he said, "and we can talk on the way."

"No, no, Martin, I am meeting another nurse a short distances from here in a little while. I will see you tomorrow night. Goodbye, my love," she said and kissed him on the side of the face.

Martin knew there was no use in protesting, so he let her go, watching her as she disappeared from his view. He threw himself on the park bench and started to fill his pipe. Martin lit it and sat there all night. He fell asleep on the bench and was awakened the next morning by the security police who asked to see his papers. He was a decorated Fallschirmjaeger, although for a time they became suspicious because of his foreign accent. They contacted his base to check out his story. One of the security men brought him to his own home because one of his sons was a wounded Fallschirm-jaeger. He was quite familiar with the details of Martin's combat experience. Martin spent the whole day at the home of the security man whose son was on sick leave. The family was very kind to Martin, and he talked all day with the wounded paratrooper. At one time they had fought within a few miles of each other.

Cleaning himself up, Martin left the security man's home. He expressed his thanks for a lovely day with such a delightful German family. When he left their home, he could not help but wonder how different it would have been if he had not been in the Fallschirm-jaeger or maybe if he had been a spy. The security man looked as though he could be quite a different person if Martin had not been what he said he was.

Martin was sitting on the park bench waiting for Contessa for over an hour when the thought came to him, "Maybe she's not coming." Patiently he waited until about 11 p.m. He knew then that she was not coming. Depressed, he left the bench and started back to his base. It took him all night and into the early morning to get there. The security seemed to be getting tighter, and he had been stopped several times, and once he was detained until his identification was confirmed. Wilhelm had shown up a day earlier from his farm, and he told Martin that he had felt smothered by his mother. She had never stopped crying from the time he got there until the time he left. Wilhelm's talk about his mother gave concerns to Martin. What must his own mother be thinking and feeling not hearing from him for such a long time? When Heinz Schroeder returned, he threw his arms around Martin, nearly knocking him down. Heinz couldn't stop talking about his sexual powers with his old girlfriend he had met on his leave. It made Martin laugh and took his mind off his mother and family in Ireland.

Mannheim hadn't returned, and the commander had to send out the military police for him. It seemed the army found Mannheim at the same *biergarten* where Martin and Heinz had left him. When the military police told him they were escorting him back to the base, Mannheim put up a ferocious fight, and two of the police were taken to the hospital. The *biergarten* was wrecked and the damages were estimated at 1000 marks. The only reason Mannheim wasn't shot was that Sergeant Keppler had informed the base commander that he needed him for the next mission. Mannheim was an experienced combat man, and the commander would need him to keep the new raw recruits under his wing when the shooting started.

Martin had little time for thinking of Contessa. The squad spent days checking their weapons and going over their different assignments. They were not told where they were going, but from the preparation for this mission it would appear to be more airfields and shipping ports that they were to secure. The German High Command was very much aware of the island of Crete, which lay off the Greek coast. The *blitzkrieg* had stormed all through Western

Europe, Yugoslavia, and Greece, but they had not secured this important base, which was capable of launching air strikes on the Romanian oil fields. These oil fields were essential to the German war effort. So the battle plans were drawn, and three weeks before the invasion of Crete, the Luftwaffe pounded the island and attacked the ships in the harbor. The German fighters strafed the defending troops and the vehicles on the roads. Leutnant General Kurt Student, commander of the Fallschirmjaeger with his 22,000 troops, was ordered to secure the island with over 700 fighter planes and bombers to support his troops. The island was defended by approximately 43,000 troops made up of British, New Zealanders, and Greeks. The commanding officer was General Freyberg of the New Zealand army.

Martin and his friends jumped out onto the northeast coast of Crete in May of 1941. They were met with murderous firing from machine guns, rifles, and other small arms by the defenders on the ground. The Fallschirmjaeger were cut to pieces, but Martin and his companions managed to get to the far edge of the Maleme airport. Most of the officers were killed or captured. Reinforcements finally reached them in the form of more paratroopers landing three miles from the airfield. A Maori battalion who were native inhabitants of New Zealand met the German paratroopers with fixed bayonets. The Germans had only their pistols and a few MP40 machine pistols. The weapon containers were out of reach. Sometime after dark the sounds of the battle grew silent. When morning came, Sergeant Keppler sent out two of Martin's squad to reconnoiter the area where the Fallschirmjaeger were dropped. They weren't gone long when they came hurrying back to report. Both men were visibly shaken. They told Sergeant Keppler that the companies that had landed, as far as they could make out, nearly all had been wiped out. Most of them had been bayoneted. It was a massacre. The Maoris gave no quarter, even when the Germans tried to surrender.

The anger spread among Martin's group. There was no German-born who was any angrier than the Irishman. Martin Connolly flew into a murderous rage and charged a group of New Zealanders and Maoris, who were behind the trees and bushes. With bullets flying all around him, he kept running towards the enemy. Firing his MP40 machine pistol, nothing seemed to deter him. When he came close enough to the Maoris and the New Zealanders in the bushes, he let out a burst of obscenities and proceeded to fire into their ranks. Within minutes the Maori and the New Zealand soldiers were lying dead all over the ground. They found Martin sitting with his back to a tree. He was bleeding from a head wound. Heinz and Wilhelm gently lifted his head before they bandaged his wounds. Wilhelm, the strongest of the group, put him over his shoulder, and with Heinz and Mannheim, brought him back to one of the transports that were used to evacuate the dead and wounded. After some of the most intense fighting of World War II, the Germans finally captured the island. The Germans had lost a little fewer than 7,000 men. Fifteen to sixteen thousand defenders escaped with the help of the British navy.

i have not forgotten thee

Stalingrad

chapter nine

The Fallshirmjaeger (paratroopers) had sustained very heavy casualties, and the German High Command would never again use the German paratroopers on such a scale as they did at Crete. Martin's head wounds were superficial, so he was returned to the same infantry unit within a few days. He reported for duty to Leutnant Schaefer who was in command of a slug (platoon). Martin asked in a respectful tone about his old comrades, would it be possible to join up with them. Leutnant Schaefer took a few steps back and stared at Martin. "You Fallshirmjaeger think you are too good for the regular Wehrmacht soldier. Right away you come in here looking for favors. Well, you will be treated like a regular Wehrmacht soldier. Your parachute days are over. From now on you will receive no more special favors than the rest of us."

Martin started to smile. "In all due respect, sir, I wish someone would have informed me of the luxury that you intimate that I was receiving as a Fallshirmjaeger. It would have been some consolation to me while I was in the hospital recovering from wounds received on the battlefield."

Leutnant Schaefer's face turned red with anger. The arrogance of this foreigner was too much, yet he must show the respect due to a soldier who had been wounded for the Fatherland. Once again he glanced at the well-decorated Irishman and decided not to press the issue. "Come with me," he said in a threatening manner. They entered one of the barracks, and there lying on the army cots were Heinz, Wilhelm, Mannheim, and Sergeant Keppler. Even the Leutnant understood the greetings that are given to old comrades that have fought together. Leutnant Schaefer could not resist some sarcastic parting words. "Listen," he said to the other soldiers in the barracks, "keep your eyes on these heroes. They will show you how it's done." Unfortunately he was the only one to see his own humor. These men knew they were looking at the best that Germany could muster. They had given their lives and blood on every battle field they fought on. The Wehrmacht were deeply respectful of them. The German respects strength, and it takes great inner strength to fight well in combat.

Martin asked Sergeant Keppler after the Leutnant left, "Where are we headed?"

"We aren't heading anywhere. We are to be retrained in infantry tactics and weapons. Then we will become instructors to the new recruits."

Mannheim started to shout, "I will not become nursemaid to any man. I am a Fallshirmjaeger." Martin could see the pride that Mannheim had in belonging to this elite fighting unit.

Martin hadn't time to think very much about what was happening to him. Mannheim's outburst brought Martin to realize that he was also proud of their group, yet they were Germans and should think of themselves as patriots for their country. But what was Martin fighting for? He wasn't German. He was an outsider, yet he had grown very fond of the German soldier. Martin believed that their reasoning was that they were soldiers defending their homeland, and their duty was to obey without question. Martin also saw in the Germans a loyalty to each other, great courage, and bravery on the battlefield. He watched the hard shell that surrounded the German soldier crack when they were confronted with a comrade dying in combat. He also listened to them reading their letters from home and watched the softness in their eyes when they talked about their wives and children. They had treated him like one of their own. He had trusted his life with them just like he would a fellow Irishman. Heinz, Mannheim, and Wilhelm, each in their own turn, had risked their lives for him. For the time being he pushed these thoughts out of his head.

Next to the training base was a prisoner of war camp. The Germans had taken prisoners from all over Europe. One afternoon Martin was walking past the barbed wire fence that kept the prisoners confined when his eye caught a group of what appeared to be British soldiers. Some of them were wearing patches that indicated that they were members of an Irish brigade. Stopping and looking among them, he saw one young lad and asked him if this was part of an Irish brigade. The Irishman was stunned by the Irish accent coming from a German soldier. "Come here, lads," he shouted out. "You won't believe this!" A group of them gathered quickly around the young Irish lad. "Would you believe this bastard is Irish?" he said.

This incited the others, and they started calling Martin names and threatening him. The yelling came swiftly to a halt when a deep voice could be heard above the group. "Well Martin, you certainly scraped the bottom of the bowl when you joined up with this lot."

Martin tried to focus into the crowd to see who the caller was who was moving towards him. He was standing in front of him on the other side of the fence when Martin finally recognized him. "Mike Murray!" he said. He had forgotten all the name-calling and abuse he had been taking, and an anxiety started to grow as he asked question after question to Mike. "What have you heard about back home? How is my mother?"

Mike was trying to make up his mind if he should answer these questions when he decided he was going to have his revenge on him. He'd give him all the bad news he could. "Your mother's dead. You broke her heart, you lousy specimen of manhood. She hadn't heard from you for over two years when she decided there was no point in living any more. Mrs. Connolly assumed you were most likely dead because you would never go that long without writing to her. She went up to the bedroom one day and never left it. She refused to eat or drink, and she died shortly after." Martin gasped for breath. He wanted to fall down on the ground and cry, but he understood what Mike was trying to do to him. So he weathered the storm by asking him how his sisters were. "I married Maureen and left her after a year. Your mother was right. I was no good. I went over to England and joined up with this Irish outfit attached to an English regiment. I've been killing Gerries like your friends since I joined up. I'm only sorry I didn't run across you. I would have loved to put the bayonet to you."

Martin turned away and walked back to his barracks. Sitting outside the barracks, he lit up his old pipe and filled it with German tobacco. He had long ago run out of his precious Irish fill. His first thought was who was managing the farm. Poor Bridget, he guessed, was doing it all. Mike's words about his treatment of his mother were true because he couldn't tell her where he was. No excuse could clear his conscience. One more burden of guilt to carry through his life. "What life?" he thought. He would never see Ireland again. He was a dead man.

Sergeant Keppler, Martin, Heinz, Mannheim, and Wilhelm reported to Captain Reischman on the morning of June 22nd, 1941. "Germany has launched operation Barbarossa (the invasion of the Soviet Union)." Shocked and surprised they listened until the captain had finished. They were informed that they would be assigned to train all new recruits who would pass through the training camp. Because they were combat experienced, they would be used to guide and prepare these young recruits for the battlefield.

Martin and his comrades were disappointed for they wanted to join the fighting with their former Fallschirmjaeger unit. Mannheim was the first to speak up. "Sir, I am Fallschirmjaeger, and I wish to return to the Fallschirmjaeger."

"The Fallschirmjaeger are being reassigned to other German units, mostly the infantry and the Panzer divisions. In the future they will be used in small operations. My personal opinion is they will eventually be disbanded. The four of you under Sergeant Keppler can expect to spend one year at this base training new recruits, and there will be thousands of these recruits passing through this base. Their lives will depend on how well you train them. Because you are Fallschirmjaeger, you will have to be retrained yourselves. We cannot teach you anything in combat. You could most likely teach us. You are our showpieces, all decorated heroes of the Third Reich. These men will look up to you and follow you anywhere. After a year you will be assigned to an infantry division for further combat. Next week you will begin your training." Captain Reischman dismissed them, and off they went talking among themselves.

Martin expressed his concern with Germany's attacking Russia. "They have never been defeated by armies that have invaded them. Russia was full of frozen French bodies when Napoleon tried to take Moscow. Russia has defeated many armies that have attempted this task. I don't believe we'll waltz through Russia like we did Western Europe."

Mannheim spoke up, "The Führer will lead us to victory. He is a military genius. And if you were German, you would believe this. It is Germany's destiny to rule the world."

Martin looked at Mannheim with sadness in his eyes. "Is this what it's all about, ruling the world?" Heinz and Wilhelm moved in between the two men and eased them apart. Heinz said, "There must be some lonely woman in this town who is in need of my service." They all laughed and headed for the biergarten. Yet Martin's head was still full of what Mannheim had said. The words "Germany's destiny is to rule the world" stayed with him.

The year 1941 was a significant one for Germany. Roosevelt signed the Lend Lease Act; Germany invaded Yugoslavia and Greece; there was heavy fighting back and forth in North Africa; Germany invaded the Soviet Union; war broke out in the Pacific; Germany became allies with Japan and Italy; and Germany declared war on the United States. Martin and his Fallschirmjaeger comrades spent an entire year training the new German recruits. Even though they were all in their middle to late twenties, the Sergeant being the exception at thirty-two years of age, it was grueling work—long hikes, many hours of exercise, nights and days in the field practicing maneuvers. They would send one trained group off after the other to the battlefields. At night Martin and Mannheim, Heinz and Wilhelm would fall asleep exhausted in their bunks. Rarely did they go into town on leave. Mannheim had become restless, and during the year he made several requests of Captain Reischman for a transfer. Once he got into a heated argument with the Captain who warned him he could have him shot for the manner in which he spoke to a German officer. Mannheim always replied in the same way. "Go ahead," he would shout. "I don't much care if I live or die." This Captain couldn't afford to shoot a hero of the Third Reich in front of new recruits, yet he was seriously thinking of transferring Mannheim out and having him shot somewhere else.

The war with Russia had been going on since June of 1941, when Captain Reischman in June of 1942 informed Martin and his Fallschirmjaeger comrades that they would be reassigned for duty with the Sixth Army under the command of General Friedrich von Paulus. The Sixth Army was in Beligorad and was heading towards the Don River. This was the beginning of an offensive to take Stalingrad. They would receive transportation in the morning. "Well, Mannheim," the Captain said, "you are getting your wish, and it is time to take out that bad temper you have on the Russians."

Mannheim smiled. "I shall miss your warm and kind concern for me, sir."

The Sixth Army on July 8, 1942, with Martin and his Fall-schirmjaeger comrades were establishing bridgeheads across the river in the Karagh area. A month later the Sixth Army crossed the Don River. September 3, 1942, the Sixth Army joined up with the Panzers. In October heavy fighting broke out with units of the Sixth Army surrounding a tractor factory. During the fighting Heinz was wounded in the shoulder, and Wilhelm went out to bring him back to safety. He was killed by machine gun fire.

The weather had grown cold, and it was snowing. Martin was asking, "When are we going to get our winter uniforms?" They were still dressed in their light summer clothing.

One of the Wehrmacht officers told him not to worry. "You'll be back in Germany in a month. Our reinforcements will be here shortly." Martin's gut feeling told him this was not to be.

No one could talk about Wilhelm Strauss. It was too painful. Heinz wrote a letter to Wilhelm's mother telling her that Wilhelm had saved his life and was killed doing it. He told her she had a hero for a son who died to save his comrade, and all the Fallschirmjaeger were proud of him.

The end of 1942 produced some heavy fighting for the Sixth Army. They pushed back the Soviet troops towards the Volga River. Martin had never experienced such cold in his whole life. Such significant amounts of snow would fall that it staggered his imagination. It was all too consuming to him. His whole life in Ireland had little or no snow. The weather was always damp, but never the fierce cold that the Russian winter had brought him. The Germans were accustomed to heavy snow and very cold winters, but even to them this was unbearable. They were frost bitten, and thousands of them froze to death in the snow. They slept on one single blanket at night, and their rations were cut to one third. They killed and ate their horses and still the winter clothing had not reached them. They fought in light uniforms in this hostile climate that in the past had defeated the might of some of the most powerful armies in the world.

November 11, 1942, the Sixth Army launched a major attack to capture Stalingrad. They fought from house to house, building to building. It was all small arms, grenades, rifles, machine guns, and mortars. The city was in rubble from the constant bombing by the Luftwaffe. Each street had to be taken one by one. The Soviets had snipers in all the bombed out buildings and machine gun nests in the streets and in the craters. They placed their men anywhere they could conceal them. On November 22, 1942, the Sixth Army was surrounded by the Soviets who had put in one army after another to reinforce their losses.

Heinz was patched up and caught up with Martin and Mannheim. Sergeant Keppler, who had been separated during the fighting for about a week, joined them again, this time with a patrol of infantrymen. He brought some Russian cigarettes and a bottle of Russian vodka. To Martin it was a pre-Christmas gift. Mannheim got drunk and charged one of the craters killing five Soviet soldiers. He was awarded the Iron Cross First Class. He couldn't remember what had happened. This was one of the few laughs Martin got in this horror of places. Sergeant Keppler told them the news was that reinforcements were on their way. They called it Operation Winter Tempest. This was never to be. The reinforcements were not able to get through to the Sixth Army.

The month of December found Martin and his comrades fighting off the attack of the Soviet troops. The Soviets were determined to take back the city. On Christmas Day Martin, Heinz and Mannheim were trapped in one of the buildings. Heinz and Mannheim told Martin that they had made up their minds that they were not going to die like trapped rats. They were going out fighting. They advised Martin to escape while they created a diversion for him. "You are Irish. This is not your country." And they praised him on how bravely he had fought for their country. He had done his duty.

Martin watched them as they marched out towards the Soviets, these men with whom he had faced death on foreign battlefields, who had shared their last rations with him. Martin thought of the cold nights they had clung to each other to keep from freezing to death. "No, no, wait!" he cried out. "I'm coming with you," and out he went after them. He was just about a few yards behind them when a loud explosion blew him, Heinz and Mannheim into the air. It was a Soviet grenade. Martin hit the ground hard, and his rifle fell next to him. He tried to see out of his blood soaked eyes. The blood was coming from a wound on his forehead. Trying to clean his eyes for a moment, he looked around him to see what had happened to Heinz and Mannheim. On his left was Mannheim. His broken body laid twisted on the ground. And looking quickly to his right, he saw Heinz's battered, bloody body on his back. He tried to crawl over to him. Heinz seemed to disappear from his eyes, and what now appeared to be many shadows blocked his view. He tried once more to wipe the blood from his eyes to see if he could get a better look at what was happening. He saw that the shadows were Russian soldiers as his eyes regained their focus. He heard a shrieking yell that came from Heinz's direction. He watched as a Russian soldier removed his bayonet from Heinz's chest. "You Russian bastard!" he cried and tried to raise himself up. He had cried out in English, which probably saved his life. The Russian soldiers came towards him and once again he tried to raise up, but this time he fell back into darkness.

The Russians interrogated Martin. They were trying to establish why an Englishman, who they believed Martin was, had fought with the Germans against his own British allies. They believed him to be a spy. The other prisoners who were captured were marched to a concentration camp in Siberia. Martin was kept outside of Stalingrad in a makeshift hospital they had for their own wounded. Martin had suffered a head wound and concussion from the grenade.

On January 8, 1943, the Russians offered to let General Paulus surrender with honorable terms. Hitler ordered Paulus to fight to the last man and not to surrender. The fighting continued until they were forced to surrender on February 2, 1943.

It was a week later when a Soviet officer came to Martin's bedside and started asking him questions. The Russian was a young lieutenant who looked to Martin as if he hadn't learned to shave yet.

"Why do you fight for the Germans, Englishman?" was his first question.

An angry Martin shouted back at him, "I am no damn Englishman, you stupid bastard. I am Irish, and the last country that I would fight for is Mother England."

Martin was met with a slap across his face. The Russian had a fair knowledge of English and understood him. "You're here to answer questions, and I could have you shot this very minute."

It was too much for Martin. He lost all control. His comrades were dead. He was wounded and still exhausted from the Russian cold and snow. He reached over and caught the Russian by the neck and proceeded to throttle him. Where he got all his strength he would never know, but it didn't last very long. The Russian drew his pistol and beat him on his wounded head until Martin fell back into the bed unconscious.

A few weeks later Martin was transferred to a prisoner-of-war camp at Vologda, which was in northwestern Russia. This region was about three hundred miles from Moscow. The area had cold snowy winters and short summers with periods of rain that could be as much as 31 inches. Martin would remain in this camp until the surrender of Germany in May 1945, a little over a year and three months. This prisoner of war camp was not run like Mrs. Dougherty's B&B in London, and how often he thought about her Irish breakfast in the morning. After a while he could actually taste her breakfast, or at least he believed he could. The cold Russian winters and very little food took its toll on Martin. The days and nights became unbearable. There wasn't much chance of escape, although if one could escape, where would one go? He would probably freeze to death in the Russian snow. The best chance was in summer, but where again would he go? The Vologda territory is 146 thousand square kilometers, which would be equal to Belgium, Denmark, the Netherlands and Switzerland altogether, a considerably long way to travel before you could even get out of the region.

The prisoners' time was spent working twelve to fourteen hours a day in hard labor. Martin's life was changed completely during this time. He met with Father Christopher Roche, an Irish chaplain in the German Wehrmacht. There were many Catholics in Germany. Hitler tried his best to get along with the Catholic

Church. He knew it wasn't a good move to isolate so many German Catholics from their faith. He had placed some restrictions on the Church, but they were not enough to concern the German people. Fr. Roche had served in Germany for years before the war. Like Martin he had grown fond of the German people. They met while waiting in a long line for their meals. The prisoners were given only potato soup and a slice of bread, which was the only big meal they received all day. Towards the end of the war, even that was not forthcoming. Martin was directly behind Fr. Roche in line, and when the priest spoke in German, there was no mistake it was done with a Cork accent. Martin reached over his shoulder. "You're a long way from Cork, boyo." The priest nearly cried with pure joy when he heard Martin's west of Ireland accent. The priest caught him around the shoulders. "Thank God! I never thought I would hear an Irish voice again before I died. What in the devil are you doing here, boy?"

"I've been with the Fallschirmjaeger, and I was captured at Stalingrad."

They became fast friends, and at every chance they got, they would talk to each other. This was mostly during meals. Martin and Father Roche made the most of this time. Martin spoke of his constant fits of depression and not being able to justify his actions from the past. The guilt of all that killing was slowly eating away at his insides. He had developed migraine headaches and would spend hours in pain. There were times he could not see for a while from the migraines. This was dangerous when he was working outside. The blindness lasted only about five or ten minutes, but it was enough to panic Martin, especially when he was doing heavy work.

The priest tried to console him, and secretly he thought that Martin had the making of a good priest. So he began to work on Martin. Father Roche fully convinced Martin that he could make up for his guilt by becoming a priest. He had Martin reading his Bible, which Martin had never done in school in Ireland. A peace started to come over him.

At that time one of the Russian guards took a liking to Martin and asked him to teach him English. During the time that Martin taught him, the man became friendlier. He gave Martin some stale Russian tobacco that Martin filled his pipe with. He hadn't had pipe tobacco in over a year. Martin found the Russian tobacco was even too much for him. This friendly guard began teaching Martin a little Russian. One morning before they went to work, the guard handed Martin a Russian newspaper. "Try to read what you can," the guard told him. Martin was browsing through the paper when he saw a picture of a couple being decorated with the Red Star of the Soviet Union. Martin strained his eyes because he believed that the man in the picture was Karl Gunter, and at his side was Contessa Garcia. There were no titles under the picture, so he really didn't know. He finally drove the thoughts out of his head and was about to throw the paper away when he remembered the guard telling him to save it so he could practice reading in Russian. He told Martin that by reading over and over the words in the paper, it would produce a small vocabulary for him. In one of the sessions with the guard he told Martin that it was strange to him that the German officer pictured in the paper was working against his own people. Martin asked him, "Why do you say this?"

"The article said that the man was a high German official working with his lover for Russian intelligence, not the profile of a hard Nazi." Martin looked again at the picture, but there was no way he could conclusively identify the man in the photo.

Martin started to accompany Father Roche in his rounds ministering to the sick and wounded and felt good about helping the priest. At first the German prisoners didn't trust him. They thought he was a spy that the Russians had planted among them. After a while they could see that Martin was doing his best to comfort their sick and wounded. Father Roche also noted that Martin had a way about him that people would trust and accept. Martin spent many hours and days with those who were about to die, even sharing the few morsels of food he had with them. He was losing his strength more and more each day. Then one night he had a dream that his mother came to him and told him that the old fellah loved him. He woke up crying. Even though it was only a dream, it meant so much to him that Martin thought it was the sign he was looking for. The next morning he went directly to Father Roche to tell him that he had made up his mind that he was going to be a priest.

Father Roche trained him to be an altar boy. This would give Martin the experience of watching and participating with the priest in Mass. Their biggest problem was finding bread for the hosts. No one wanted to give up even a piece of bread when they could eat it. Martin was always the first to give up his bread to Father Roche. Quietly he began to teach Martin how to say Mass. This was to help him catch up with the students at the seminary when he returned to Ireland. He also taught Martin some theology, and he would go over the laws of the church with him. Towards the end of the year Martin had been fully convinced that when the war was over, he would return to Ireland and become a priest.

Sometime in January 1945, Father Roche took sick, and Martin took over his duties but could not say Mass or give out sacraments because he wasn't a priest. He did the best he could to comfort the men although there wasn't much he could do for them. It was mind boggling to Martin to even try to understand how the human body and mind could survive this misery and still be able to rise in the morning and work all day into the evening. They wore nothing but rags on their backs, no food in their stomachs, and most of them were very sick. There were times when they received some brutal beatings from their guards who hated them. If a prisoner would give a wrong look or wouldn't respond quickly enough to a guard's orders, he was beaten with rifle butts. Even at night there were cases of their own comrades attacking them while they slept to take whatever few possessions they had left. The attackers would see them with a small piece of bread they had saved or some extra clothing they had taken off a dead man they were burying. Cannibalism was not unheard of. Anything and everything was done to survive.

Father Roche's health grew worse, and Martin tried to keep him alive by giving him his own food, which was very little. After a week Martin also became very weak, but he still couldn't save this gallant Irish priest. He felt guilty because he could continue eating the little meals that he was given and would not have to share them with Father Roche anymore. Part of him was actually glad that the priest was gone. He fought with this demon of guilt in his soul. Martin kept asking himself how he could justify his feelings. What kind of a man had he become? There was no one to tell him that it was not unusual for combat soldiers to feel guilty about being alive after a battle when they saw their dead comrades alongside them. Martin would find out years later that men who have been in combat, no matter how old they grew, would never know such fear again. Their eyes and ears would never again experience the horror they had seen and heard on the battlefield. These men would never show the white feather in civilian life. They were too proud. They had proven to themselves that they had stood fast in the ranks of the most terrifying fear of all, the battlefields of war.

Never a day went by that Martin didn't see Contessa's face in front of him. He continued to wonder about the picture in the paper of the spies, but he couldn't confirm who they were. He had no way of proving it was them.

One night he dreamt again of his lovely green fields in the Connemara hills. He drew great strength from this dream. He would live somehow so he could see those hills once more.

In May 1945, the Germans surrendered. The original German troops that were trapped by the Soviet Army in Stalingrad were estimated at between 285,00 and 300,000. Some 91,000 surrendered, and they were sent to Siberian concentration camps. At the end of the war, only 5,000 returned to Germany. And Martin Connolly was one of them, but since he was an Irish citizen, he was transferred to Ireland after many months in Germany. It took time to straighten out all the paperwork. His birth certificate had to be certified proving that he was an Irish citizen, and there was an investigation by the Irish authorities to determine if he had broken any Irish laws while serving with the Wehrmacht.

The Irish authorities had no information on his spy activity in Ireland, nor did they have any evidence to tie him into the disappearance of McCarthy. Martin Connolly returned to Ireland at the end of September 1945. The rugged Irish hurler now was but a shell of a man, both physically and mentally. He was spent. The Irish authorities but him up at a B&B in Dublin near a local hospital and gave him some money to live on. He spent most of his days in Dublin and would report to the hospital in the morning for treatment. And when he had finished, he would take the bus out to old Dun Laoghaire where he would sit for the rest of the day on a bench at the west pier. This was fine when he first arrived in September and even October, but during the months of December, January, and even the beginning of February, it was bitter cold and raining. He bought some fisherman's rainwear for a few pounds from an old sailor who was retiring from the sea. This kept him dry. This particular old man would spend the day at the pier talking away to him. Somehow it made Martin feel better just talking to someone, even though this old man could not know or even imagine the horrors he had gone through.

By February 1946 Martin's physical wounds had healed, but his mind was still in bitter conflict with his soul. Once again he was united with his favorite Irish tobacco for his old pipe, which was his only joy. Waiting no longer, he headed for his beloved Galway hills. The train trip down to Galway was about three hours, and Martin sat by the window watching as the train hurried by the little green patches, with the old cows wandering along the grass and the sheep grazing in the fields. Once in a while he would see a sight that excited him the most, the fine sturdy Irish horses standing in the green grass of Ireland. A businessman sat opposite him, reading the paper. Putting the paper down, he said to Martin, "What do you think about these war crime trials that are going on in Germany? My God, they must have been a pack of murdering bastards if what they say is true about them. The whole damn German race should be eliminated," he said.

Martin looked at him. "Then, sir, if you took part in this elimination, you would have been no better than they were."

The man's face grew red. "Ah," he said, going back to his paper. "A lot you'd know about these people."

Martin smiled and ignored the man for the rest of the trip. When the train came into Galway City, Martin was the first one off. He stood there breathing in the Galway sea air. It gave him great pleasure just to be in the middle of the Galway accents. He thought to himself, "What a fine looking people they are!" He had always taken them for granted. His money nearly gone, he hired a taxi to take him to Connemara. The days were gone for him to handle that ride on horseback. Maybe he could do it some day in the future when he felt strong again, but not now. When he arrived at Connemara, he stood in the grass looking at the smoke coming out of his house. The Irish blue sky was over his head, but this time there was no rainbow. He fell to the ground and, straightening out his body, clung to the grass with both hands. Sobbing aloud, he thought the pain would never leave him. At one point he thought he was having a heart attack, but a good psychologist would have told him all of the years of that pent up emotion was finally coming out on him. The guilt had finally taken its toll. After a while, he managed to sit up from the ground. He was extremely weak in his legs, and both of them were shaking under him. It took a little while before he got to his house. Martin knocked and knocked on the door, but there was no answer. Finally the door opened, and it was Bridget, staring in amazement. "Martin, my God," she said, "I thought you were dead. Come in, come in. And from the looks of you, it would appear like you nearly made it."

Sitting him down by the warm fireplace, she removed his coat and hat. Martin sat there for a while, just staring into the fireplace. Just being home and by the warm fire seemed to work miracles. After a while he took out the old pipe and started to fill it. Once the pipe was lit, a peace seemed to settle over his face. Puffing away he could hear Bridget asking questions of him. It wasn't long before the questions were getting through to him.

"Martin, you look very bad," Bridget said. "May I get you a cup of tea?"

"Yes, please," Martin replied, "I'd love a cupa."

"I have some brown bread. How about a big chunk of that with lots of butter?"

"Hurry up woman," he said. "You're torturing me with the waiting." It had been months since any form of humor had passed from his lips.

Bridget watched with delight as Martin gobbled down the brown bread and tea. When he had finished, all the brown bread was gone, and about four cups of tea had joined the brown bread. The pipe was lit again, and Martin started to tell Bridget where he had been all these years and what had happened to him. Bridget shed tears at what she was hearing. Her young handsome brother had gone away to war and had come back an old man with multiple scars on his face, and what about the wounds he had told her about on the rest of his body. He asked about Grainne and Maureen. "Maureen is over in England," she said. "She left after Mike Murray left her. She is living with an English soldier in Manchester, and they have a child." Martin shook all over. "Grainne is in

Dublin, and working in the bank. She's going with a lovely fellow named Kiernan McCafferty. He is working in the bank with her."

Martin looked at her as only a brother who is concerned could. "Bridget, are you taking on all of this farm work by yourself?"

"Ah, sure," she said, "it's no bother to me. I'm used to it by now. Besides, when Ma died, it released me from all that time taking care of her. It gave me more time to work the fields."

While he was talking to Bridget, he fell asleep in the chair. The warm fire put him into a deep sleep. The morning had come and gone when Martin awoke to the smell of rashers and eggs. There was no brown bread left. He had eaten it all the night before, but he dove into the eggs and rashers until nothing was left but a shine on the plate.

Bridget was laughing at him. "Don't worry, Martin. You can stay here with me, and I'll take care of you until you get your strength back." He smiled at her. She had the makings of a fine woman.

I have not forgotten thee

Monastery

chapter ten

In the spring of 1946 Martin left the farmhouse to go to Cork. He wanted to visit Fr. Roche's seminary. When he arrived there, he was met by Monsignor McDonagh. He was the head of the seminary for young men for the priesthood. They hit it off well from the beginning. What they had in common was the affection they both had for Fr. Roche. The Monsignor invited him to stay for a few days, and Martin accepted at once. He felt peace and a sense of well-being under the roof of this seminary. He ate with the young men who were a delight to be with, all of them devoted to their God. Full of good humor, they made him laugh. They questioned him for hours at a time on his experiences in Spain and his service in World War II. What was it like in a strange country? What was life like in the battle at Stalingrad? Did you kill men? And so on. Martin became exhausted from the questioning. There were times he couldn't answer the questions himself. At night he sat for hours with Monsignor McDonagh, talking about life in general. "What will you do," he asked Martin, "with the rest of your life? You're still a young man. How old are you?"

"I'm thirty-two," he said.

"Well, you're still young enough to find your calling whatever it might be."

"I am very happy here, Monsignor. It's been years since I've felt at peace with my inner soul. Would you have a job here for me?" he asked. "I'd be more than glad to work just for my room and board."

The Monsignor smiled at him like a father would at a child who has said something funny to him. "I've got twenty pairs of young strong hands to take care of whatever has to be done around here." The Monsignor changed the conversation and asked about Fr. Roche and his work with the prisoners. It was obvious to the Monsignor that Martin had a lot of respect for Fr. Roche, and he listened with interest in how Martin had assisted the Cork priest. "Did you like what you were doing?" he asked Martin.

"I did," Martin replied. "It made me feel good inside, and I needed that for all the killing that I had done."

Martin had told the Monsignor the whole story of his life that first night they met. They had talked into the morning hours. "I think," the Monsignor said, "you were brave to go over to Spain to fight for the Faith. That took a bit of doing."

"I told myself I was going to fight for the Faith, but after a while I came to the conclusion I was running away from my father."

The Monsignor took a long look at him before he spoke again. "That took a lot of honesty, boyo, to come to that conclusion. It would seem to me, Martin, that you have never lied to yourself about the wrongs you have committed. And from what you tell me, they have been a series of mortal sins and grievous offenses to your God. But you are man enough to tell it the way it is. I also can understand your loyalty to your young German comrades, and why you would continue to fight alongside them. The cause you were fighting for was wrong, but I say this now as a man and not as a priest. I have respect for you for the loyalty you have shown for the German Fallschirmjaeger. These are the qualities that I would look for in someone for the calling of the priesthood. Your character and sensitivity in helping Fr. Roche in that concentration camp was admirable. You could have sat back like all the others and tried to stay alive and ignored the pleas of help from the sick and wounded. The quality of loyalty is a necessity in the priesthood, a complete unconditional loyalty to God and the Church. You possess that rare quality of being able to judge yourself and not hide your faults and not make excuses for your actions.

"Martin," he continued, "you have experienced every kind of temptation that exists in this old world. You've been exposed to death and destruction, mortally wounded, both in the body and the mind. There are very few of us who would be able to bring this kind of experience in life to our young seminarians. Nearly all of these young boys are taken directly from their homes to the seminary, and they have never lived anywhere in the outside world except the safety of their own homes. This would be so valuable to them to have someone like you able to share these experiences with them. We have all been taught that we are given a vocation from God to enter the priesthood, but there are many of us who had to pray for that vocation. It didn't just come to us in a dream."

He smiled at Martin. "Do not think badly of me for expressing my own opinions. I know it's not what you have learned in school. I have chosen to speak out on many occasions on the church's policy on certain issues. I've been blessed with having a good friend in Rome who has saved me many times from disciplinary action. Martin, I'd like you to stay for a little while here, and we could talk quite a bit during your stay. I must tell you that my instincts tell me you'd make a good priest."

Martin was absolutely stunned. He was speechless at what the Monsignor was proposing. They said no more, and Martin returned to his room for a long and sleepless night.

The next few days Martin didn't see much of the Monsignor who was quite busy in the classrooms teaching his young eager prospects for the priesthood. There were four other teaching priests with whom he would have his meals. To Martin they were all reasonably happy, and they all seemed to get along together quite well. After classes, they would go out on the field and play football and hurling with these young hopefuls. Watching them lining up for hurling practice one day, he saw one young lad who couldn't put the ball over the bar with his hurling stick. Martin went over to him, and within ten minutes or so he had the young fellow hitting it right over the bar. The priest who was out there with them asked Martin to have a go at it himself. Martin hadn't used the stick in a good few years, but he started to walk about sixty yards away from the goal post when he heard laughing from the group. It seems the other priests were making some humorous remarks about Martin thinking he was a member of the Galway senior hurling team. Martin put the ball in the air and sent it straight as an arrow through the uprights. There was dead silence for a few moments, and then the whole group ran towards him. Martin glanced over to the corner of the doorway of the classroom building just in time to see

Monsignor McDonagh move his head to the side with a sign of approval, the typical gesture of the Irish way of saying. "Good man yourself."

Martin spent days thinking over what Monsignor McDonagh had told him. He knew he wouldn't see Contessa again, and it was more than likely it was she in the Russian paper with Karl that he had seen in the prisoner-of-war camp. There wasn't anything back home for him, and Bridget deserved the farm. She had worked hard for it, and he believed she could handle it on her own. He believed that there was good work for him to do. He owed it to his God. There was no way of repaying his God, but he could serve as a proof of his gratitude for sparing his life. Martin knew that by becoming a priest he would be able to say Mass for his father and mother, and he reasoned he owed them this, especially his mother for whom he felt responsible for her premature death worrying about him. His biggest doubt was if he could handle the huge studies that were necessary to become a priest. He had only finished secondary school, and he hadn't done well in school at all. Monsignor McDonagh met with Martin in June and could see that Martin hadn't made up his mind yet. "Go home, boy, to your sister, " he said, "and think about the conversations we had together, and if you decide to become a priest, we will start you in classes in September. God love you, and I shall pray for you, and I hope God will send you back to us. It is my firm belief that you have found your destiny, Martin Connolly."

If Martin had met another priest who was in charge of this seminary, he would have been advised to go back to farming. This Monsignor was a special kind of priest with an exceptional instinct and foresight for bringing young men into the priesthood. He saw in Martin not only the qualities that would make him a good priest, but he thought that Martin could become an exceptional priest. Martin returned to Galway to the surprise of Bridget. "I thought you were gone again for good. What happened this time?"

Martin explained where he had been, and Bridget became quiet. After a while she turned to him. "I think you will make a fine priest, Martin Connolly. I remember one night with Ma talking about you. She had expressed to me how she would have wished you had become a priest. Mrs. Burke started her thinking the day she delivered you. After Mrs. Burke had washed you off and wrapped you in a blanket, she gave you to Ma. 'Ah, this one,' she said, 'will be a priest.'" Bridget looked at the expression on Martin's face, and she started to laugh. "I know what you're thinking. It was some kind of an omen. Well, it wasn't. Go away with yourself. Every mother in Ireland is praying for her son to become a priest, and if they all got their wishes, there'd be no one for the likes of me to marry." Turning towards the kitchen, she spun back around, "and if I don't find a man soon, I'll be joining the priesthood meself." She left Martin laughing.

Bridget's remarks got him thinking. She must be very lonely here on the farm by herself. Martin felt bad for her. It was very insensitive of him not to speak to her about that particular subject. He remembered asking her when he first arrived how she was managing the farm, but nothing about being alone by herself. They sat down to eat at the table, and Martin once again noticed all the empty chairs. How lonely this place would be if he stayed, and eventually Bridget would leave. She had always wanted to go to Dublin to that culinary school. Martin realized at once that he could not live alone, no matter how much he loved his Connemara hills. It has to be shared with someone, and he knew he could never love another woman like Contessa. So he probably never would marry and would end up a grouchy old farmer, living by himself. While they were eating, Martin asked Bridget if she had any suitors who she was interested in. "Oh, my dear brother, there were plenty of local lads courting me when Ma died, but unfortunately for me, they were actually courting the old farm."

Martin smiled. She had a great wit about her. Who else but an Irish woman could make fun of her own misfortunes? The summer days went by quickly, and Martin prayed for guidance. Frequently he'd go back in his thoughts to the old Cork nun he had met on the bus going to Galway City years ago. If he was to become a priest, then he wanted to be a missionary.

The end of august came, and Martin tearfully kissed Bridget goodbye. He promised to write to her. If he made it to the priesthood, she would be invited to his ordination. Soon Martin stood before Monsignor McDonagh and advised him that he was ready for the priesthood. "Good boy. We'll go to the chapel and say a prayer that God will guide you through the seminary to the priest-hood."

Martin had trouble with Latin from the very beginning. He clashed with the Church opinions on how to handle different situations with the clergy. Even understanding some of the rules of the Church seemed to give him trouble. On quite a few occasions the Monsignor told him he'd have to change his thinking or he would not be ordained.

One of the classes on self-control nearly cost him his ordination. The Monsignor was furious at him. It seems one of the teaching priests who taught this class on self-control was very fond of demonstrating the lessons on turning the other cheek. So he would bring up one of the seminarians before the class and without any warning would strike the student very hard across the face. Then he would watch carefully the reaction of the student. "We must never react to violence with violence," he said. "We are taught to turn the other cheek. Violence for any reason is wrong. For a priest to display a violent reaction is wrong, and there's always someone present who will see how he responds. You must show a good example wherever you go."

One of his students had pointed out to him that in his parish he watched the local priest display anger at Mass many times, giving out to everyone in the place. "And sometimes," the seminarian said, "he looked so mad I thought he would come down off the altar and have a go at half the parishioners." The response was not forthcoming. The teacher instead began talking about the assignments for the week.

The same priest had Martin in one of his classes and brought Martin up in front of the class, and with a little more power to the blow, knocked Martin down. It took four of the seminarians to carry the teacher to the infirmary. The Monsignor was looking out his window and saw this strange parade of pall bearers carrying the body to the infirmary. He ran out to see what was happening, and one of the lads who was holding the teacher's leg, dropped it on the ground. This panicked the rest of the pall bearers when they saw the Monsignor coming at them at full speed. "What has happened here?" the Monsignor demanded. He was not getting too far with his inquiry so he started to scream at them.

One of the lads developed a stutter and told the Monsignor that Mister Connolly had laid out the teacher. He said, "H-h-he f-f-flattened his n-n-nose."

The Monsignor went nearly mad. "Where is he?" he shouted. This time he scared the hell out of the four of them, and they dropped the teacher on the ground. "Pick him up! Pick him up!" he shouted at them, and he started shoving the seminarians all over the place. The Monsignor was beside himself. He spotted Martin leaving the classroom, and he ran towards him calling out his name. "Martin, you bloody eejit, what kind of example have you shown these young seminarians? I am having second thoughts about you becoming a priest. After this incident today on the lesson on self-control, it would seem to me that this lesson has gone by the wayside." He was so excited that he started to pass wind. "Well," he said with a very serious face, "you've got me so mad that I can't stop farting."

They both looked at each other, each one afraid to laugh. The forbidden word had passed through the Monsignor's lips, and it was too late to recall it. So they both started to laugh. And the more the Monsignor would laugh, the more wind he would pass. The seminarians were watching in dismay when the Monsignor started to run to the WC holding two other cheeks in an area that had no bearing on the lesson.

The years went by very quickly for Martin who spent them in constant reading and studying for the priesthood. There were times when he thought he would never pass all his exams. He was constantly disagreeing with his teachers on the rules of the Church. He would plead with them, telling them the Church was too rigid on their rules governing the clergy. Poor Monsignor McDonagh would spend hours with him trying to convince him that he must not rebel against the teachings of the church or he would never become a priest. His duty was to obey the Church without question. Martin also had difficulties with his studies. Martin was continuously failing in Latin, and the old Monsignor would spend hours tutoring him. During the different seasonal breaks, he would go home to Bridget, and they had become very close.

Shortly after the holidays the old Monsignor was confined to his bed, and Martin spent many hours at his bedside. Martin had made up his mind that he could not be a priest. The academic schedule was too much for him. The time was drawing near for him to tell the old Monsignor he was leaving. The Bishop kept asking the Monsignor when Martin was going to finish up his studies. Martin didn't want to leave his old friend alone and made one excuse after another to stay with him. He informed the Bishop that the Monsignor wouldn't last too much longer, and he'd like to stay with him until the end. The seminarians were all having dinner one evening when Martin was summoned to the old man's room. There was no doubt he was dying. Martin had to bend over to hear him speaking. He was whispering. He told Martin how proud he was of him, and that he hoped Martin would fulfill his destiny. The very last words he spoke to Martin were to tell him that the crowning jewel of his priesthood would be Martin's ordination. He smiled at him and closed his eyes. Once again Martin Connolly had lost a friend to old Sergeant Death.

After the Monsignor's funeral Martin informed the Bishop that he was no longer considering the priesthood, and the bishop understood how he felt. However, the Bishop asked him if he would be part of a clergy committee that was being sent to Berlin, Germany, to a conference that was being set up to look into the possibility of raising funds to rebuild the Catholic Church presence in Germany. Martin readily agreed and returned to Berlin the following month, but this time, it was under different circumstances. He was not wearing the German Fallschirmjaeger uniform, but was returning as a civilian.

Berlin was still full of bombed out buildings and a few huge craters in the middle of the streets. The Abwehr building was one huge crater. He remembered so well meeting Karl Gunter there for his assignments. He walked along the streets of Berlin until he found the little café where he had last met Contessa. The café had been rebuilt and was still on the same site it had been before it was bombed out. He ordered some coffee and once again watched the people walking along the main streets. He made note that they were not dressed as well as they had been when he was last there. They still looked to him as people with despair in their eyes. They had been through hell and back. The German is resilient and hard-working, and Martin knew that they would be back on their feet again. The German would fight and crawl all the way up again. These people were not losers—the war yes, but not their will. They would never remain at the bottom of the heap, and he would live to see Germany become a big player in the European community again.

As he sat there, all the faces of the past came before him— Karl, Contessa, Heinz, Mannheim, Wilhelm, Greta Stein, Leutnant Muller, and the submarine captain, Captain Reischman, and the German officer who got him on the sub from Spain to Germany, he had never known his name. He wondered what had become of Sergeant Keppler. He had disappeared at the Battle of Stalingrad. Most of these Germans he knew were dead. They had been hated by the world, and many bad things had been written about them. To Martin these men he had fought with were the type of men he would have gladly died with, and at times nearly did. No matter what was said about the Germans, he would always be a Deutsch Fallschirmjaeger.

The conference had gone on for nearly a week with some definite proposals being made. He himself was not moving mountains, but he was able to project the German point of view with this group that had come from all around the world.

One evening he stopped in an old German restaurant that had been there for years. It was partially destroyed in the war, but the owner had rebuilt it, and it took him over seven and a half years to do it. It had now been open only about six months. Martin had developed a taste for the German potato salads and large knockwurst sausages, and he loved the sauerkraut. He ordered this with some apple strudel from the menu. Martin was delighted with himself as he gave his order to a cheery waitress. When she had left, he filled up his old pipe and laid it down on the table. He was going to be ready after his meal for that morsel of pleasure that the old pipe brought. Looking dreamily at his old pipe, he thought to himself, "This old pipe has been with me through thick and thin. It almost has a life of its own." He had kept it in his mouth all the time he was in the prisoner-of-war camp even though he had no tobacco.

He was brought out of his trance by a hand on his shoulder. "Hello, my Irish friend." Martin looked up. It was Karl Gunter, and standing alongside him was Contessa.

Martin stood up, but his attention was not on Karl. He couldn't keep his eyes off Contessa. His mind was relaying messages back and forth to him. "She is still beautiful. Why am I now, above all times, feeling this sensuous feeling about her? I shouldn't have any thoughts about this woman."

While he was wrestling with his feelings about her, she spoke to him. "You're looking well, Martin. While I was taking care of some soldiers who had come back from the battle of Stalingrad, all ex-war prisoners from Siberia, I found out one of them knew you. He was one of the Fallschirmjaeger. His name was Sergeant Keppler. He told me how much he admired your courage on the battlefield and that he would have fought alongside you anytime."

Martin grew excited. "Where is he?" he asked.

"I'm sorry Martin. He didn't make it. The men who survived these concentration camps were walking miracles." Martin wanted to cry. Sergeant Keppler had been the only link left to his Fallschirmjaeger comrades. He had always hoped inside that he'd find Sergeant Keppler alive.

The two sat down and ordered a meal. Karl had not lost his taste for the finer things in life. After the waiter had gone with their order, Martin said, "You'll understand that I won't be able to pay for this type of meal."

Karl laughed. "Don't worry, my Irish friend. I will take care of everything. Isn't that right, Mrs. Gunter?"

Martin wasn't quite sure he had heard him correctly. "*Bitte* (please)?" he said in German. "This is your wife?"

"Yes," Karl said, jokingly. There was no smile from Contessa. She had seen the painful look in Martin's face.

"How long have you been married?" Martin asked.

"I believe it's eighteen years, isn't it, Darling?" Martin nearly exploded, but before Martin could say anything, Karl continued. "I met her at Moscow University when she was a student and I was a military attaché in Moscow at the time. I fell in love with her and subsequently joined the Communist Party."

Martin couldn't fathom what he was hearing. "My God," he thought to himself. "These two set me up. Contessa was married to him while she was seducing me." The next thought that came to him was that Karl had been the enemy all along. Martin stared directly into Karl's eyes. Karl Gunter could see the hate that Martin had for him. He found it very unnerving. Martin's eyes gave him a reason to be concerned. He hoped that if he could explain it all to Martin, he might get him to understand why it had happened.

The meal arrived, but no one seemed to be interested in eating. Karl began by philosophizing on the Communist beliefs and explaining how he had been caught up in the excitement of a new order and his disenchantment with the German leadership. He had known that Hitler was wrong for Germany and that Communism was the only hope to save Germany. He continued. "I was in a very good position to serve the Party, and my uncle, Field Marshal Gunter, was of the same thinking as myself. He hated the Little Corporal. At the time my uncle was in Ireland meeting with Sean McCarthy, an Irish-born German agent. During his time there, my uncle also met with a Russian agent, and McCarthy came upon their meeting by accident. This worried my uncle because this McCarthy might report back to the Germans about the meeting. He ordered me to eliminate McCarthy. When I realized that you were not capable of killing him, I followed you that night on board the Irish ferry to Holyhead, Wales. I had informed McCarthy that you were going to kill him that night on the ferry, so he was waiting for you. I came up behind him and shot him while he had you covered with his pistol. I knew you wouldn't be able to eliminate McCarthy or Pulaski, so you were of no further use to me. I didn't get a chance to finish you off that night because after I shot McCarthy, I thought someone would discover me on deck. It had taken too long to get McCarthy in position for a shot.

"As far as Pulaski was concerned, if you remember, he was translating messages from a French agent planted in Moscow by the English. He was also passing this information on to us in Germany. I informed my Russian contact that there was a leak. While they were trying to uncover the French agent, they ordered me to eliminate Pulaski. Contessa met with you the night before we had set up the date with you and Pulaski at his apartment. She informed me that you couldn't kill Pulaski. Contessa followed you that day to his apartment and was lucky enough that Pulaski had forgotten to lock his door after you. She knocked you out from behind and killed Pulaski. She told me later that you had the gun raised to the back of his head, but that you couldn't pull the trigger, so she did what she had to do."

Martin said to Karl, "So all that crap you told me was lies."

"It had to be done," Karl told him.

Looking over at Karl again, Martin asked him, "After saving your life, you would have killed me because I couldn't kill an unarmed man? What a hard SOB you are! I really didn't know you or this woman, did I?"

"Martin," Karl replied, "I would have killed my own mother for the party."

Martin smiled at him and said, "I believe you would have." Martin got up to leave the table. Karl rose with him and put out his hand. "No hard feelings, Martin. I know you will understand."

"Oh, yes," Martin said, "I understand all right," letting go with a short right cross on Karl's jaw. With that he left the restaurant.

He was awakened by a knock on his hotel room door at about three o'clock in the morning. Half asleep, he opened the door. It was Contessa looking very upset. She asked if she could come in. Martin sarcastically asked her, "And how much are you looking for, honey?" Even after he said it, he felt bad about it. She sat on the chair near his bed, and at that moment it took him back to another night in a hotel room when he was very much in love with her.

She started quickly, "Martin, I must tell you that at first I felt nothing for you. It was just an assignment for the Party. All my life the Party had come first. I know you have never known the all-consuming passion, feelings, and dedication one can have for a cause. Communism to me was my life, a workman's world run by the workers. It's what I believed in. I thought it would save the world."

Martin brought his finger to her face. "Yes, if the leaders of this great revolution were capable of following this philosophy themselves."

"Karl and I never had any real love for each other. We blended well in our love for the sake of the Party. I had never been capable of loving anyone until I met you. My childhood, as you know, hardened me for the world. When I met you with your innocence and your strong values on the taking of life, it touched me, and soon I found myself in love with you. The love I gave you was sincere. Yes, I used you. But remember. I had a chance to kill you that day at Pulaski's flat. That choice was given to me—you or the Party. And I chose you, my love."

Martin's head was spinning. He couldn't think. He did what is usually done when one is in love. He reached over and kissed her, and they were immediately in each other's arms. They lay that way for the rest of the night in silence, and they both watched the dawn come through the window. Finally, when morning arrived, Martin asked her what Karl would say about her being out all night. After all he was still her husband. "Karl isn't saying anything. At the moment his jaw is wired shut. It seems he ran into a big Irish fist." And they both started to laugh. "He's in the hospital at the moment, so I'll have to go see him this morning.

"What will happen to us, Martin?" she asked. "Karl and I are living in Leipzig, East Germany. We are training young Communists to infiltrate the western countries. Many of them are Germans who were disillusioned with losing the war. They are looking for some ideals to cling to. The Cold War is heating up, my love, and soon it will engross all of us. Karl and I will be going back as soon as he gets out of the hospital, and I will try to contact you before we leave."

Martin said, "Ill be leaving myself in two days for Ireland."

"What I wouldn't give to go with you."

"Well, you can," he said. "Let's go now."

"Martin, you don't quite understand these people. They would think nothing of killing me. Karl himself would have me killed without hesitation. I'll miss you when you go, and I will try to see you before you go." She dressed quickly and left, not giving Martin a chance to put his thoughts together.

Martin didn't attend the morning session of the church committee, but instead sat around on a park bench for hours trying to clear his head. He was wondering if it was possible to escape with her. His thoughts were all about her again. Martin had forgotten all the hurts that Contessa had given him. All he knew was that he loved her dearly, no matter who or what she was. It was unconditional love for him. He knew no other way. She was his first love, and to him, his last one.

chapter eleven

he next few days for Martin dragged on. There was no word from Contessa. Even up to the last minute before he boarded the plane for Ireland he had hoped she would appear at the airport terminal. It seemed to him that since he had met her, life was a waiting process that never ended.

Something seemed wrong to Martin as he approached his Connemara house. The long journey had tired him, and he passed the feeling off as being overly tired. "Funny," he thought, "Bridget doesn't have the fire on. There's no smoke from the chimney." The door wasn't fully closed, and he pushed it open and shouted in, "Bridget, I'm home." There was no answer. So he tossed his bags and coat in the living room chair and went into the kitchen to make himself a cup of tea. "Good girl, yourself, Bridget," he said out loud for she had made the brown bread. He started to cut the full loaf of bread when he noticed that the bread was stale. "It must have been here for days," he thought. "That's not like Bridget. Maybe she went into Galway city for a few days shopping." He finished his tea and lit a fire for the house was quite cold for that time of the year. The fire blazing away, he lit his pipe and sunk into the armchair near the fire. Tired from his trip, he fell asleep and woke up to see the sun setting in the distant fields.

Gathering up his bags and coat, he went to his room. The fire had gone out again, and he felt a chill in the air. He promised himself that he would go to bed early that night, and after unpacking, he turned down his bed that was always made for him by his sister who had taken over the chores that his mother had done for him.

The Irishman's sister fusses over her brother as though she were his mother, especially if the mother is gone from them. Mothers, sisters, wives, sweethearts spend most of their lives catering to their men folk. It becomes a rude awakening when the Irishman leaves their company and is faced with the world of reality.

He took a quick look into Bridget's room to see if her bed was slept in, and seeing the bed had not been made, he started to leave. "That's funny," he thought, "that's not like her to leave her bed unmade. She must have been in a hurry leaving." His nose caught a whiff of a strong odor, and the more he sniffed it, the worse it got. Looking around the room, he noticed that there were items of Bridget's things on the floor. He hadn't noticed that when he first looked into her room. Her hairbrush and comb and some personal things were on the floor, but were lying on the other side of her bed by the window, so one could not see these things by just looking into the room from the doorway. Her sheet was strung over the bed off to one side. It was as though someone was trying to hide that side of the bed. Pulling back the sheet, he saw that the bed was covered with dried blood. "By God," he shouted out, "what's going on here?" Blood, guts, and parts of bodies were not new to Martin Connolly. He had seen plenty of them slung all over the battlefields of Europe. This was different. Something had happened to Bridget, but what?

He began to search the room, and finally he opened the closet where she kept her clothes, and when he did, he found his beloved sister Bridget, crumpled up on the closet floor. He pulled her from the closet and placed her on her bed. He knew this would disturb any investigation by the police, but he couldn't leave her on the floor. It was too much for him to bear. It took him a while to assimilate what had happened to her. To Martin it appeared that the blood that was on the bed and in the closet was due to a beating. She must have been beaten on the face because it was so badly smashed up. He could see that her neck was broken. He thought that this bastard must have been very strong. At that moment Martin's mind snapped. All he remembered later was waking up in the Galway City hospital. He was told that the local postman found him on the road to Galway City. He remembered nothing of how he got there.

The guards (police) came around later in the day to question him. The doctors told them he had suffered a complete breakdown and to be careful with the questions. To the guards it was a matter of cleaning up some loose ends. The killer had turned himself in a few days after Martin had discovered Bridget's body. It was a month later that Martin was released from the hospital. He was supposed to continue his therapy with a local psychiatrist until he was fully recovered. Martin stayed in town. He couldn't handle going back to the old farmhouse. No one had spoken to Martin about Bridget's killer, and she had been buried while he was out of it in the hospital. Grainne and Maureen had arranged for her funeral. They had both been to see Martin, but he didn't recall either of them visiting him. The doctors told Martin it was the many months of everything coming together at once that had caused his mind to snap. He was not able to handle another tragedy. After all he'd been through and finally confronted with his sister's dead body, the brain overreacted and blacked out. Later on when Martin felt strong enough to handle his sister's murder, he went to the police station. A Sergeant Timothy Hussy was assigned to the case, and he met with Martin one afternoon in town. They had lunch together, and during the conversation, Martin asked the sergeant if he was any relation to Katherine Hussy in town. "I am," the sergeant said. "She's my sister. Do you know her?"

"I do," Martin said. "She's a lovely girl. Did she ever marry?"

"No," the sergeant replied, "she became a missionary nun, and she's out in Brazil, South America."

Martin was taken back, but said nothing. Somehow he had wished that she were still in Ireland. He would have loved to talk to her about his own troubles. She had been so easy to talk to. He needed someone to confide in. Grainne and Maureen had their own lives to contend with, and they wouldn't be the ones to sort out his troublesome thoughts.

Martin's first question to Sergeant Hussy was who had killed his sister.

"He's one of the lads outside of Galway City. I believe you know him, Mick Murray." Martin's face grew red with anger. The sergeant continued. "It seems when he returned from the war, he had become bitter and had long fits of depression. As you know, he had left your sister, Maureen, his wife. The local pubs had been complaining about him for a good while because of his violence. We arrested him twice for breaking up some of the local pubs here in Galway City. In one of these fights he nearly killed one of the locals with his fists. Well, as near as we can piece this together and from his own confession, he went to your house during the time you were away at the Church conference. Bridget let him in because, I suppose, he had been her sister's husband, and even though she didn't like him, to her he was just drunk. She probably thought he wouldn't do her any harm. He left that night and returned in the morning. Breaking in as she lay asleep, he entered her room, approached the bed and started punching her in the face. She tried to fight back, and was knocked unconscious. While she lay unconscious, he sexually assaulted her. She came to during the assault, tried to fight back, and he broke her neck. He had learned how to do this when he was in the army. I understand he had been in some serious battles in Europe and spent some time in a concentration camp."

Martin decided there was no point in telling the sergeant that he had met Mick Murray in a German prisoner-of-war camp. Martin asked when the trial was coming up, and the sergeant told him it would be a little while. "There is a lot of paperwork and investigation connected to a murder trial."

"Well," Martin replied, "he'll probably spend the rest of his days in jail." Hearing no comment from the sergeant, he pushed for an answer. Finally the sergeant told him that it was doubtful that he would receive any real punishment because his barrister was going to appeal for him on the grounds he was mentally unbalanced from the War. Hate came across Martin's face. Sergeant Hussy had seen this expression a few times in his police career, and he knew it meant trouble. Martin thanked him and said goodbye. Before he left the sergeant, he asked him for Kathleen's address in South America, and the sergeant, being a good policeman, had his notebook handy, full of personal and professional addresses in his little black book. Martin put the address in his pocket without even looking at it.

Martin returned to the farm and started to work it. The months went by, and working on the farm restored Martin's mental health. The beginning of 1956 brought a date for Mick Murray's trial. It proceeded rapidly and Mick's barrister pleaded temporary insanity for his client. Martin went into Galway City each morning to attend the trial. To Martin it seemed that Mick Murray was out of it. He just sat there staring into space. Martin was asked to testify when and how he had found his sister's body. Martin kept looking at Mick to see if he would get any reaction from him, but Mick just kept staring. They found Mick Murray guilty of manslaughter, and he was recommended for psychiatric care while in prison. As he passed Martin by on his way out of the courtroom, he shouted, "You bloody traitor and Nazi lover who fought against the Free World." Martin could tell from the reaction of the crowd in the courtroom that he had gotten them thinking. Martin thought to himself that Mick couldn't be that insane not to realize what his remarks had done. It was deliberate.

Martin made up his mind to keep vigilance over Mick Murray's activities. He might very well get off with less time for good conduct, and if he did, Martin would be waiting for him when he came out.

Back on the farm Martin read with interest the continuing heating up of the Cold War. Waiting and hoping that Contessa would be able to contact him, he continued his hard work on the farm. After a while he became increasingly doubtful if Contessa was telling the truth that she really loved him. One day while he was working in the fields, he saw a figure in the distance approaching him. Stopping his work, he tried to concentrate on identifying the figure coming towards him. Finally he made this figure out to be a man, but he couldn't put a face on him. When the visitor finally came face to face with him, he still didn't recognize him. "*Wie geht's*, my friend?" the man said. Martin was still trying to remember who he was. "Don't you remember me? I'm Fritz Wagner." Martin would have never recognized him. He looked like hell. He told Martin he had gone back to Germany and fought in the Battle of Berlin and spent time in a Russian prisoner of war camp. He finally returned to the widow in Kerry where he had met with Martin some fifteen years before.

Martin became irritated with him because he was talking around what he was there for. Finally Marin burst out, "Get on with it. What is it you want?"

"Hard times have come upon me," Fritz said. "The widow wants to throw me out."

"Yes, yes, go on," Martin said.

"Well," he said, "since we were comrades in the War, I was wondering if you could spare a few pounds."

Martin reached into his pocket and gave Fritz a twenty-pound note. Looking at the money Martin had given him, he smiled and said, "This is not what I had in mind."

Martin grew angry, "What did you have in mind?"

"Well, I was thinking about five hundred pounds to start with, and a permanent arrangement of twenty pounds every week."

Martin exploded. He caught Fritz by his neck and began to shake him. "Why, you're trying to blackmail me!" and he threw Fritz on the ground. "Get out of here before I throttle you."

Fritz slowly got up from the ground. "Oh, I think you'll pay me, my friend. I'm sure that the Irish authorities would be most interested in why you were working with a German agent in 1937 and 1938 here in Ireland." Martin knew that Fritz Wagner any other time couldn't have done much damage to him, but with Mick Murray's comments at the trial, it could anger some of the locals, even maybe lead to some investigation. That outburst in the court-room by Mick Murray about Martin fighting with the Germans dur-ing the War had some people talking already, especially those who had lost their loved ones fighting with the British during the War.

"Well, Fritz," Martin said, "I'll need some time to get the five hundred pounds. I will have to sell some livestock, and that will take a little time."

Fritz, seeing Martin had calmed down and looked quite docile, agreed to wait for three weeks but no more. When Fritz had left, Martin sat down on a rock in the field and lit his old pipe and started to smoke it. He had to come up with a way of silencing Fritz, but he knew he couldn't kill him. Martin had never changed his mind about killing outside of war or self-defense. This part of his character had been well reinforced by his years in the seminary. At the moment he was only interested in keeping track of Mick Murray.

Martin was not able to concentrate on the farm, and he decid-ed one night to leave and find Contessa. He had been heartsick over the loss of Bridget, and his interest in the farm had left him. Even the revenge on Mick Murray was not strong enough to keep him from Contessa. He now had to deal with Fritz Wagner in three weeks. He decided he was going to Leipzig, Germany, to find his love. "To hell with Fritz Wagner," he thought, "and what he has to say about me." He would go into Galway City in the morning and buy his air tickets to Germany. Then he would go back to Connemara and see Mrs. Burke's young son, Paddy Burke, and make some arrangements for him to run the farm while he was gone. This had to be done quickly without Fritz Wagner getting on to him that he was leaving Ireland. Although Fritz was back in Kerry with his lover, he might just come back unexpectedly to Galway to keep an eye on Martin. After all, it was only three weeks until the deadline.

In two days Martin was packed and on his way from Shannon Airport to Frankfurt, Germany, where eventually he would fly from Frankfurt to Leipzig. During his flight he went over in his mind the arrangements he had made with Paddy Burke to run the farm while he was away. Burke had only agreed to work the farm for one year, and after that he was gone. Martin thought that if he didn't find Contessa within a year, he never would. His first priority when he got to Frankfurt was to make some good connections to be able to work in the Russian section of East Germany. He chuckled to himself about Fritz Wagner. He would be in for a surprise when he faced Paddy Burke at the farmhouse. Young Paddy had a very bad temper, and in a minute he'd put Fritz into the hog trough.

He found a B&B place in Frankfurt that suited him. There were all kinds of construction still going on in Frankfurt. It had taken a terrible pounding during the War. He spent a few days getting back to the German ways of doing things while he was practicing up on his German. He took a plane to West Berlin hoping to find someone that he had known from the war who would help him, but this was very unlikely. Everyone he had fought alongside was dead. When he got to West Berlin, he traced his steps back to the time he had last met Contessa in a Berlin café. After he got leave from the Belgium campaign in 1940, he remembered falling asleep on the bench opposite the café they had eaten in. He tried to remember the name of the security officer who had checked his papers and then brought him to his home to eat. Martin recalled that his son had been a Fallschirmjaeger, too.

The area had changed dramatically during the Battle of Berlin. Martin found the police station that was responsible for that particular area where he had met the security guard. He must have talked to at least thirty police officers asking about this security man who had shown him kindness during the war. Not having his name made the task more difficult. While talking with a group of policemen in another station house, a policemen came over to Martin and asked him, "Don't I know you?"

Martin also thought his face was familiar, but he couldn't place the man either. It was only when Martin explained who he was looking for that the police officer remarked, "I know who you are now. You are looking for my father. I remember my father bringing you to the house to eat, and we talked most of the day about the Fallschirmjaeger because we were both within a few miles of each other during one of the campaigns.

"Yes, yes," Martin said excitedly. "Where is your father?"

The policeman said, "He died during the war."

"I'm sorry to hear that," Martin said. "He seemed like a fine man." The officer had given his name as Peter Hoffman. He had become a policeman like his father. Martin explained what he was looking for, and indicated Karl and Contessa's names and that they were living in Leipzig, Germany, working for the Communist Youth Party. Peter Hoffman had friends in the East German police station whom he would ask to help find Karl and Contessa. Martin was delighted with his luck, and Peter would prove to be a good contact for him. It took Peter Hoffman two days to receive back the information on where Karl and Contessa were. It seems they were in the East German Communist Youth Party Headquarters in Leipzig.

Peter informed Martin that he would have to get the necessary papers to cross over into East Germany, but this would not be a problem for him. Martin must have some legitimate reason for being in Leipzig during his stay. They discovered that the Leipzig Agricultural Fair was to start the following week. This would be perfect cover for Martin. It consisted of the presentation of farm machinery and different lectures on new methods of increasing production of farm crops, and also any subject connected to farming. His cover would be that of an Irish farmer visiting the Leipzig Agricultural Fair seeking out new thinking on how to manage a farm. It was a subject that they couldn't trap him on. He had been farming most of his life. Peter Hoffman secured the necessary papers for Martin to enter East Germany and procured an invitation from the Farm Committee itself for Martin. This invitation was thanks to a West German who had done business with one of the East German machinery companies. Its president was on the fair committee.

On the train to Leipzig, he made friends with some of the West German farmers going to the fair. So when he arrived, he had a fair idea of what he was about to experience at the fair. When the train entered East Germany, his visa and passport were inspected. Although they had very little suspicion of an Irish passport, they still remained vigilant, and he was questioned about why he had come so far just to see a German agricultural fair. If he wanted new information on farm machinery, why not attend the British or French shows? Martin was starting to worry, so he gambled. He produced his Fallschirmjaeger ID card that he had kept after the War, with papers indicating that he had won the Iron Cross First Class and two second classes, and the wounded badge three times. His interrogators, all first class Communists, had served in the Wehrmacht during the War and were impressed with this foreigner who had shown such courage for the Fatherland. Martin fully explained to them he had grown to admire German ingenuity and would therefore always seek out German products. Martin was permitted to enter Leipzig, and he headed for the Hotel Leipzig where he went straight to bed and slept until midmorning. After breakfast he took a taxi to the Leipzig fair, and on the way discreetly asked the taxi driver for the location of 15 Wilhelmstrasse. The taxi driver looked at him suspiciously. "Do you know what's at that building?" the driver asked him.

"Yes," Martin replied, "it's a German machine company that produces farm equipment."

The driver laughed. "I'm afraid not. You have the wrong address. It is a building that houses the East German Communist Party Headquarters."

This is what Martin was leading his taxi driver to tell him. Sometimes one has to appear stupid to ascertain the answers to sensitive questions by letting the other party show him how smart he is. Martin apologized for his mistake and told the driver when he got back to the hotel he would check the address again. So it passed off with no more thought given to it by the driver.

The Leipzig fair was the biggest exhibition Martin had ever been to. He had attended a few in Dublin, but they were never as big as what he was looking at here in Leipzig. He couldn't help but look at the farm machinery in the stands and think to himself that he wished he could afford this type of equipment. It was Shank's mare for him, and he would just have to break his ass the old fashioned way. The old fellah, he thought, would have had something to say about this fair. Martin knew his answer to it. "Ah, sure, it'll never work. You'd be spending all your time getting the damn machinery to run. Meanwhile, I'd have a day's work done and sitting by the old fireplace smoking me pipe when you would be dragging your weary ass in from the fields." Martin caught himself laughing because he could hear the old fellah saying it. A few men standing next to him were wondering what the hell he was laughing at because they saw no one around them.

Martin kept walking around to the different booths and would stop and ask different questions on what he had seen. It was during this time that he saw a large map of Leipzig on one of the walls. It took him a little while to find 15 Wilhelmstrasse on the map. The building seemed to be by itself. He noticed across the street from the building on the map it looked like a series of small stores. He left the fair and went straight to his hotel where he ate supper and stopped on a couch in the lobby to smoke his pipe before he retired to his room. In a little while a very pretty woman in her late thirties sat next to him. She began to converse with him in German which Martin had no problem understanding, but when he replied in German, she recognized that his German was that of a foreigner. She proceeded to question him at great length about his business, and Martin soon realized she was trying to decide if he was a big spender or not. Finally she came to the point. "I am very much attracted to you," she told him, showing off her baby blues, "and I would very much like to make love to you."

Martin smiled at her. "Is this for love or money?" he asked with a twinkle in his eyes.

The lady was taken back. "Well," she said, "if you put it that way, it's for money."

Martin rose from his seat. "I'm afraid not," he said. "I never pay for what I can get for nothing." As he passed her by, he was privileged to discover some new flattering words in German he had not encountered before, not even in the Fallschirmjaeger.

Martin woke up the next morning and dressed, but didn't eat his breakfast. The map he had seen at the Leipzig fair indicated some sort of eating places opposite the building of the Young Communist Party's headquarters. Taking the bus to 50 Wilhelmstrasse, he walked back to stop directly in front of 15 Wilhelmstrasse, but on the opposite side of the street. There was a small coffee shop there. The coffee shop was crowded, but he saw a table at the window with an old man sitting there drinking his coffee. "*Bitte?*" he said to the old man, pointing to the empty chair. The old man just nodded his head. The waiter came by shortly and took his order. The breakfast consisted of some cold cuts, different kinds of cheese and fresh fruits. He was in Germany, so there was no big Irish breakfast for him. It made him smile. How did he ever live without his old Irish breakfast?

While he was eating and observing the Young Communist Party building across the street, he couldn't help but watch the old man whose face was scarred and full of deep wrinkles across his brow. The wrinkles went with old men that age, but the scars indicated he must have seen the terror of war. Martin knew shrapnel wounds when he saw them. Nearly finished with his breakfast, he was watching a busload of tourists parking in front of 15 Wilhelmstrasse. It emptied out, and a group of about 15 people walked across the street and into the coffee shop where Martin was eating. The tour guide was young and perhaps a university student working his way through school. The group came into the coffee shop, and the owner was trying to seat them all, but there was no room. Looking for space for his customers, he approached Martin's table and standing over the old man, he told him to get up and get out. He didn't need his kind of business. "You've been here all morning nursing that lousy cup of coffee in front of you."

The old man rose from the table and left quietly. Martin figured that he was probably sitting there to keep warm because he had no other place to go and maybe where he was living, it was cold and damp because there was a big shortage of fuel in East Germany. What a change, Martin thought, from the prosperous Germany he had known long ago. Whatever was said about the Führer, he had built up the German economy from the ruins of World War I. It was a shame he wasted so many German lives.

Martin went over to the young guide who was standing against the wall drinking his coffee. He expressed his desire to join the tour, which he knew was visiting the Communist Youth Party building, and the guide informed him this was not possible because he would have had to join the tour at the beginning and finish with it. These were security rules for the tour company. Martin took a hundred West German marks from his pocket and slipped it to the young guide who was delighted with his newfound fortune. This was a very large amount of money at that time, especially for a young university student. Martin had guessed right about him being just that.

Leaving with the group, a tourist tag on his coat that the young guide had provided for him, he came upon the old man standing outside the coffee shop. The old man was standing in the cold, shivering and shaking. Martin gave the old man a hundred marks and told him in German, "*Deutschland, Deutschland Uber Alles.*" This drew a tear from the old man, and even though he was living in the Communist controlled East Germany, he knew which Germany Martin meant.

Martin entered the Communist Youth Party building and moved from floor to floor with the tour, always watching for Contessa, but there was no trace of her. It was a long shot, but he tried, hoping against hope he would see her, his Spanish love. The tour ended, and as they were leaving the building, they received pamphlets and leaflets on the Communist Youth Party, which included policies and different functions. As he came to the exit, Martin looked up at the building directory, and there in plain sight, listed on the fourth floor, was the name of the director of the Communist Youth Party of East Germany, Karl Gunter. Why not? There was nothing secret about the Communist Party any more. Everyone knew now how they were trying to spread their philosophy through the whole world. If Karl was here, then the chances were that Contessa, who was working with him, was probably on the same floor or even in the same office. He thought later going back to his hotel that all he had to do was call the building and ask for Contessa. Maybe it was not that simple, but it seemed logical enough to pull this caper off. The main number for the building was on the pamphlets that were given to the group. Martin dialed the number, an operator answered, he asked for Frau Gunter, and he was immediately connected with her. She was at first speechless when she heard his voice. He told her that he was in Leipzig.

"Where are you staying?" she asked.

"I'm at the Hotel Leipzig, and my room number is 602," he answered.

"I will be there tonight at seven," and she hung up. When she hung up, she told Karl who was sitting across the room from her, that the call came from a young member of the party who had some information about a high party official where she was working as a maid. The party had sent her there because they weren't sure of his loyalty. She was sent to spy on him, taking note of any unusual behavior deviating from party policy. She told Karl that she wouldn't be long and would see him at home later on.

"Should I wait for you for dinner?" he asked.

"No, no, I'm having dinner with her."

The hours dragged on for Martin. He couldn't wait to see Contessa. Finally seven o'clock came, but there was no sign of Contessa. Maybe she had told Karl. It might be a trap for him. By eight o'clock Martin had begun to worry. He was about to go down to the lobby and have a drink when a knock on his door took him by surprise. He opened the door with great enthusiasm, but was greeted by two East German policemen. "Oh," he thought, "she has betrayed me. It's all over for me."

Without saying a word, the two policemen came right into the room. Looking around, the older policeman, who seemed to be in authority, asked him for his passport. After what seemed to be forever to Martin, the policeman finally put the passport down.

"You are in Leipzig on business, *ja*?"

"Yes," Martin replied, "I'm here to see the machinery at the Leipzig fair."

This drew no reply from the policeman. "If you don't mind, my man here would like to inspect your room."

Martin said, "What you mean is that you would like to search my room. What is all this about?" Martin protested. "I am an Irish national. I am here on business. Why are you here searching my room?"

The older policeman brought his forearm across Martin's face, knocking him to the floor. "You capitalist pig! When you are here in my country, you will show some respect for authority. *Verstehen Sie*?"

Martin got up from the floor, and he tried to stop the bleeding from his mouth. He was about to say more, but it dawned on him that if Contessa had sent the two policemen, he would be sitting in a police wagon by now. This was routine with this lot.

The younger policeman brought him a towel from the bathroom to clean him up and stop the bleeding. The older man became polite. "I'm sorry that I lost my temper, but you must realize that we live here in East Germany in difficult times, and we are under heavy tension when we are in the presence of foreigners who may come here to spy on us. We must be constantly on guard."

Martin said no more and watched them leave the room. The relief he felt compensated for his swollen jaw, knowing that it was just a routine procedure. At eight-thirty there was a knock on the door. Martin was hoping as he opened it that it wasn't the two policemen, back again to have another go at him. Standing there was his love and his life. Contessa explained to him that she had been there in lobby since seven-thirty and was about to come to his room when she saw the two policemen in the lobby talking. She couldn't be sure if they might be coming for him. "So I waited. I knew it mustn't be serious, and I thought they were probably not even coming for you but someone else."

He hung on every word she spoke, not listening to the words she was saying, just the way the words left her lips. Waiting no longer, he caught hold of her and kissed her. She collapsed in his arms, and the time melted away with their passion for each other. It was going on 11 p.m. when she told him that she must go or Karl would grow suspicious.

"There is no life for me without you," Martin told her. "We must get out of Germany together. We must form a plan."

Contessa looked at him and said, "You are a crazy Irishman if you think we can escape this fortress."

"It's been done before," Martin told her. "I'm leaving tomorrow. We must meet to discuss our plans to escape. We don't have much time. When you go home tonight, list the people in your mind that we can trust to help us. I have some good contacts in West Germany who have excellent connections here in Leipzig. We must try unless you feel that you would prefer to continue here with Karl."

"I do love you, Martin," she said, "and I will try to figure a way out, but it's my firm belief we will die trying."

"Yes," Martin said, "you are probably right, but at least we will die together, my love."

She kissed him goodbye, and agreed to meet him during her lunchtime at a local department store at the other end of the city. She would tell Karl the next day when she was going for lunch that she was going to go shopping in a particular department store just in case she was seen there. Martin had told her that Karl would think that was a little unusual for her to travel all the way to the other side of the city during her lunchtime.

"Martin," Contessa said, "I will tell him that I need some special hair shampoo that is only found in that department store. This is East Germany, not West Germany. It is almost impossible to get anything here, and Karl knows this too well. Don't you worry about Karl," she said. "I can take care of him."

Martin looked at her. "Karl Gunter is a clever man, and don't ever underestimate him."

"Ah, yes," she laughed, "my Irish lover, but who was married to him for all these years, you or me?"

Martin tried to smile, but he had his doubts. He stayed up all night trying to lay out the plan. This time it was Contessa who was waiting for Martin in the department store, a novelty for him. There was a small restaurant in the store, and they sat down and began to discuss their plans. Martin stopped her in the middle of her proposal. "No, no, Contessa, there is only one way to go, and that's out through East Berlin into West Berlin."

In the mid-fifties it was possible to walk across the border from East Berlin to West Berlin, so Contessa would have no trouble. They decided that Martin would take his five o'clock train to West Berlin. Contessa would follow him as soon as she could. She told Martin she could try it the next day. Karl was leaving for a three-day conference, but she didn't know where he was going. Sometimes he didn't inform her of his travel plans. She believed it was due to some covert activities that he was engaged in. Their stay was brief in the coffee room. It was better not to spend too much time together, so he parted with one last look at her, and he hurried on.

He had no problem leaving Leipzig. He arrived at his hotel in West Berlin in a matter of hours. The next morning he went to the area where the East Berliners would start to cross over to the West. The crowds started early in the morning and lasted late into the night as they came across by the thousands. The year The Wall went up, over 1,600,000 people had escaped into West Berlin. Martin waited all morning, and by afternoon he finally saw Contessa among the crowd. She was about 25 yards out of the East Berlin border when he saw two men in civilian clothes grab hold of her. He borrowed some field glasses from a tourist. He could see that the two men were struggling with her to get her back to the East Berlin border. Then he noticed a third man coming out of the crowd towards her. It was Karl Gunter. Martin dropped the field glasses and ran into the coming crowd. He progress was painfully slow for he was running against the tide of East Berliners with suitcases and boxes and all kinds of paraphernalia. As they dragged her across to the border, Karl saw Martin fighting his way through the crowd. He turned and threw his arm into the air in an obscene gesture at Martin. It was too late. They had made it back to the border and were pushing her into an awaiting car. Martin turned and slowly walked back with the crowd. There was nothing he could do. She was gone.

When he reached the West Berlin border, he found a spot and sat all night looking at the crowd moving across to West Germany. Martin knew that she was going to be sent to prison or maybe even shot. Karl Gunter was not a man who took betrayal easily.

Somehow he must have found out. Maybe she didn't listen to Martin's warning. She appeared too confident in knowing her man. But Martin also knew him. Karl Gunter was capable of deceiving anyone no matter how close they were to him. Martin contacted Peter Hoffman and asked him to obtain for him an extension on his visa in West Berlin. This was not an easy task for Peter. He finally got Martin a temporary visa to stay in West Berlin for another year. He also arranged for Martin to be employed as a concierge in a new hotel that had just opened that catered to western businessmen. During the long years that followed, Martin's hopes were dashed by rumors and false information coming out of East Berlin. West German agents coming across the border brought word of a Spanish woman held prisoner for years in a Siberian work camp, but no proof that is was Contessa. Martin never gave up. He waited patiently over the long years for his love. Many times he thought of going back to Ireland, and why not? She might even be dead. This is all quite possible. But when he proceeded to leave Germany, something deep inside him wouldn't let him go. He grew old waiting for his Spanish love. The years were lonely and empty for him. After he finished his work at the hotel each day, he continued to work diligently for the Catholic Church, helping where he could with the poor and sick in the area. No one else came into his life over all the long years of waiting for Contessa.

In 1969 Martin went back to Ireland on holiday. He was then 55 years of age, and his hair had turned a gray-white. He still bore that physical presence about him. The signs of middle age were coming upon him, and after being away so long, he had nearly lost his Connemara accent. When he stopped at the immigration office in Dublin, he was asked what his business was in coming to Ireland. Martin tried some of his Irish wit, saying, "I'm here to plow the Rocks of Bawn." He was met with a serious and sultry expression from the immigration officer. After Martin had passed through the immigration line, the officer leaned over to his comrade, "What do you think of that Kraut? He tells me he's here to plow the Rocks of Bawn."

The other officer responded to his comrade in Irish. "Well, he doesn't look like he could plow my old granny's garden in Stillorgan."

Martin took a taxi from the Dublin airport to the Huston train station. Boarding the Dublin to Galway train, he took a seat next to a window. Shortly after, a woman with her little girl, who appeared to be about six years of age, sat down opposite him. Martin couldn't help but notice the little girl. She was very pretty. The Galway accent was music to his ears. It seems the two had come up from Galway to spend a few days with the mother's family. While talking to the child's mother, she told him that her father was with Civil Service and had been transferred up from Galway to Dublin. Martin listened with interest to what the little girl was saying to her mother.

"Why is Granny so old? Sure, she's old, Ma, isn't she? Granddad has no hair, has he not?" The Irish have a habit of making a question out of a statement.

Martin had forgotten what would have been normal conversation of a child with her mother, and it was extremely funny to him. The mother was trying to read her paper, but the little one kept on interrupting. The mother put down the paper. "Emer," she spoke quietly and softly to the little girl, and in one breath she was able to answer the child's questions, something Martin suspected she had plenty of practice at. "Granny is old because we all get old, and Granddad has no hair because Granny was like myself. We both ended up with two baldy beans."

"What's a baldy bean?" the child asked.

"Oh, please, Emer, will you ever shut up?" Turning to Martin, she said, "She's the image of her father. You couldn't get two words in with him. After we were married for about six months, I went to the ear doctor because I thought I was going deaf." She said this laughingly. "Are you married yourself?"

Martin told her that he wasn't. The conversation ended with her going back to her paper.

When Martin got off at Galway City, he headed for the Old Salt pub. When an Irishman is looking forward to his pint, it is not a good idea to delay giving it to him. The bartender was Japanese and kept asking him the same question, "What you have? What you have?" and Martin kept telling him that he wanted a pint. The Japanese man didn't seem to understand him, so Martin looked around the bar to seek help from one of the Galway lads who were drinking there.

"What the hell do I have to do to get a pint here?" he asked. Finally one of the young lads who was dressed up in a suit came over to him. "A suit!" Martin thought. "My God, what a change." If you'd worn a suit in his time, you would have been laughed out of the pub. The young Galway lad spoke quietly to the Japanese bartender in Japanese. Martin seemed stunned. "You mean to tell me," Martin said, "to get a pint in this pub, you have to speak Japanese? And by the way, what the hell is a Galway man speaking Japanese for?"

The young lad laughed at him and said, "Normally, this Japanese bartender will serve you a pint with no problem, but in your case he said to me you made him nervous the way you asked for it. He thought you were going to beat him up. And as far as speaking Japanese, I've been taking this course at Galway University for the last three years. Ireland is changing. We are becoming more and more adapted to dealing with foreign countries, including the Far East." The young man left, and Martin resumed listening to the conversations among the young Galway men. There wasn't a word about farming; it was all talk of big buy-out deals and mergers of different companies. Martin would have liked another pint, but the thought of another confrontation with the Japanese bartender turned him off.

He left the pub, and as he entered the street, he passed a remark to an old-timer passing by about the pub. "I know what you mean," he said to Martin. "This Galway City lot has become too grand for me. I don't know what the hell they're talking about. It's like Japanese to me."

"Yes," said Martin, laughing, "it sounds like Japanese to me, too," trying hard to be serious as he said it.

The old-timer started to tell him about a great pub in Salt Hill where you could meet with the old timers and have a good craic for the night. The old-timer stood back and took a strange look at Martin. "For a minute there," he said, "I thought you sounded like a Connemara man."

"I am," Martin said. "I've been away for years, and I suppose I've lost most of my accent."

"Well, it so happens that I'm a Connemara man myself. What's your name?" he asked Martin.

"Connolly," he said.

"I know the Connolly's farm," he said. "My farm is a little way from Pat Burke's farm. Do you know the Burkes?"

"Sure, Paddy Burke's mother brought me into the world."

The old-timer told Martin he was heading home, and Martin asked if he could hitch a ride with him. Martin found out along the way that Maureen had moved back from England and was living on the farm with her daughter. When he finally got to the farmhouse, he stood and looked at it for a while. It was in need of repairs. Looking over the fields, he thought they hadn't been worked. He remembered when he was last here that Bridget had the farm in great shape, and a small tear fell from his eye. Maureen wasn't much of a farmer. She liked the city life too much. He knocked on the door, which was strange to him because it had always been open. After a little while, a girl about twelve years of age appeared. "Yes?" she asked.

Martin smiled at her. "I'm your uncle, Martin. Is your mother at home?"

"Mum," she called out with a very distinct English accent. "There's a man here who says he's my Uncle Martin."

Just for a moment Martin thought that the woman coming towards him was his mother. "My God," Martin said, "you look like Ma. It's unbelievable."

"How are you, Martin?" Maureen said as she put her arms around him. "I wouldn't know you. What happened to you?" She noticed his hair was pure gray, and his face was very wrinkled for a man in his fifties.

"Well," Martin said, "you put a few miles on your own face. I'm afraid we're both no spring chickens anymore," and they both laughed.

Maureen had Martin sit down on a chair in the kitchen while she was cooking dinner. "I'm making spuds and stew and a vegetable in this old pot. How does that sound to you?"

"Fine," Martin said. "It's been a long time since I ate out of that old pot. As you know, I stayed with Bridget for a while after the War, and she made many a meal for me in that old pot. Ma must have got that pot from Granny. It's that old."

After dinner Martin sat near the fireside, smoking his pipe. He tried a few times to start a conversation with Maureen's daughter, whose name was Eileen, but she would have no part of it. She was a very unhappy child, and he heard her sass her mother more than once that night. Martin tried talking about her English father, whom Maureen had been living with. This brought a response from the child. "Well," Martin said, "I understand your father was English."

"Yes," she broke in, not giving him a chance to finish, "I'm English. I was born in England."

"Well," Martin replied, "your Ma is Irish, so you got a bit of both in you."

"Don't say that," she screamed at Martin. "I'm not like your lot over here. I want to go home to England. I hate it here in Ireland. We're stuck here on this dirty old farm," she said and ran out of the room.

"Wow," Martin said. "She's a real piece of work."

"Don't be too hard on her," Maureen said. "She's been through a lot with her father and me. He was no good. Thank God she never met Mike Murray."

"Do you know if he's still in jail?" Martin asked.

"Yes, he is," she said, "and I hope he rots there. My poor sister Bridget. Ma was right about him, but we didn't listen to her.

"Will you be staying, Martin?" she asked.

Martin told her about Contessa and that he was going back for her. She told Martin that was foolish. She was probably dead by now. Martin paid no attention to her. Nothing could change his mind about waiting for Contessa, and when she came back to him, he would bring her back to Ireland.

After a few days, Martin became restless and headed back to Germany. Looking back towards his Connemara hills, he said softly, "I will be back, even if it's only to rest beneath your green shade." He got into a taxi and headed for Galway City. When Martin arrived back in Germany, he went straight back to work in the hotel and continued to wait for his Spanish love.

chapter twelve

Contessa had aroused Karl's suspicion when she arrived home that night after meeting Martin. Karl had no idea that Martin was in Leipzig. He had suspected that she was having an affair with someone. Over the years after meeting with Martin she had changed. Contessa had followed Karl's orders in seducing Martin and spied on him for Karl. Yet he noticed that she was becoming less and less enthusiastic with her assignment. There were times that he could see the expression of dislike for it on her face, but what bothered him the most was when he noticed how her face lit up when she would talk about Martin. These unguarded facial emotions gave her away, and it was obvious to an old pro like Karl Gunter that she wasn't even aware of her true feelings for Martin.

Karl left his home that morning that Contessa was leaving to meet Martin. He let her believe that he was going on the pre-arranged three-day meeting that he had told her about. When Contessa left their home, he followed her car to the East Berlin border. He could not believe his eyes. She was going to cross over to the other side! Quickly he identified himself to the border guards, and two plainclothes intelligence officers caught up to her as she made her way to the West Berlin border. Karl himself also followed her, and he helped subdue her. It was only then that he saw Martin coming towards her from the opposite direction. "So," he said to himself, "she's leaving me for that Irish peasant. Well, she'll pay dearly for her little folly."

Contessa was taken to an out of the way police station where two sultry East German intelligence officers interrogated her. She was beaten within an inch of her life, thrown into a small dark cell with no windows and left in her own blood for three days. When the door of the cell finally opened, she was blinded by the light and only saw three figures entering her cell. One of the men asked her if she was ready to talk about why she had been fleeing to West Germany. Contessa tried to speak but her mouth was so swollen that nothing seemed to come out but unrecognizable sounds. Another man knocked her to the floor, and then the third man reached out and pulled her to her feet. She couldn't make out his face, but when he told the other men to leave, she knew immediately that it was Karl.

"Would you like a cigarette?" he asked her.

She jumped at the opportunity. "Yes, yes, please," she said.

He placed the cigarette in her mouth and lit it for her. When she tried to remove the cigarette to exhale the smoke, her swollen lip got caught on the cigarette and tore a small piece of the skin of her lip off. She started to bleed, and Karl, being the proper gentleman, gave her his handkerchief. Hope sprung up inside her. Karl was going to get her out. He still was in love with her. So she thought. But after all those years of being married to him, she still had no idea what he was capable of.

Karl started his conversation by addressing her as his dear *Liebchen.* "I would have thought all the years you spent with me would have taught you to have some style and class, but when you try to run away with an Irish farmer, it tells me that I was wrong. You came to me as the daughter of a prostitute, and your manners were as bad as I've ever seen. I spent years making a lady out of you. No one would ever have known what you came from. At least not when you were ordering at a first class restaurant. I dressed you in the best, and nothing was too good for you. But I suppose I never thought that you would finally come down to the social level of a peasant farmer. Did you really believe that you two could out think your betters?

"My position with the Party could have been compromised by what you have done, but I can assure you, it won't be. I was the one that helped capture you. It may even enhance my position in the

Party. After all, not many men would turn in their own wives. No, *mein Liebchen*, you will be sent to the furthest prison in Siberia that we have, and you will soon lose those beautiful looks and voluptuous body. Yes, you will grow old and sick, and you will pray for the luxury of death. Knowing human nature for what it is, your Irish lover will go back to his native land and marry a nice proper Irish girl and have many children. He will probably enjoy his remaining years in marital bliss while you rot in a cell in Siberia."

She was sitting in the cell looking up at him when within in one swift motion he slapped her across the face. "You are no better than your whore of a mother." Then he knocked on the cell door to be opened. Glancing back at her, he left. She never saw him again. Her world had ended, and she did for a moment in time believe that what he had said about Martin going back to Ireland and marrying an Irish girl was probably true. After all, he was always praising the girls in Ireland.

After Karl had left Contessa, he went straight to the police commandant. A short squat individual sat at the desk. Karl told him to ship Contessa out as soon as possible.

"There is a train full of Jews that is due here in a few weeks," the Commandant said. "I will personally see that she is on it." Looking at Karl, he said, "You realize that she will be going to her death. I believe she's your wife. This must be very difficult for you."

Karl lit up a cigar and blew the smoke out through his nose and mouth. "Don't waste my time with this sentimental talk. Get her on that train, and don't let me hear that you haven't obeyed my orders."

Karl left the Commandant's office. As he went through the door, he slammed it behind him, which in turn smashed the Commandant's glass partition to pieces. Karl had come to the police station by motorcycle. He loved to ride it in his spare time. Getting on it, he revved up the engine and took off. He was soon out of the city limits and on the local two-lane highway, one lane going east and the other west. Moving his motorcycle at great speed, he zigzagged in and out of the lanes, and at one such turn in the road his misjudged the opposite car coming toward him. He crashed into the oncoming car at full speed. He was killed instantly.

The days went by for Contessa and nothing happened. She hoped that Karl was trying to teach her a lesson and that he would be back to deliver her from this nightmare, but she would soon learn that this place was a luxury compared to the places she was going. One very cold morning she was taken from her cell and put aboard an open truck with some other prisoners and taken to a railroad station. When the train was loaded with hundreds of people— men, women, and children—the doors were finally locked. There was no place to sit down because they were jammed so tight, so they all stood until they reached their destination. The smell and foul air made Contessa sick. The train traveled for days without the doors opening. The stink was overwhelming, and Contessa could see at least ten bodies lying dead on the train floor. The bodies were starting to decay. She had fainted a few times. Being a nurse, she tried to comfort as many of the unfortunate wretches as she could, but she could do very little because she had no means on hand to give them relief.

Finally the train stopped, and they got out. The only identification of where they were was a sign with the number Camp 109. At her first glance of the outside she saw piles and piles of snow along the ground with more snow falling and harsh winds that smashed into her face, but being off that nightmare of a train was a relief. The guards were dressed in heavy fur coats, fur hats, and high boots, and they all carried rifles. The boxcars were soon empty, and after approximately fifteen minutes standing out in the blinding snow, they were loaded into trucks. She stood up on the back of the truck, and she was watching the guards throw the dead bodies off the train, leaving them strung along the tracks. Some of the women started to scream at the guards to bury the dead, and they were immediately shot. It was not less or more than she expected because she had heard from Karl what the death camps were like. The whole area was strung up with barbed wire fencing, and there were guards in the towers with machine guns. There was no need for any more deterrents. If one made it through the gates, there was no place to go. Some had escaped, but their dead bodies were discovered days later. The weather was brutal.

They stood at attention in the bitter cold for thirty minutes waiting for the Commandant. When he finally arrived, the group was all covered with fallen snow. They looked like a row of snowmen. They gave no appearance of being human. The Commandant told them that most of them were here for life. "Make any trouble here, and you will die a slow, brutal death."

They were housed in broken down buildings with hundreds of prisoners jammed into barracks that contained bunk beds, one on top of the other. One would have to squeeze into the bunk at night, which was quite confining. Many lives were saved by living in such close proximity because the warmth of their bodies kept them from freezing to death. The women and children were separated from the men, which didn't stop them from copulating. There wasn't very much of that because every ounce of energy was lost working twelve to fourteen hours in the harshest winter conditions that anyone could imagine. This once proud and beautiful woman, whose presence would command the attention of everyone in a restaurant when she would appear, was now carrying the welts and scars she had received from that terrible beating in the police station.

The first night she lay asleep in her bed, she was awakened by one of the trustees who told her very quietly that he would like to invite her to his room. These trustees were given privileges that included extra food, housing, and other amenities in exchange for controlling their fellow prisoners. Contessa asked him why he wanted her to go to his room, and he told her that he would like to treat her to some dinner. The trustees were given a choice of the most beautiful women who passed through these camps. This particular trustee explained to Contessa that unless she had someone to protect her, she would find herself preyed on by the guards and the other trustees. He pointed out to her that if she refused his offer, she would be back to him on her hands and knees for his protection, so she'd better make up her mind quickly. Contessa bit her lip and buried her head on the bed trying to fight back the tears. She motioned him to go. When he left, she lay on the bunk thinking of what she had just done. She knew she had no chance of surviving on her decision, but being a very proud Spaniard, she could do no less.

The next day Contessa was called to the Commandant's office. He informed her that he had looked at her file and understood that she was a nurse with a university degree. He would like to put her to work in the dispensary. "This can be easily arranged." He stood up from his desk and moved towards her. Placing his arms around her shoulders, he kissed her on the back of the neck.

Contessa's Spanish temper got the best of her, and she lashed out at him. "Keep your filthy hands off me," she shouted.

In an awful rage the Commandant told her to stand at attention and went outside his office to where one of the guards was standing. Taking the guard's rifle, he went back into the office and smashed Contessa on her back with the rifle butt. She was taken out of the office unconscious and placed in the dispensary. When she came to, she had to fight back the tears from the excruciating pain. She had never experienced such pain before. The sudden blow had been a shock to her system. The injuries were so severe in her back that she was never able to stand up straight again. All through the years she never recovered from this injury. She was constantly in severe pain. There were no painkillers, not even an aspirin, nothing available but the pain itself.

Contessa lay in the bed for weeks. She got little or no sleep with the pain. Trying her best to survive, she played mind games with herself. She started back over her whole life from the beginning to the present trying to recall everyone she had ever met from the time she could remember. She tried to put this in chronological order. Sometimes she would concentrate so strongly on this that she would get a few minutes of peace from the pain. She never knew what it was to pray. Oh, how she envied those who sought refuge in prayer. Contessa had never believed in God, so why now try to pray to a God that she never believed existed? She could taste the hate in her mouth for this Commandant.

One afternoon the Commandant came to the dispensary and with him a medical officer who had been sent down to check his administration. It was only a routine visit that meant nothing. This Commandant was a loser who was sent out to pasture because of his past. The medical officer examined Contessa's back and asked her how she got hurt. Without hesitation she pointed at the Commandant. "That fine upstanding gentleman decided he'd have some rifle butt practice on my back." The Commandant never said a word, and the medical officer finished his examination. She knew it was a bad move. No one would do anything about this brutality. That was one of the reasons he was in charge.

The next day the Commandant came back by himself. "That was a foolish outburst, my dear," he said. "It was a waste of time. Now since you appear to be much better, you will be assigned to hard labor in the fields starting tomorrow." He looked directly into Contessa's eyes and smiled, and then he turned and walked out of the room.

The first day out in the fields she was asked to carry wood to the standing truck that was being filled for fuel. The pain got so bad that she fainted. The guards threw her on the truck and left her there for most of the day where she developed a cold and finally pneumonia. The pneumonia probably saved her life because she was returned to the dispensary. While she was recovering from the pneumonia, she was receiving a certain amount of rest for her back. It gave it more time to heal. Meanwhile the Commandant had been called back for reassignment because his uncle was promoted to Fieldmarshall. While he was away, Contessa thought of how she could pay him back for what he had done to her. It was one of the few things that kept her spirits up during her recuperation.

The Commandant returned from Moscow to collect his belongings, and with him came his new replacement. He was an elderly man with the rank of Colonel, and from his chest full of medals, it indicated he had seen more than his share of action in the late war.

Visiting the dispensary with his new replacement, he spotted Contessa lying in bed. Pointing to her, he said, "This is a typical case of imaginary back pains that do not exist."

Looking at her medical chart, the colonel remarked, "It says here that she had pneumonia and that she suffers from an unknown back injury."

The Commandant's reaction was, "Well, what did I tell you, Colonel? It's listed as an unknown back injury because no one can find this so-called injury. Get out of bed, you lazy bourgeoisie. She is the educated intellectual type that looks down her nose at the common man. This was exactly why we fought our revolution, to eliminate her kind."

Contessa was having difficulties getting out of the bed, and losing patience with her, the Commandant hit her on the back of the head, knocking her to the ground. While she was down, he started to kick her in the ribs. The colonel stepped in between the Commandant and Contessa and just stared the Commandant down. "Please, Commandant, let's give her a chance to get on her feet."

The Colonel leaned forward and put his arm under Contessa's arm helping her up from the floor. What he saw in Contessa's eyes was very familiar to him. It was the same look that many of his men had when they had captured German soldiers in Stalingrad. Contessa was sent back to her barracks, and she was told to report to the Colonel's office in the morning. All night she tried to come up with a plan to kill the Commandant before he left, but how?

The next morning she reported to the Colonel's office. He was very polite and seemed to want to talk to her. "Contessa, I see you have a degree from Moscow University and that you have served in the late war in a German medical unit."

"And I see, Colonel," Contessa said, "from your war ribbons that you were at Stalingrad. I served on the front lines with the Wehrmacht nurses at Stalingrad. My husband was also there as a German officer, and we were captured by a Russian patrol and released when it was confirmed that we were both Russian intelligence agents. We were both decorated in Moscow."

"What are you doing here?" he asked. "Your file says you have committed crimes against the state."

Contessa explained her story to him at great length. Although he was sympathetic to her, there wasn't very much he could do. However, he was going to have her assigned to a mobile medical unit roving from camp to camp. These forced labor camps were strung all over Siberia, and were usually set up in local timber areas. When the timber resources had been exhausted, the camp would be moved to another timber enterprise area. The prisoners spent many hours in brutal weather conditions in a timber felling and cutting operation.

The Colonel leaned back in his chair and offered her a cigarette. She was caught by surprise because he was behaving so decently to her, and she thought he had some ulterior motive. Still the look in his eyes was very kind, and he appeared to be a man who was completely spent from the war even after many years. It had not left him. She told him about her Irish love, that he was a Fallschirmjaeger. He could have very well been a few miles from where she had been nursing at Stalingrad. The Colonel told her it was very possible because he had encountered the Wehrmacht Sixth Army, and the Fallschirmjaeger were integrated into the regular Wehrmacht. "They fought like tigers, and we had to kill the majority of them because they refused to surrender. In one such area we fought a single Fallschirmjaeger unit, and they held back our tanks. When they were out of ammunition, they came at us with nothing more than their bayonets. We Russians have respect for bravery. You can be sure that your Fallschirmjaeger fought bravely." The tears fell from Contessa's eyes. She knew Martin Connolly, and she knew by now that the Irish soldier is as brave as they come.

Before Contessa left, she asked about the Commandant, and the colonel told her he was bound for Moscow. She had lost her chance, at least for now.

Contessa worked in the Colonel's dispensary for over a year before she was able to get reassigned as a mobile nurse to the labor camps. Over the years she moved from camp to camp, and most of the time it was in Siberia. The cold and brutal weather and the constant pain from her back took its toll on her. Now in her middle fifties, this once beautiful Spanish maiden was moving fast towards premature old age. Because of the lack of mirrors in the labor camps, she could go for one or two years without seeing her own face, and when she finally would find a mirror, the shock to her was devastating. Contessa often wondered how much Martin had changed. They were nearly the same age. Would he still love her after she had changed so much?

As the years went by, she was slowly giving up the thought of escape. Twice she made plans but at the last minute decided against it. If she got caught, she would lose her present position of nurse to the camps, and she knew there was no way she could survive becoming one of the labor camp prisoners. One of the only reasons she was able to function with her back pain was her access as a nurse to drugs. Over the years she became dependent on the drugs. They were used for treatment of the camp prisoners. There wasn't very much of these drugs, but there was just enough to keep her from losing her mind from the pain in her back. So she couldn't take any risks. The odds for escape were against her.

In the 1970s she was assigned to a camp that was expected to stay in that area for years. It was set in the deep forest, which contained an area of rich timber. This was close to the Mongolian border. The weather was so hazardous to the laborers that there were constant accidents, and cases of pneumonia were rampant. The Commandant was the usual deadbeat, sent there for his past blunders. Contessa had by now adopted a way of dealing with these misfits. She knew that these Commandants depended on the nurses to keep the prisoners in good shape so that the Commandant could continue to meet his quotas and the State would make money. A profitable camp would secure his position.

After settling in, Contessa made her routine check of the patients who were in the dispensary. She saw a bed tucked away in the corner, apart from the other patients. As she approached the bed, she saw a grey haired male who appeared to be in his forties. She took his hand to take his pulse and was surprised to hear him speak in English. "I'm sorry," she said, "but I find your accent strange to me. Where are you from?"

"I'm an American, and I'm from New York."

Contessa was taken aback, but she said, "What are you doing here?"

I was captured in the Korean War with some other American soldiers and never released."

"My God," she said, "that's almost twenty years ago. That war has been over for years. Why haven't you been released?"

"No one knows I'm here," he said. "There are Americans in these camps all over Russia, but no one back home realizes that we are here. As a matter of fact, we understand that they've been told we're all dead. I have no parents or family. I'm an orphan, so there's no one looking for me."

The next three years Contessa became very close to the American soldier. He was always able to make her laugh, something she hadn't done for years. She once told him he must have had Irish blood in him because he was so funny. His wit reminded her of Martin.

The prison Commandant was retiring, and his replacement was to arrive within a couple of days. Contessa was always uneasy when a new Commandant would be sent to replace the present one. It took her quite a few months to break them in. The Commandant who was leaving had let Contessa run the dispensary without any interference. Three days later a guard brought word to Contessa that the new Commandant was waiting in his office to see her.

She went straight to his office and knocked on his door. "Come in," a deep voice said. After she walked into the office, she stopped dead in her tracks. There sitting at the Commandant's desk was her old enemy from way back. "I see," he said sarcastically, "that your back has never straightened out. How unfortunate." And then he smiled.

She knew he was talking to her, but she was in such shock that she wasn't connecting the words from his mouth to her brain. She made a motion to sit in the chair opposite him. She was so used to doing this with the old Commandant. "You will always stand in my presence," he said. "Do you understand?" She didn't answer him. "I see you have done well for yourself here, but we'll soon take care of that. Now get out of my office. I have not forgotten you." Later Contessa found out from one of the guards, who had talked with his driver, that once again the Commandant had fouled up in Moscow, and this would be his last assignment.

One afternoon the Commandant came to the dispensary and went directly to the American soldier. Contessa was working with another patient, her back to the soldier when she heard a crash. When she turned, the American was lying on the floor near his bed. The Commandant was cursing at him. Later the American told Contessa that the Commandant had wanted to know if he was ready to become a Communist. "I laughed at him, so he got angry and punched me out."

The next morning when Contessa came to the dispensary, she found the American soldier's bed empty. She made inquiries of the guard, but no one knew what had happened to him. Contessa headed for the Commandant's office, but on the way she met him. She asked what had happened to the American. The answer to her question was a slap across her face nearly putting her on the ground. "Your life is in my hands," he shouted, "and if I get any more insubordination from you, then you shall get what your American friend got."

She waited until he disappeared into one of the buildings. She said to herself, "If it's the last thing I do, I'll kill him."

Contessa walked slowly back to the dispensary, trying to come up with a final solution for this Commandant. She realized it would have to be something that would not lead back to her. The answer was that she would wait for the right time. When the opportunity occurred, she would strike without any mercy. That opportunity did not come until nearly a year later when an old man was committed to the camp. His name was Vladimir. He was a man in his late seventies who had been a political prisoner for over twenty years. The labor camp he had been in had been closed down, and he was transferred to Contessa's campsite.

Vladimir made his first mistake when he was being questioned in the Commandant's office. Annoyed at his response to one of his questions, the Commandant beat the old man unconscious, and he was taken to the dispensary where Contessa took care of him. There was a time she thought the old man would not survive. She finally nurtured him and brought him back from the brink. Contessa spent hours talking to him and she found out that he hated the Commandant and would like to kill him. He believed that the Commandant had received orders to finally get rid of him for good. He told her he would gladly give his life if he could take the Commandant with him. He explained to Contessa that he didn't believe his life was worth very much, but to take someone out like the Commandant before he died would have some meaning.

Contessa pondered this for a while, always coming to the conclusion that the old man would not have the physical strength to kill him. The next few weeks Contessa and Vladimir went through many scenarios on how to eliminate the Commandant, but nothing seemed feasible. The old man told Contessa that the only way he saw it possible would be at night, so he suggested that if she could provide him with a sharp instrument, he would sneak into the Commandant's quarters at night when he was asleep and kill him. The only sharp instrument that Contessa could give him was a pair of large scissors that was used to cut bandages. It was sharp enough, but would the old man have strength enough to push it into the Commandant's chest?

There was another problem—the guard who stood watch over the Commandant's quarters. So Contessa spent some time talking to this guard, giving him small doses of the dispensary's alcohol that he drank eagerly. There was nothing else to drink at the camp, and so the guards would drink anything. She also found out that the guard hated the Commandant, and that he himself would like to kill him if he could do it without being caught.

Finally she put the plan into operation. One night Vladimir sneaked off to the Commandant's quarters to kill him with the scissors from the dispensary. Meanwhile Contessa put the guard out of action by feeding him large doses of the alcohol while he was on watch. The guard passed out, and the old man went into the Commandant's quarters and stabbed him in the chest. The Commandant was too strong, and even with the scissors in his chest, a struggle ensued. The old man died of a heart attack during the struggle. The Commandant managed to crawl to the dispensary where Contessa was on duty that night. Staggering into the dispensary and bleeding profusely, he laid on the floor looking up at her. "Please help me," he said.

"Help you?" Contessa said. "Yes, *mein Liebchen!*" Taking a pillow off the bed and bending down, placing it over the Commandant's face, she said, "Oh, yes, I'll help you straight into Hell." It wasn't very long before the Commandant was on his journey to warmer places. An investigation was conducted, and it was determined that the old man stabbed the Commandant and that he died of his wounds in the dispensary. The guard was transferred for drunkenness on duty, and Contessa figured that he himself was in one of the labor camps. The guard never did have any suspicion of Contessa. He believed it was his fault that night that he got drunk and neglected to protect the Commandant.

The new Commandant was an educated man and immediately got along with Contessa. He gave her complete control of the dispensary, and until the year she was released, she ran the operation. The Wall came down in 1989, and it took Contessa three months to get to East Berlin. She still believed that Martin was alive and waiting for her. No funds, no one to help her, she worked her way across Siberia to East Berlin, many times washing and scrubbing floors along the way. Plagued with the continuous pain in her back and now with no drugs to ease the pain, she suffered the tortures of hell. Now in her seventies and not able to straighten up her back, she still carried on. The only hope that kept her going was to see her Irish love. She had to stop many times along the way to rest, so her travels were delayed. And there were times when she couldn't even rise from her bed.

Finally, on a very dark and damp night she crossed over from East Germany to the West. It was dark with no moon. She could see that she was the only one walking across the border. It seemed to her that it took forever.

Now 75 years of age, Martin was prepared to retire from the hotel where he had worked for over 30 years. He had lived in one small room in West Berlin and had become very quiet and subdued. His religious faith and his charitable work had kept him going. Martin spent long hours praying in church. In 1989 the Wall was torn down, and West Germany was swamped with East Germans crossing over the border. Every night for months after the wall was torn down, Martin stood at the crossover, watching the groups of East Germans coming over. Even in the snow and cold he waited patiently for Contessa. Somehow he knew that she was alive. He felt it, and nothing over the long years of waiting could discourage him from that thinking.

On one of these damp and rain-soaked evenings he was a little late in coming to the crossing area. It appeared that everyone who was crossing that night had come over already, when his old eyes saw a lone figure coming toward him. The figure appeared to Martin to be a crouched older woman having difficulty walking. She was about five yards away from him when he decided to help, and coming up close to her he took hold of her arm. "May I help you, Madam?" Martin asked, and looking closer he could see she was old like himself with gray-white hair that even at that age was as full as any young woman thirty years her junior.

The old woman's hand reached out and touched his face. "Martin, don't you know me? It's your Spanish love. I knew somehow you would be waiting for me."

Martin couldn't speak. He choked in his own tears as he clung to her. Finally he whispered into her ear, "I have loved only you." To a passerby they were just two old people clinging onto each other. There was nothing that appeared to the naked eye that could detect anything unusual about them. Yet they both had lived lives that few people would deem possible. Holding hands and talking very quietly to each other they disappeared into the fog and dampness of the German night.

They stood on the rain-soaked streets waiting for a cab, Martin with his arms around Contessa tightly. "I will take you to my room, and we will talk."

Contessa smiled at him, "Maybe you will get arrested for bringing a woman to your room for the purpose of illegal sex."

Martin, who up to now was quite solemn, broke out in laughter. "Well," he said in his Irish whit, "Adolf Hitler would have a better chance of rising up than this old boyo."

"It doesn't matter," Contessa said. "You weren't too good at it anyway."

"Oh," Martin said, "you are starting already." Again they laughed.

A taxi came right up to them. "Get in, Martin," the taxi driver said. "You will get your death of cold on a night like this." Martin, after 30 years as a concierge in the hotel, knew every taxi driver in Berlin.

Contessa was impressed. "You must be a very big man here in Berlin when all the taxi drivers know you."

"Some day I will tell you about my success in the hotel business." He had trouble keeping a straight face when he said it.

The taxi driver was looking into his rear mirror at Contessa. "I see you have a lovely lady back there with you."

Martin again could not resist the Irish humor. "Yes," he said, "she is one of the ladies of the night. I picked her up a little while ago, and she promised me a real good time."

Contessa hit him on the arm, "Go away with yourself."

Martin's laughter stopped abruptly. "You haven't forgotten." He reached over and kissed her tenderly on the mouth. He turned himself away for he was too embarrassed for her to see an old man crying.

Just before they came to Martin's apartment, the taxi driver broke the two of them up. "Martin," he said, " do you think you should stop at the chemist first? You wouldn't want to get this lady in trouble."

When Martin got to the apartment house, he got out of the taxi and shoved some Deutschmarks into the taxi driver's hand. Turning back to the driver he said, "The only trouble I get into these days is going to the bathroom."

They entered his room still laughing at the taxi driver. When Contessa saw the room, she broke down. Martin saw this and said to her, " I knew it was bad, but I didn't think it was that bad."

"No, no," she said, "it is lovely and warm. If I could die right now, I would like to die in this room."

"Well," Martin said to her, "you keep this talk up, and you might get your wish." He went over to his little stove and made her coffee. Martin had given up his tea over the years because tea was hard to get, and coffee was always available because Germans preferred coffee. Martin noticed she was shivering. He went over to his bed and removed the blanket and put it around her shoulders. It was then that he noticed her face. She had grown old like himself, but hard living had made her much older-looking than Martin. He found it hard not to stare at her for he didn't want to make her self-conscious. They sat and talked most of the night. He told her how he had read about Karl Gunter's death in an East Berlin paper.

"Good," she said. "This makes me eligible for marriage. I would like a long white dress and white lace veil to hide this beat up old face." It was amazing how she could joke after all she'd been through. They were both strong individuals and were not given to complaining.

Martin's last 30 years had been a walk in the park compared to what his Spanish love had gone through. The night grew colder, and they both went into bed with all their clothes on. Contessa cuddled up to Martin with her head on his chest. She had never felt that much contentment in 30 years. Feeling safe and secure in Martin arms, she fell into a deep sleep, a sleep that would last her for all eternity. That night her need to survive to see her Irish love was fulfilled. Her long journey was over.

An old man stood facing the hills of Connemara. It appeared as though he was talking to himself. "Well, my Spanish Love, what do you think of my Irish Hills? I knew I could never make an Irish woman out of you. But that's fine, because I loved you the way you were." He stood silent for a moment as if he received an answer. He started to walk away and then suddenly turned and said, "Ah, go away with yourself!"

Many miles away in a West Berlin cemetery lies a small headstone with the inscription:

Contessa Garcia
The years have come and gone,
But I have not forgotten thee,
My Spanish Love.
Martin

I have not forgotten thee

This book was set in Adobe Times and Bitstream Libra types
on Apple Macintosh equipment
using QuarkXpress
by Michael Höhne
in 2002